BUDDHIST TALES
for
YOUNG and OLD

Volume 2

Stories of the Enlightenment Being
Jātakas 51–100, 514

BUDDHIST TALES
for YOUNG and OLD

Volume 2

Stories of the Enlightenment Being
Jātakas 51–100, 514

Interpreted by
KURUNEGODA PIYATISSA MAHA THERA

Stories Told by
Todd Anderson

Illustrated by
JOHN PATTERSON

2nd Edition, Revised and Enlarged by
Kurunegoda Piyatissa Maha Thera and
Stephan Hillyer Levitt

Buddhist Tales for Young and Old

Volume 1: STORIES OF THE ENLIGHTENMENT BEING, Jātakas 1–50.
Interpreted by Kurunegoda Piyatissa Maha Thera. Stories Told by Todd Anderson. Illustrated by Sally Bienemann, Millie Byrum, Mark Gilson. 2nd edition, revised and enlarged by Kurunegoda Piyatissa Maha Thera and Stephan Hillyer Levitt. Parkside Hills, New York: Buddhist Literature Society, Inc., 2013. (1st edition, under the title PRINCE GOODSPEAKER, STORIES 1–50, 1995.)

Volume 2: STORIES OF THE ENLIGHTENMENT BEING, Jātakas 51–100, 514.
Interpreted by Kurunegoda Piyatissa Maha Thera. Stories Told by Todd Anderson. Illustrated by John Patterson. 2nd edition, revised and enlarged by Kurunegoda Piyatissa Maha Thera and Stephan Hillyer Levitt. Parkside Hills, New York: Buddhist Literature Society, Inc., 2013. (1st edition, under the title KING FRUITFUL, STORIES 51–100, 1996. 2nd ptg. of the 1st edition, together with KING SIX TUSKER AND THE QUEEN WHO HATED HIM, CHADDANTA-JATAKA (NO. 514) appended, [2004].)

Volume 3: STORIES OF THE ENLIGHTENMENT BEING, Jātakas 101–150.
Interpreted by Kurunegoda Piyatissa Maha Thera. Stories Retold by Stephan Hillyer Levitt. Parkside Hills, New York: Buddhist Literature Society, Inc., 2007.

Volume 4: STORIES OF THE ENLIGHTENMENT BEING, Jātakas 151–200.
Interpreted by Kurunegoda Piyatissa Maha Thera. Stories Retold by Stephan Hillyer Levitt. Parkside Hills, New York: Buddhist Literature Society, Inc., 2009.

Volume 5: STORIES OF THE ENLIGHTENMENT BEING, Jātakas 201–250.
Interpreted by Kurunegoda Piyatissa Maha Thera. Stories Retold by Stephan Hillyer Levitt. Parkside Hills, New York: Buddhist Literature Society, Inc., 2012.

"Suddenly the water demon stuck his head up above the water.
He exclaimed, 'In all the time I've lived here, I have never seen anyone,
man or beast, as wise as this monkey!...'"

Pariyatti Press
an imprint of
Pariyatti Publishing
www.pariyatti.org

First Pariyatti Edition, 2024
Published with the consent of Buddhist Literature Society, Inc.

ISBN: 978-1-68172-658-8 (Print)
ISBN: 978-1-68172-678-6 (PDF)
ISBN: 978-1-68172-679-3 (ePub)
ISBN: 978-1-68172-680-9 (Mobi)
Library of Congress Control Number: 2024936371

Cover illustration by Sally Bienemann, assisted by Arlene Yellen and cover design by Nalin Ariyarathne.

Foreword to the 2nd Edition

This 2nd edition of vols. 1 and 2 of *Buddhist Tales for Young and Old* was undertaken so as to bring the format of these volumes in line with that adopted in vols. 3–5.

These Jātaka stories as they have been handed down to us are accompanied in Buddhaghosa's text with "stories of the present" which narrate the circumstances under which the Buddha is reputed to have told the various fables and parables, and which grew up around these stories in the course of their transmission.

It is apparent that the "stories of the present" are integral to at least some of the stories in that some of the stories take their titles from these. Thus, for instance, the *Losaka-Jātaka* (No. 41), the two *Sāketa-Jātaka*-s (Nos. 68 and 237), the *Telapatta-Jātaka* (No. 96), the *Samiddhi-Jātaka* (No. 167), the *Kāmanīta-Jātaka* (No. 228), and the *Palāsa-Jātaka* and *Dutiya-Palāsa-Jātaka* (Nos. 229 and 230). In several instances, the main characters in the fables and parables take their names from the person in the "story of the present" about whom the story is told. So, for instance, in the *Rohiṇī-Jātaka* about a servant girl of the millionaire Anāthapiṇḍika named Rohiṇī (No. 45), and in the *Kālakaṇṇi-Jātaka* (No. 83) about a friend of Anāthapiṇḍika's named Kālakaṇṇi.

The fables and parables themselves, of course, in at least many instances pre-date the Buddha and at times can be found elsewhere in South Asian literature, as well.

Buddhaghosa's text also includes the "connection" between the "stories of the present" and the fables and parables – referred to as "stories of the past," which "connection" identifies the characters in the "stories of the present" with those in the "stories of the past" – the fables and parables as told here by Todd Anderson. The "connection" appears at the end of each Jātaka tale.

In vols. 3–5 we related the "stories of the present" and "connections" along with the Jātakas proper. We have here added them to the stories in vols. 1 and 2.

In vols. 3–5, we generally followed closely the late 13th c. – early 14th c. C.E. Sinhalese translation of the Jātaka stories by Virasiṁha Pratirāja for both the "stories of the present" and the "stories of the past," and for the "connections." In vols. 1 and 2, though, with the exception of the narration of the *Chaddanta-Jātaka* (No. 514) that was appended to vol. 2, the stories were more abbreviated. We have therefore in the main followed this practice here as well for this 2nd edition of vols. 1 and 2, abbreviating the "stories of the present" and the "connections."

On the whole, we have not altered here the text as told by Todd Anderson except for a few stylistic revisions here and there, and except that in a few places, mostly in vol. 2, additions and changes were necessitated on account of the addition of the "stories of the present" and the "connections." Also in a few places in vol. 2, changes had to be made in the specifics of a repeated story or in the specifics of two stories the telling of which had been here combined.

We have as well added here the Pāli titles of the various Jātaka stories for more ready recognition of the different stories. We have also added the Pāli names of the various characters the names of which were characterized in English by Todd Anderson earlier – giving these the first time the name is mentioned only; and for the purpose of clarity, in brackets, we have added various Pāli technical terms which terms were earlier characterized here in English only. When Pāli names were given in the translation earlier, we have added the appropriate diacritics. And we have added in footnotes points of general interest.

Further, for the sake of uniformity with vols. 3–5, we have here changed the way in which vols. 1 and 2 were titled.

The Pāli story titles, which Radhika Abeysekera, currently of Winnipeg, Manitoba, Canada, had also earlier suggested be added, very often focus on different points in, or aspects of the stories than the English titles given to characterize the stories in vols. 1 and 2. On account of layout, an English rendering of these Pāli titles could not be given in place. We give here an English rendering of these titles for the stories in vol. 2:

51. *Mahāsīlava-Jātaka* – The Story of Mahāsīlava (One With Great Virtue)
52. *Cūḷajanaka-Jātaka* – The Little Story of (King) Janaka (Fruitful)
    [539. *Mahājanaka-Jātaka* – The Story of (King) Janaka the Great]
53. *Puṇṇapāti-Jātaka* – The Story of Full Containers
54. *Phala-Jātaka* – The Story of Fruit
55. *Pañcāvudha-Jātaka* – The Story of (Prince) Pañcāvudha (One Possessing Five Weapons)
56. *Kañcanakkhandha-Jātaka* – The Story of a Bulk of Gold
57. *Vānarinda-Jātaka* – The Story of the Monkey King
58. *Tayodhamma-Jātaka* – The Story of Three Qualities
59. *Bherivāda-Jātaka* – The Story of the Sound of a Drum
60. *Saṅkhadhamana-Jātaka* – The Story of Blowing a Conch
61. *Asātamanta-Jātaka* – The Story of the Secret Saying About Unhappiness
62. *Aṇḍabhūta-Jātaka* (*Andhabhūta-Jātaka*) – The Story of a Foetus / The Story of One Who Was Mentally Blindfolded
63. *Takka-Jātaka* (*Takkāriya-Jātaka*) – The Story of Buttermilk (or, The Story of Dates) / The Story of Takkāriya (= Takkapaṇḍita, The Buttermilk [or, Date] Holy Man)
64. *Durājāna-Jātaka* – The Story of Something That Is Difficult to Understand
65. *Anabhīrati-Jātaka* – The Story of Discontentedness
66. *Mudulakkhaṇa-Jātaka* – The Story of Mudulakkhaṇa (One With a Tender Character; or, Tenderhearted)
67. *Ucchaṅga-Jātaka* – The Story of a (Woman's) Hip[1]

---

1   In South Asia, women carry young children on their hip. In this Jātaka story, the main character is protective of her brother as if she were an older sister carrying her younger brother on her hip. She thereby saves not only her brother, but also her husband and son.

68. *Sāketa-Jātaka* – The Story of Sāketa
69. *Visavanta-Jātaka* – The Story of a Poisonous Snake
70. *Kuddāla-Jātaka* – The Story of a Spade
71. *Varaṇa-Jātaka* – The Story of a *Varaṇa*-tree
72. *Sīlavanāga-Jātaka* – The Story of a Virtuous Elephant
73. *Saccaṁkira-Jātaka* – The Story of a Solemn Oath
74. *Ruddhadhamma-Jātaka* – The Story About the Nature of Trees
75. *Maccha-Jātaka* – The Story of a Fish
76. *Asaṅkiya-Jātaka* – The Story About There Being Nothing to Fear
77. *Mahāsupina-Jātaka* – The Story of an Important Dream
78. *Illīsa-Jātaka* – The Story of Illīsa
79. *Kharassara-Jātaka* – The Story of a Rough Sound
80. *Bhīmasena-Jātaka* – The Story of Bhīmasena (A Fearful Person)
81. *Surāpāna-Jātaka* – The Story of Drinking Alcohol
82. *Mittavinda-Jātaka* (*Mittavindaka-Jātaka*) – The Story of Mittavinda (or, Mittavindaka)
83. *Kālakaṇṇi-Jātaka* – The Story of Kālakaṇṇi (One With Black Ears)
84. *Atthasadvāra-Jātaka* – The Story of the Doors to Well Being
85. *Kiṁpakka-Jātaka* – The Story of a *Kiṁpakka*-tree
86. *Sīlavīmaṁsana-Jātaka* – The Story of Examining Virtue
87. *Maṅgala-Jātaka* – The Story of Auspicious Signs
88. *Sārambha-Jātaka* – The Story of Sārambha (Tit-for-Tat)
89. *Kuhaka-Jātaka* – The Story of a Knave
90. *Akataññu-Jātaka* – The Story of Ingratitude
91. *Litta-Jātaka* – The Story of Gambling
92. *Mahāsāra-Jātaka* – The Story of Something Most Precious
93. *Vissāsabhojana-Jātaka* – The Story About Trustingly Accepting Gifts
94. *Lomahaṁsa-Jātaka* – A Story of Horripilation
95. *Mahāsudassana-Jātaka* – The Story of (King) Mahāsudassana (Clear-sighted the Great)
96. *Telapatta-Jātaka* – The Story of a Begging Bowl Filled With Oil
97. *Nāmasiddhi-Jātaka* – The Story of the Consequence of a Name

98. *Kūṭavāṇija-Jātaka* – The Story of a Cunning Merchant

99. *Parosahassa-Jātaka* – The Story of More Than a Thousand

100. *Asātarūpa-Jātaka* (*Aghātarūpa-Jātaka*) – The Story of Something Unpleasant / The Story of Taking a Nonviolent Posture

*   *   *

514. *Chaddanta-Jātaka* – The Story of One With Six Tusks

The transliteration system used for Pāli words and names is that of the U.S. Library of Congress Cataloging Service for Sanskrit and Prakrit languages in *Devanāgarī* script as in their Bulletin 64 (February 1964), with a few minor but standard variations. That for Sinhalese words and names, when these are given, is that of the U.S. Library of Congress Cataloging Service Bulletin 88 (January 1970). A guide to the pronunciation of Pāli words and names is given in vol. 1 following the Foreword in that place.

We would like to thank Namal Kuruppu for preparing a JPEG file of the illustrations that accompany the stories in these vols. 1 and 2 so that they could be included here expeditiously. We would also like to thank the Ven. Sirisumana of the New York Buddhist Vihara for his instruction on incorporating the images in the text.

We hope our readers will receive this revised and enlarged edition of vols. 1 and 2 as well as they have received the earlier edition of vols. 1 and 2, and as well as they have received vols. 3–5.

Peace and health to all!

Kurunegoda Piyatissa Nayaka Maha Thero

Stephan Hillyer Levitt, Ph.D.

June, 2012

Buddhist Literature Society, Inc.

New York Buddhist Vihara

214-22 Spencer Avenue

Parkside Hills, New York 11427-1821, U. S. A.

A Guide to the Pronunciation of Pāli Words and Names

Vowels

a	as *u* in but	u	as *u* in pull	ā	as *a* in father
ū	as *u* in rule	i	as *i* in pin	e	as *ay* in say
ī	as *i* in machine	o	as *o* in go		

Consonants and Nasals

k   (guttural) like the English *k* in take or pick. kh as *kh* in lakehouse. g as *g* in pig. gh as *gh* in doghouse. The nasal ṅ is used with k, kh, g, and gh.

c   (palatal) similar to *ch* in chalk, but unaspirated. ch as *ch* in chalk or church.

j   like the English *g* in page. jh as *j* in joy, but even more aspirated. The nasal ñ as in Spanish Español is used with c, ch, j, and jh.

ṭ   a retroflex sound, pronounced with the tongue curled back so that it touches the roof of the mouth. ṭh is the same sound, but aspirated. ḍ and ḍh are the voiced counterparts of these sounds. ṇ is the retroflex nasal. The difference between these sounds and the dentals, without dots, is not important for the general reader.

t   (dental) similar to *t* in French or Italian. th as *th* in anthill. d similar to *d* in pod or paid. dh as *dh* in roundhouse. The nasal n is used with t, th, d, and dh.

p   (labial) as *p* in English up. ph as *ph* in uphill. b as *b* in rub. bh as *bh* in clubhouse. The nasal m is used with p, ph, b, and bh.

ṁ   as *ng* in sing. This is a nasal sound that lacks the closure of the organs required for the other nasal sounds.

Semivowels

y, r, l, v similar to their English counterparts. ḷ is a retroflex variant of l.

Sibilant

s   as *s* in saint or hiss.

Aspirate

h   as *h* in hit.

Contents

Foreword to the 2ⁿᵈ Edition vii

A Guide to the Pronunciation of Pāli Words and Names xii

1ˢᵗ Edition Acknowledgements xvii

Interpreter's Introduction to the 1ˢᵗ Edition xviii

From the Storyteller to the Listeners xxv

51 - King Goodness the Great [Perseverance] (*Mahāsīlava-Jātaka*)............. 1

52, 539 - King Fruitful and Queen Sivali (*Cūḷajanaka-Jātaka,*
  Mahājanaka-Jātaka)...9
  Chapter 1. Rebirth of the Bodhisatta 10
  Chapter 2. Gaining Power 14
  Chapter 3. Giving Up Power...23

53 - A Gang of Drunkards [Sobriety] (*Puṇṇapāti-Jātaka*) 32

54, 85 - The What-not Tree [Prudence] (*Phala-Jātaka, Kiṁpakka-Jātaka*)..36

55 - Prince Five-Weapons and Sticky-Hair [The Diamond Weapon]
  (*Pañcāvudha-Jātaka*)..39

56 - A Huge Lump of Gold [Moderation] (*Kañcanakkhandha-Jātaka*).........44

57, 208, 224 - Mr. Monkey and Sir Crocodile [Good Manners]
  (*Vānarinda-Jātaka*) 46

58 - A Prince of Monkeys [Carefulness] (*Tayodhamma-Jātaka*) 49

59, 60 - Two Ways of Beating a Drum [Excess] (*Bherivāda-Jātaka,*
  Saṅkhadhamana-Jātaka)...54

61 - Two Mothers [Renunciation] (*Asātamanta-Jātaka*) 55

62 - The Priest Who Gambled With a Life [Misguided Morality]
  (*Aṇḍabhūta-Jātaka, Andhabhūta-Jātaka*) 60

63 - The Wicked Lady and the Buttermilk Wise Man [Seduction]
  (*Takka-Jātaka, Takkāriya-Jātaka*)....................................67

64, 65 - Country Man and City Wife [Adultery] (*Durājāna-Jātaka,*
  Anabhirati-Jātaka) 73

66, 251 - The Wisdom of Queen Tenderhearted [Lust]
  (*Mudulakkhaṇa-Jātaka*) 76

67 - A Wife and Mother Who Was a Sister First [An Intelligent Woman]
  (*Ucchaṅga-Jātaka*)..81

68, 237 - 3,000 Births [Rebirth] (*Sāketa-Jātaka*) 83

69 - The Strong-minded Snake [Determination] (*Visavanta-Jātaka*) 85

70 - The Shovel Wise Man [Renunciation] (*Kuddāla-Jātaka*) 87

71 - The Green Wood Gatherer [Laziness] (*Varaṇa-Jātaka*).....................91

72 - The Elephant King Goodness [Generosity and Ingratitude]
    (*Sīlavanāga-Jātaka*) 94

73 - Four on a Log [Gratitude] (*Saccaṁkira-Jātaka*) 100

74 - New Homes for the Tree Spirits [Wise Advice]
    (*Rukkhadhamma-Jātaka*) 107

75 - The Fish Who Worked a Miracle [The Power of Truthfulness]
    (*Maccha-Jātaka*) 110

76 - The Meditating Security Guard [Fearlessness] (*Asaṅkiya-Jātaka*)....113

77 - 16 Dreams (*Mahāsupina-Jātaka*)..116
    Chapter 1. Panic...116
    Chapter 2. Roaring Bulls With No Fight.................................119
    Chapter 3. The Frightening Sound of
    'Munch, Munch, Munch' 124
    Chapter 4. Teaching 129

78 - Illīsa the Cheap [Miserliness] (*Illīsa-Jātaka*) 132

79 - A Motherless Son [Betrayal] [(*Kharassara-Jātaka*) 141

80 - Fear Maker and Little Archer [Self-deception] (*Bhīmasena-Jātaka*)....144

81 - Forest Monks in a King's Pleasure Garden
    [Pupils Without a Teacher] (*Surāpāna-Jātaka*) 150

82, 41, 104, 369, 439 - The Curse of Mittavinda (*Mittavinda-Jātaka,
    Mittavindaka-Jātaka*) 155
    Chapter 1. Jealousy 155
    Chapter 2. Greed...160
    Chapter 3. Pleasure 162

83 - A Hero Named Jinx [Friendship] (*Kālakaṇṇi-Jātaka*) 168

84 - A Question From a Seven-year-old [Six Worthy Ways]
    (*Atthasadvāra-Jātaka*)...172

86, 290, 362 - A Lesson From a Snake [The Value of Goodness]
    (*Sīlavīmaṁsana-Jātaka*) 174

87 - A Priest Who Worshipped Luck [Superstition] (*Maṅgala-Jātaka*) 178

88, 28 - The Bull Called Tit-for-Tat [All Deserve Respect]
(Sārambha-Jātaka) 181

89 - The Phony Holy Man [Hypocrisy] (Kuhaka-Jātaka)............................185

90, 363 - One Way Hospitality [Ingratitude] (Akataññu-Jātaka).............189

91 - Poison Dice [Deception] (Litta-Jātaka) 192

92 - The Mystery of the Missing Necklace (Mahāsāra-Jātaka)................194
Chapter 1. One Crime Leads to Another 196
Chapter 2. The Mystery Is Solved 198

93 - The Careless Lion [Circumspection] (Vissāsabhojana-Jātaka) 202

94 - The Holy Man Who Tried To Be Too Holy [Extremism]
(Lomahaṁsa-Jātaka) 204

95 - Clear-sighted the Great, King of the World [Impermanence]
(Mahāsudassana-Jātaka)...207

96, 132 - The Prince and the She-devils (Telapatta-Jātaka)...................211
Chapter 1. Five Meals in the Forest 211
Chapter 2. A Feast in the Palace...216

97 - A Man Named Bad [Self Acceptance] (Nāmasiddhi-Jātaka) 219

98 - A Man Named Wise [Cheating] (Kūṭavāṇija-Jātaka) 222

99, 101, 134 - Achieving Nothing [No Thing] (Parosahassa-Jātaka).........225

100 - A Mother's Wise Advice [Nonviolence] (Asātarūpa-Jātaka,
Aghātarūpa-Jātaka)...228

Appendix A : Who Was the Bodhisatta? 231

Appendix B : An Arrangement of Morals 233

Interpreter's Introduction to the 1st Edition   239

514 - King Six Tusker and the Queen Who Hated Him
(Chaddanta-Jātaka)...241
Chapter 1. Rebirth of the Bodhisatta 241
Chapter 2. Home and Family 243
Chapter 3. The Hate-filled Queen 246
Chapter 4. The Hunt 249
Chapter 5. The Victorious Queen...253

1st Edition
Acknowledgements

The main computer system was generously provided by Thanh Van Nguyen, who also gave valuable technical assistance.

The storyteller's computer system was contributed by Karen Fazio, in memory of Beverly Vanice.

Interpreter's Introduction to the 1st Edition

This is the second volume containing fifty more Jataka stories in addition to those in Volume I issued in 1995. They highlight aspects of human character which in some respects re-enforce those emphasized in Volume I and some which are entirely new.

The Jataka stories, over millennia, have been seminal to the development of many civilizations, the cultivation of moral conduct and good behavior, the growth of a rich and varied literature in diverse parts of the world and the inspiration for painting, sculpture and architecture of enduring aesthetic value. The Buddha himself used Jataka stories to explain concepts like *kamma* and *rebirth* and to emphasize the importance of certain moral values. A Jataka *bhanaka* (Jataka story teller) is mentioned to have been appointed even as early as the time of the Buddha. Such appointments were common in ancient Sri Lanka and among others, King Ilanaga (1st century A.D.) is recorded in the *Mahavamsa*, to have heard Kapi Jataka from a bhanaka bhikkhu. It is in continuation of this noble tradition that these stories are now re-told in print to an audience which had been denied access to them by language and other cultural barriers. These stories are ever more relevant in the fragmented societies of today, where especially children, in their most formative years, seek helplessly for guidance in steering their lives to success and fulfillment.

No other civilization has been as much nourished by this rich source as that in Sri Lanka. Sinhala, the language of the people of Sri Lanka, in which script the teachings of the Buddha were written down for the first time ever, carries unerring marks of that nourishment. Both the most hallowed literary works as well as the colloquial language of ordinary present-day villagers are replete with allusions to the better-known Jataka stories. The latter would frequently refer to "King Vessantara" (who was generous to a fault), "King Cetiya" (an inveterate liar), the blind jackal (a most grateful friend), to Prince Mahaushadha (of unfathomable wisdom), to a tortoise who readily takes to water, or to the occasion when the sky fell on the hare.

There is hardly any form of Sinhala literature which has not been fed by the wellsprings of Jataka stories. Works of poetry beginning from *Sasadavata* (12th century), *Muvadevdavata* (12th century), *Kausilumina* (13th century), *Guttila kavyaya* and *Kavyashekharaya* (14th century), *Kusa jataka kavyaya* and *Asadisa da kava* (17th century) embody Jataka stories. Poems of other genre are replete with allusions to incidents and personalities drawn from Jataka stories.

Among prose works *Sulu Kalingu da vata* (12th century), *Ummagga Jataka* (13th century), *Bhuridatta Jataka* (13th century) and *Vessantara Jataka* are jataka stories re-told in inimitable fashion. Other works such as *Amavatura* (12th century), *Butsarana* (12th century) *Pujavalia* (13th century), *Saddharmaratnavalia* (13th century), and *Saddharmalankaraya* are deeply embellished with material from Jataka stories. Until quite recently, the most widely read Sinhala prose work was *Pansiya Panas Jataka Pota*, number 6 in our list of sources.

Later works of drama such as the Sandakinduru Nadagama, Vessantara Nadagama, Pabavati, Kada Valalu, Kala gola and Pemato jayati soko are based on Jataka stories.

Stories similar to Jataka stories occur in the *Vedas*. Some of the *Brahmanas* and *Puranas* are simply narrative stories. In many places, the context, the style or the core stories are altered. The same story is often told by different authors in different places, for example, *Kausilumina* and *Kusadavata* as poetry and *Pabavati* as drama are based on Kusajataka.

In Mahayana literature Asvaghosa's *Sutralankara*, Aryashura's *Jatakamala* and Kshemendra's *Avadana Kalpalata* are well-known as Jataka stories.

Indian Sanskrt works such as *Katha sarit sagara, Dasa kumara carita, Panca tantra* and *Hitopadesa* contain similar stories. These stories contributed to the later incomparable works of Kalidasa and Ashvaghosa.

There are also Mahayana Jataka stories such as *Vyaghri, Dhammasondaka* and *Seta Gandha Hasti* which do not appear in Pali at all. Some Jataka stories can be found in Jain literature, such as the story of *Isisinga* in *Suyakadanga*, which is the Nalini Jataka. They are found in even in the Mahabharata, for example Rsisringa upakhyana.

Jataka and similar other stories traveled far and wide by word of mouth along caravan routes and contributed to the literature in Persia, China, Arabia, (Arabian nights), Italy (Boccaccio's tales), Greece (Aesop's fables), Britain (Chaucer's Canterbury Tales) and Japan (Zen stories).

For developing moral conduct and good behavior, there are few more instructive foundations than Jataka stories. All Jataka stories hold out advice on how to correct our ways. They played and continue to play in some societies an enormous role in the cultivation of peace and generosity. When Buddhist monks taught children in viharas, Jataka stories took a prominent place in primary education. Young samaneras (novice monks) were required to read Jataka stories aloud after the midday meal in order that they may learn to read and preach effectively. In India these and similar other stories were a principal instrument in the socialization of children, discouraging them from selfishness and laying foundations for family had community solidarity. Jataka stories speak eloquently of those human values which contribute to harmony, pleasure and progress.

Besides literature, painting, sculpture and architecture in many parts of the world carried the message of Jataka stories. King Dutugemunu of Anuradhapura (2nd Century B.C.) had the inside shrine room of the Ruvanveliseya embellished with murals depicting scenes from Jataka stories. This practice is still carried on today in Buddhist viharas in Sri Lanka as well as in Miyanmar (Burma), Thailand, Cambodia, Laos, and Viet Nam. Fa Hien, who visited Sri Lanka in the fifth century A.D., recorded that at festival times the city of Anuradhapura was festooned with paintings from Jataka stories. This practice continues today in major cities in Sri Lanka during Buddhist days of celebration. Jataka stories are well depicted in Amaravati, Nalanda, Ajanta, Ellora, Bharhut, Nagarjunikonda, Borobudur and Angkor Vat. The late historian Mackensey in *Buddhism in pre-Christian Britain* (1928) demonstrated that there were artistic works based on Jataka stories in pre-Christian Britain.

At this point I wish to draw the reader's special attention to three stories in this collection. The first is when the Enlightened one had been born as a quail. In the forest where he lived he befriended a monkey and an elephant. They raised a question among themselves: who was the most experienced and most worthy of respect?

After discussion, they came to a conclusion: whoever was the oldest would be the most experienced and the most knowledgeable. Then they had to decide which among them was the eldest and the most respected. Pointing to a very large and well-grown banyan tree the elephant said, "Can you remember that banyan tree in whose shade we used to rest sometimes? I used to scratch my tummy rubbing on it when I was very little." Then the monkey responded "Oh, I ate its tender leaves while sitting next to it when I was very young." Finally the quail chirped in, "When I was young, I ate a fruit from an old banyan tree. Afterwards I left dropping that held a seed that grew into this banyan tree." They concluded that the oldest of them was the smallest, the quail. So they began to respect each other according to their age – first the quail, second the monkey, and last the elephant.

This story teaches respect for elders. It is an essential part of the Buddhist tradition to respect seniority. Among Buddhist monks this is strictly observed and it is an offence to violate this seemingly minor rule. It also points to the need to gain control over conceit, a minor defilement. This very same respect for seniority may have led to the development of historiography.

The second story, that of a half-blind fox teaches the value of being grateful. The half-blind fox was caught by a python in his coils and was fighting for his life. A poor peasant who was collecting wood in the forest helped the fox escape from his predator. Later the same poor peasant was the victim of a python. The half blind fox who heard the screams of the peasant ran in to a village field where a group of men were ploughing field and ran away with their clothing. The villagers chased after the fox, heard the screams of the helpless man and released him from the coils of the python.

The third story relates the fate of two parrots who were carried from their nest in a storm and one dropped in a hermitage and the other in a den of thieves. The one who fell among the hermits learned and eventually practiced generosity and became quite gentle. The one who fell among thieves grew up like them – cruel, rough and wicked. This story teaches the ill of associating with bad people and helps to cultivate the mind in many ways. Generosity, the use of gentle language, the nobility of the ways of wise people, the value of morality and the evils of unwholesome associations are all thrown into high relief. In this and many other respects, Jataka stories contributed to happiness and the development of the minds of young ones. The happiness they engendered went well beyond the mundane to reach the supra-mundane. They led mankind to all that is good in this world and to the ultimate happiness taught by the Buddha.

The sources used in this second volume are as follows:

1. *Jataka Pali* (Colombo: Buddha Jayanti Tripitaka Series Publication Board, 1983) – original Pali stanzas.
2. *Jataka Pali* (Colombo: Simon Hewavitarane Bequest, 1926) – original Pali Jataka stories in Sinhalese characters.
3. *Sinhala Jataka Pot Vahanse* (Colombo: Jinalankara Press, 1928) – Sinhalese translation of Pali Jataka stories.
4. *Sinhala Jataka Pot Vahanse*, (Colombo: Ratnakara Bookshop, 1961) – Sinhalese translation of Pali Jataka stories.
5. *The Jataka or Stories of the Buddha's Former Lives*, ed. E. B. Cowell (London: Pali Text Society, 1981), 6 vols., index – English translation of Pali Jataka stories.
6. *Pansiyapanas Jataka Pot Vahanse* (Bandaragama: H. W. N. Prematilaka, 1987) – Sinhalese summaries of Pali Jataka stories.

The sequence numbers used for the stories are in the same order as in the *Jataka Pali* and *The Jataka or Stories of the Buddha's Former Lives* (numbers 1 and 5 cited above).

The publishers of this and other volumes, The Buddha Educational Foundation of Taiwan, are making an inestimable contribution of Dhamma. I offer my thanks to the Director of the Board and to all donors as well as to the office staff. They are making an essential contribution that the world badly needs today.

Since its inception The Buddha Educational Foundation has contributed to a marked rise in the reading of the Dhamma. While many kinds of reading material are cheap and widely available, the precious and valuable works on *DHAMMA* that can instruct the minds of the people are scarce and costly. The Buddha Educational Foundation and its donors have eased the severity of these problems considerably. I wish to thank them all and say, "Much merit to them". May they all be well and happy and live long. May the merit they acquired through this noble Dhammadana cause them to attain the ultimate happiness of Nibbana!

I would also like to thank John Patterson for his talents, skills and insights to create the marvelous illustrations. I wish him the greatest of success in the future.

I also take this opportunity to appreciate and thank my good-hearted friends (kalyana mitta), Todd Anderson, for his tireless effort and Tanh Van Nguyen and Dr. G. Uswattearatchi. My colleagues Ven. Higgoda Khemananda, Heenbunne Kondanna and Aluthgama Dhammajothi are also especially thanked for their assistance in our work. May they be able to realize the Dhamma and attain Nibbana!

May all beings be well and happy!

Kurunegoda Piyatissa
November 30, 1994

Buddhist Literature Society Inc.
New York Buddhist Vihara
84-32 124th Street
Kew Gardens
New York, N.Y. 11415, U.S.A.

From the Storyteller to the Listeners

When you read or listen to these very old stories, if you wonder how much is really true, the Buddha gave some advice that might help. He said that when you listen to what a monk says you should test the meaning, weigh or consider it, and depend on your own insides to know the truth of it. Then follow and practice what you know to be true.

Let us praise the Exalted, Worthy,
Fully Self-Enlightened One
and follow the Truth

(51)

King Goodness the Great
[Perseverance]
(Mahāsīlava-Jātaka)

The Buddha told this story while he was dwelling in Jetavana temple with regard to a certain monk who was lax in meditation, and who was thinking of giving up monkhood. In order to show the value of perseverance, the Buddha said to the assembly of monks gathered together in the preaching hall that in ancient times there was a king who had lost his kingdom. But through perseverance, he regained it. The monks then requested that the Buddha tell the story. And the Buddha told this story of the past:

Once upon a time, in Benares in northern India, the Enlightenment Being was born into the royal family. When he became king he was called Goodness the Great [Mahāsīlava]. He had earned this title by trying to do good all the time, even when the results might not benefit him. For example, he spent much of the royal treasury on the building and running of six houses of charity. In these houses food and aid were given freely to all the poor and needy who came along, even to unknown travelers. Soon King Goodness the Great became famous for his patience, loving-kindness and compassion. It was said that he loved all beings just like a father loves his young children.

Of course King Goodness observed the holy days by not eating. And naturally he practiced the 'Five Training Steps' [pañca-sīla-s, the first five sikkhā-pada-s], giving up the five unwholesome actions [akusala-kamma-s]. These are: destroying life, taking what is not given, doing wrong in sexual ways, speaking falsely, and losing one's mind from alcohol. So his gentle kindness became more and more pure.

Since he wished to harm no one, King Goodness the Great even refused to imprison or injure wrongdoers. Knowing this, one of his highest ministers tried to take advantage of him. He cooked up a scheme to cheat some of the women in the royal harem. Afterwards it became known by all and was reported to the king.

He called the bad minister before him and said, "I have investigated and found that you have done a criminal act. Word of it has spread and you have dishonored yourself here in Benares. So it would be better for you to go and live somewhere else. You may take all your wealth and your family. Go wherever you like and live happily there. Learn from this lesson."

Then the minister took his family and all his belongings to the city of Kosala. Since he was very clever indeed, he worked his way up and became a minister of the king. In time he became the most trusted adviser to the King of Kosala. One day he said, "My lord, I came here from Benares. The city of Benares is like a beehive where the bees have no stingers! The ruling king is very tender and weak. With only a very small army you can easily conquer the city and make it yours."

The king doubted this, so he said, "You are my minister, but you talk like a spy who is leading me into a trap!" He replied, "No my lord. If you don't believe me, send your best spies to examine what I say. I am not lying. When robbers are brought to the King of Benares, he gives them money, advises them not to take what is not given, and then lets them go free."

The king decided to find out if this was true. So he sent some robbers to raid a remote border village belonging to Benares. The villagers caught the looters and brought them to King Goodness the Great. He asked them, "Why do you want to do this type of crime?"

The robbers answered, "Your worship, we are poor people. There is no way to live without money. As your kingdom has plenty of workers, there is no work for us to do. So we had to loot the country in order to survive." Hearing this, the king gave them gifts of money, advised them to change their ways, and let them go free.

When the King of Kosala was told of this, he sent another gang of bandits to the streets of Benares itself. They too looted the shops and even killed some of the people. When they were captured and brought to King Goodness, he treated them just the same as the first robbers.

Learning of this, the King of Kosala began marching his troops and elephants towards Benares.

In those days the King of Benares had a mighty army which included very brave elephants. There were many ordinary soldiers, and also some who were as big as giants. It was known that they were capable of conquering all India.

The giant soldiers told King Goodness about the small invading army from Kosala. They asked permission to attack and kill them all.

But King Goodness the Great would not send them into battle. He said, "My children, do not fight just so I may remain king. If we destroy the lives of others we also destroy our own peace of mind. Why should we kill others? Let them have the kingdom if they want it so badly. I do not wish to fight."

The royal ministers said, "Our lord, we will fight them ourselves. Don't worry yourself. Only give us the order." But again he prevented them.

Meanwhile the King of Kosala sent him a warning, telling him to give up the kingdom or fight. King Goodness the Great sent this reply: "I do not want you to fight with me, and you do not want me to fight with you. If you want the country, you can have it. Why should we kill people just to decide the name of the king? What does it matter even the name of the country itself?"

Hearing this, the ministers came forward and pleaded, "Our lord, let us go out with our mighty army. We will beat them with our weapons and capture them all. We are much stronger than they. We would not have to kill any of them. And besides, if we surrender the city, the enemy army would surely kill us all!"

But King Goodness would not be moved. He refused to cause harm to anyone. He replied, "Even if you do not wish to kill, by fighting many will be injured. By accident some may die. No one knows the future –

whether our attackers will kill us or not. But we do know whether our present actions are right or wrong. Therefore I will not harm, or cause others to harm, any living being!"

Then King Goodness ordered the city gates be opened up for the invaders. He took his ministers to the top floor of the palace and advised them, "Say nothing and try to remain calm."

The King of Kosala entered the city of Benares and saw that no one was against him. He surrounded the royal palace. He found that even the palace doors were open to him. So he and his soldiers entered and went up to the top floor. They captured the innocent King Goodness the Great. The soldiers tied the hands of the defeated king and all his ministers.

Then they were taken to the cemetery outside the city. They were buried up to their necks, standing straight up, with only their heads above ground. But even while the dirt was being trampled down around his neck, the Great Being [Bodhisatta] remained without anger in his mind and said nothing.

Their discipline and obedience to King Goodness were so great that not a single minister spoke a word against anyone. But the King of Kosala had no mercy. He said roughly, "Come nighttime, let the jackals do as they please!"

And so it came to pass that, at midnight, a large band of jackals wandered into the cemetery. They could smell a feast of human flesh waiting for them.

Seeing them coming, King Goodness and his ministers shouted all at once and scared the jackals away. Twice more this happened. Then the clever jackals realized, "These men must have been put here for us to kill and eat." No longer afraid, they ignored the shouts. The jackal king walked right up to the face of King Goodness.

The king offered his throat to the beast. But before he could bite into him, the king grabbed the jackal's chin with his teeth. Not harming him, King Goodness gripped him tightly so the jackal king howled in fear. This frightened his followers and they all ran away.

Meanwhile the jackal king thrashed back and forth, trying madly to free himself from the mighty jaws of the human king. In so doing, he loosened the dirt packed around the king's neck and shoulders. Then King Goodness released the screaming jackal. He was able to wiggle himself free from the loosened earth and pull himself up onto the ground. Then he freed all his frightened ministers.

Nearby there was a dead body. It just so happened that it was lying on the border of the territories claimed by two rival demons. They were arguing over the division of the body, insulting each other in ways that only demons can.

Then one demon said to the other, "Why should we continue quarreling instead of eating? Right over there is King Goodness the Great of Benares. He is famous in all worlds for his righteousness. He will divide the dead body for us."

They dragged the body to the king and asked him to divide it between them fairly. He said, "My dear friends, I would be glad to divide this for you. But I am filthy and dirty. I must clean myself first."

The two demons used their magic powers to bring scented water, perfume, clothing, ornaments and flowers from the king's own palace in Benares. He bathed, perfumed himself, dressed, and covered himself with ornaments and flower garlands.

The demons asked King Goodness if there was anything else they could do. He replied that he was hungry. So, again by their magic powers, the demons brought the most delicious flavored rice in a golden bowl and perfumed drinking water in a golden cup – also from the royal palace in Benares.

When he was satisfied, King Goodness asked them to bring him the sword of state from the pillow of the King of Kosala, who was sleeping in the palace in Benares. With magic this too was easily done. Then the king used the sword to cut the dead body in two halves, right down the spine. He washed the sword of state and strapped it to his side.

The hungry demons happily gobbled up the fairly divided dead body. Then they gratefully said to King Goodness, "Now that our bellies are full, is there anything else we can do to please you?"

He replied, "By your magic, set me in my own bedroom in the palace next to the King of Kosala. In addition, put all these my ministers back in their homes." Without a word, the demons did exactly as the king had asked.

At that moment the King of Kosala was fast asleep in the royal bedchamber. King Goodness the Great gently touched the belly of the sleeping king with the sword of state. The king awoke in great surprise. In the dim lamplight he was frightened to see King Goodness leaning over him with sword in hand. He had to rub his eyes to make sure he was not having a nightmare!

Then he asked the great king, "My lord, how did you come here in spite of all my guards? You were buried up to your neck in the cemetery – how is it you are spotlessly clean, sweet smelling, dressed in your own royal robes, and decorated with fine jewelry and the loveliest flowers?"

King Goodness told him the story of his escape from the band of jackals. He told of the two demons who came to him to settle their quarrel. And he told how they gratefully helped him with their magic powers.

On hearing this, the King of Kosala was overcome by his own shame. He bowed his head to King Goodness the Great and cried, "Oh great king, the stupid ferocious demons, who live by eating the flesh and drinking the blood of dead bodies – they recognized your supreme goodness. But I, who was lucky enough to be born as an intelligent and civilized human being – I have been too foolish to see how wonderful your pure goodness is.

"I promise never again to plot against you, my lord – you who have gained such perfect harmlessness. And I promise to serve you forever as the truest of friends. Please forgive me, great king." Then, as if he were a servant, the King of Kosala laid King Goodness the Great down on the royal bed, while he himself lay on a small couch.

The next day the King of Kosala called all his soldiers into the palace courtyard. There he publicly praised the King of Benares and asked his forgiveness once again. He gave back the kingdom and promised that he would always protect King Goodness. Then he punished his adviser, the criminal minister, and returned to Kosala with all his troops and elephants.

King Goodness the Great was sitting majestically on his golden throne, with its legs like those of a gazelle. He was shaded from the sun by the pure white royal umbrella. He taught his loyal subjects saying, "People of Benares, wholesomeness begins with giving up the five unwholesome actions once and for all. The highest qualities of the good person, whether ruler or subject, are loving-kindness [*mettā*] and compassion [*karunā*]. Filled with these qualities, one cannot harm another – no matter what the reason or the cost. No matter how dangerous the threat, one must persevere until the greatness of the good heart wins in the end."

Throughout the rest of his reign, the people of Benares lived peacefully and happily. King Goodness the Great continued performing wholesome works. Eventually he died and was reborn as he deserved.

The Buddha then identified the births in this way:

"The bad minister in those days is today Devadatta. The king's good ministers are today the Buddha's disciples. And I, myself, was King Goodness the Great."

The moral: "Refusing to harm others, the good heart wins over all."

$$\boxed{52, 539}$$

King Fruitful and Queen Sivali
(Cūḷajanaka-Jātaka)

The Buddha told this story while living in Jetavana temple with regard to a monk who had given up persevering in his vows. The story was told to illustrate perseverance in the face of troubles. The story is similar to the *Mahājanaka-Jātaka* [No. 539]. At the end of this story, the wavering monk attained sainthood [Arahant-ship]. Both the background behind the telling of the story, and the story itself, will come later on.

* * *

Mahājanaka-Jātaka

The Buddha told this story while living in Jetavana temple about his renunciation of lay life. The Buddha said that he gained wisdom after renouncing worldly pleasures, and after renouncing his kingdom, in former times, too. And the monks assembled in the preaching hall asked the Buddha to tell the story of the past. The Buddha told the story in this way:

Chapter 1. Rebirth of the Bodhisatta

Once upon a time in the city of Mithilā,[1] there was a king who had two sons. The older one was named Badfruit [Ariṭṭhajanaka], and his younger brother was called Poorfruit [Polajanaka].

While they were still fairly young, the king made his older son the crown prince. He was second in command and next in line to the throne. Prince Poorfruit became commander of the army.

Eventually the old king died and Prince Badfruit became the new king. Then his brother became crown prince.

Before long, a certain servant took a disliking to Crown Prince Poorfruit. He went to King Badfruit and told a lie – that his brother was planning to kill him. At first the king did not believe him. But after the servant kept repeating the lie, the king became frightened. So he had Prince Poorfruit put in chains and locked up in the palace dungeon.

The prince thought, "I am a righteous man who does not deserve these chains. I never wanted to kill my brother. I wasn't even angry at him. So now I call on the power of Truth [Saccaṁ]. If what I say is true, may these chains fall off and the dungeon doors be opened!" Miraculously the chains broke in pieces, the door opened, and the prince fled to an outlying village. The people there recognized him. Since they respected him they helped him, and the king was unable to capture him.

Even though he lived in hiding, the crown prince became the master of the entire remote region. In time he raised a large army. He thought, "Although I was not an enemy to my brother at first, I must be an enemy to him now." So he took his army and surrounded the city of Mithilā.

He sent a message to King Badfruit – "I was not your enemy, but you have made me so. Therefore I have come to wage war against you. I give you a choice – either give me your crown and kingdom, or come

---

1   Mithilā was once the capital of Videha, the kingdom of the traditional father-in-law of the Hindu god Rāma. Like the main character of the story here his name, too, was King Janaka. By the time of the Buddha, the kingdom of Janaka had disappeared and its capital city Mithilā had lost its importance.

out and fight." Hearing of this, most of the city people went out and joined the prince.

King Badfruit decided to wage war. He would do anything to keep his power. Before going out with his army, he went to say good-bye to his number one queen. She was expecting a baby very soon. He said to her, "My love, no one knows who will win this war. Therefore, if I die you must protect the child inside you." Then he bravely went off to war and was quickly killed by the soldiers of his enemy brother.

The news of the king's death spread through the city. The queen disguised herself as a poor dirty homeless person. She put on old rags for clothes and smeared dirt on herself. She put some of the king's gold and her own most precious jewelry into a basket. She covered these with dirty rice that no one would want to steal. Then she left the palace carrying the basket on her head. It was still before sunrise and no one recognized her.

She left the city by the northern gate. Since she had always lived inside the city, the queen had no idea where to go from there. She had heard of a city called Campā.[2] She sat down at the side of the road and began asking if anyone was going to Campā.

It just so happened that the one who was about to be born was no ordinary baby. This was not his first life or his first birth. Millions of years before, he had been a follower of a long-forgotten teaching 'Buddha' – a fully 'Enlightened One'. He had wished with all his heart to become a Buddha just like his beloved master.

He was reborn in many lives – sometimes as poor animals, sometimes as long-living gods and sometimes as human beings. He always tried to learn from his mistakes and develop the 'Ten Perfections' [*dasa-pāramitā-s*].[3] This was so he could purify his mind and remove the three root causes

---

2 Campā was the capital city of the Aṅga kingdom on the northwest border of modern-day West Bengal. It was a river port of considerable importance. From it, ships would sail down the Ganges and coast to such places as Burma and South India, returning with jewels and spices.

3 The 'Ten Perfections' of an Enlightenment Being are giving (liberality), morality, renunciation, wisdom, energy, patience, truthfulness, resolution,

of unwholesomeness [*akusala-mūla*-s] – the poisons of craving, anger and the delusion of a separate self. By using the Perfections, he would someday be able to replace the poisons with the three purities [*ti-pārisuddhi*-s] – nonattachment [*alobha*], loving-kindness [*adosa*] and wisdom [*amoha*].

This 'Great Being' had been a humble follower of the forgotten Buddha. His goal was to gain the same enlightenment of a Buddha – the experience of complete Truth. So people call him 'Bodhisatta', which means 'Enlightenment Being'. No one really knows about the millions of lives lived by this great hero. But many stories have been told – including this one about a pregnant queen who was about to give birth to him. After many more rebirths, he became the Buddha who is remembered and loved in all the world today.

At the time of our story, the Enlightenment Being had already achieved the Ten Perfections. So the glory of his coming birth caused a trembling in all the heaven worlds, including the Heaven of 33 ruled by King Sakka. When he felt the trembling, being a god he knew it was caused by the unborn babe inside the disguised Queen of Mithilā. And he knew this must be a being of great merit. So he decided to go and help out.

King Sakka made a covered carriage with a bed in it, and appeared at the roadside in front of the pregnant queen. He looked just like an ordinary old man. He called out, "Does anyone need a ride to Campā?" The homeless queen answered, "I wish to go there, kind sir." "Come with me then," the old man said.

Since the birth was not far off, the pregnant queen was quite large. She said, "I cannot climb up into your carriage. Simply carry my basket and I will walk behind." The old man, the king of the gods, replied, "Never mind! Never mind! I am the cleverest driver around. So don't worry. Just step into my cart!"

Lo and behold, as she lifted her foot, King Sakka magically caused the ground under her to rise up! So she easily stepped down into the carriage. Immediately she knew this must be a god, and fell fast asleep.

---

loving kindness, and equanimity.

Sakka drove the cart until he came to a river. Then he awakened the lady and said, "Wake up, daughter, and bathe in this river. Dress yourself in this fine clothing I have brought you. Then eat a packet of rice." She obeyed him, and then lay down and slept some more.

In the evening she awoke and saw tall houses and walls. She asked, "What is this city, father?" He said, "This is Campā." She asked, "In so short a time? I heard it was a long way to Campā." King Sakka replied, "I took a short cut. Now that we are at the southern gate of the city, you may safely enter in. I must go on to my own far-off village." So they parted and Sakka disappeared in the distance, returning to his heaven world.

The queen entered the city and sat down at an inn. There happened to be a wise man living in Campā. He recited spells and gave advice to help people who were sick or unfortunate. While on his way to bathe in the river with 500 followers, he saw the beautiful queen from a distance. The great goodness of the unborn one within gave her a soft warm glow, which only the wise man noticed. At once he felt a kind and gentle liking for her, just as if she were his own youngest sister. So he left his followers outside and went into the inn.

He asked her, "Sister, what village are you from?" She replied, "I am the number one queen of King Badfruit of Mithilā."

He asked, "Then why did you come here?" "My husband was killed by the army of his brother, Prince Poorfruit," she said. "I was afraid, so I ran away to protect the unborn one within me." The wise man asked, "Do you have any relatives in this city?" She said, "No sir." Then he said, "Don't worry at all. I was born in a rich family and I myself am rich. I will care for you just as I would for my own young sister. Now you must call me brother and grab hold of my feet and cry out."

When she did this, the followers came inside. The wise man explained to them that she was his long-lost youngest sister. He told his closest followers to take her to his home in a covered cart. He told them to tell his wife that this was his sister, who was to be cared for.

They did exactly as he had said. The wife welcomed her, gave her a hot bath, and made her rest in bed.

After bathing in the river the wise man returned home. At dinnertime he asked his sister to join them. After dinner he invited her to stay in his home.

In only a few days the queen gave birth to a wonderful little baby boy. She named him Fruitful [Mahājanaka, Fruitful the Great]. She told the wise man this was the name of the boy's grandfather, who had once been King of Mithilā.

Chapter 2. Gaining Power

The baby grew into a little boy. His friends took to making fun of him for not being of high-class birth like they were. So he went and asked his mother who his father was. She told him to pay no attention to what the other children said. She told him his father was the dead King Badfruit of Mithilā, and how the throne had been stolen by his brother, Prince Poorfruit. After that, it didn't bother him when the others called him "son of a widow."

Before he was 16, the bright young Fruitful learned all there was to know about religion, literature and the skills of a warrior. He grew into a very handsome young man.

He decided it was time to regain his rightful crown, which had been stolen by his uncle. So he went and asked his mother, "Do you have any of the wealth that belonged to my father?" She said, "Of course! I did not escape empty-handed. Thinking of you, I brought pearls, jewels and diamonds. So there is no need for you to work for pay. Go directly and take back your kingdom."

But he said, "No, mother, I will take only half. I will sail to Burma [Suvaṇṇabhūmi], the land of gold, and make my fortune there." His mother said, "No my son, it is too dangerous to sail abroad. There is plenty of fortune here!" He said, "I must leave half with you, my mother, so you can live in comfort as a queen should." So saying, he departed by ship for Burma.

On the same day that Prince Fruitful set sail, his uncle King Poorfruit became very ill. He was so sick that he could no longer leave his bed.

Meanwhile, on the ship bound for Burma there were some 350 people. It sailed for seven days. Then there was a violent storm that damaged and weakened the ship. All except the prince cried out in fear and prayed for help to their various gods. But the Bodhisatta did not cry out in fear; the Enlightenment Being did not pray to any god for help. Instead he helped himself.

He filled his belly with concentrated butter mixed with sugar, since he didn't know how long it would be before his next meal. He soaked his clothes in oil to protect himself from the cold ocean water and help him stay afloat. Then when the ship began to sink, he went and held on to the mast, for it was the tallest part of the ship. As the deck sank underwater, he pulled himself up the mast.

Meanwhile his trembling praying shipmates were sucked underwater and gobbled up by hungry fish and huge turtles. Soon the water all around turned red from blood.

As the ship sank, Prince Fruitful reached the top of the mast. To avoid being devoured in the sea of blood, he jumped mightily from the tip of the mast – in the direction of the kingdom of Mithilā. And at the same time as he saved himself from the snapping jaws of the fish and turtles, King Poorfruit died in his bed.

After his mighty leap from the top of the mast, the prince fell into the emerald-colored sea. His body shined like gold as he swam for seven days and seven nights. Then he saw it was the fasting day of the full moon. So he purified his mouth by washing it out with salt water and observed the 'Eight Training Steps' [*aṭṭhaṅgika uposatha*].[4]

---

4   These are the *pañca-sīla*-s, the 'Five Rules of Morality,' or first five of the ten (*dasa-*) *sikkhā-pada*-s 'Training Steps,' not taking life, not taking what is not yours, not engaging in sexual wrongdoing, not speaking falsely, and not losing one's mind from alcohol, to which are added: not eating at improper times; avoiding dancing, singing and playing music; and not wearing garlands and using unguents, perfumes and makeup. Together, these are the first eight

Once upon a time in the very distant past, the gods of the four directions had appointed a goddess [Maṇimekhalā] to be the protector of the oceans. They had told her that her duty was to protect especially all those who honor and respect their mothers and other elders. All such, who did not deserve to fall into the sea, were to be protected by her.

of the ten (*dasa-*) *sikkhā-pada*-s. The lay Buddhist community is supposed to observe the first five at all times, but on new, full and half moon days, eight *sikkhā-pada*-s, or 'Training Steps' are observed. Hence, *aṭṭhaṅgika uposatha* 'a fast day with its eight constituents.'

It just so happened that Prince Fruitful was one who deserved the protection of the ocean goddess. But for the seven days and seven nights that he had been swimming through the sea, the goddess had not been paying attention and doing her duty! She had been too busy enjoying heavenly pleasures to remember to keep watch on the oceans.

Finally she remembered her duty and looked over the oceans. Then she saw the golden prince struggling in the emerald sea after seven days and seven nights of swimming. She thought, "If I let this Prince Fruitful die in the ocean, I will no longer be welcome in the company of the gods. For truly, he is the Enlightenment Being!"

So she took on a form of splendor and beauty, and floated in the air near him. Wishing to learn Truth [Dhamma] from him, she asked, "Without seeing the shore of the ocean, why are you trying to reach the ocean's end?"

Hearing those words the prince thought, "For the seven days I've been swimming, I have met no one. Who can this be?" When he saw the goddess above him he said, "Oh lovely goddess, I know that effort is the way of the world. So as long as I am in this world, I will try and try, even in mid-ocean with no shore to be seen."

Wishing to learn more from him, she tested him by saying, "This vast ocean stretches much farther than you can see, without reaching a shore. Your effort is useless – for here you must die!"

The prince replied, "Dear goddess, how can effort be useless? For he who never gives up trying cannot be blamed, either by his relatives here below or by the gods above. So he has no regrets. No matter how impossible it seems, if he stops trying he causes his own downfall!"

Pleased with his answers, the protecting goddess tested him one last time. She asked, "Why do you continue, when there really is no reward to be gained except pain and death?"

He answered her again, like a teacher to a pupil, "It is the way of the world that people make plans and try to reach their goals. The plans may succeed or fail – only time will tell – but the value is in the effort itself in the present moment.

"And besides, oh goddess, can't you see that my actions have already brought results? My shipmates only prayed and they are dead! But I have been swimming for seven days and seven nights – and lo and behold here *you* are, floating above me! So I will swim with all my might, even across the whole ocean, to reach the shore. While I have an ounce of strength I'll try and try again!"

Completely satisfied, the ocean goddess who protects the good said, "You who bravely fight the mighty ocean against hopeless odds, you who refuse to run from the task before you, go wherever your heart desires! For you have my protection and no one can stop you. Just tell me where I may carry you to."

The prince told her he wished to go to Mithilā. The goddess gently lifted him like a bouquet of flowers and laid him on her chest, like a loving mother with her newborn babe. Then she flew through the air, while the Enlightenment Being slept, cradled against her heavenly body.

Arriving at Mithilā, she laid him on a sacred stone in a garden of mangos, and told the garden goddesses to watch over him. Then the protector goddess of the oceans returned to her heaven world home.

The dead King Poorfruit had left behind only a daughter, no sons. She was well educated and wise, and her name was Princess Sīvalī.

When the king was dying, the ministers asked him, "Who will be the next king?" King Poorfruit said, "Whoever can satisfy my daughter Sīvalī; whoever recognizes the head of the royal square bed; whoever can string the bow that only a thousand men can string; or whoever can find the 16 hidden treasures."

After the funeral of the king, the ministers began searching for a new king. First they looked for one who could satisfy the princess. They called for the general of the army.

Princess Sīvalī wished to test him, so Mithilā could be ruled by a strong leader. She told him to come to her. Immediately he ran up the royal staircase. She said, "To prove your strength, run back and forth in the palace." Thinking only of pleasing her, the general ran back and forth until she motioned for him to stop. Then she said, "Now jump up and down." Again the general did as he was told without thinking. Finally the princess told him, "Come here and massage my feet." He sat in front of her and began rubbing her feet.

Suddenly she put her foot against his chest and kicked him down the royal staircase. She turned to her ladies in waiting and said, "This fool has no common sense. He thinks the only strength is in running around and jumping up and down and following orders without thinking. He has no strength of character. He lacks the will power needed to rule a kingdom. So throw him out of here at once!"

Later the general was asked about his meeting with Princess Sīvalī. He said, "I don't want to talk about it. She is not human!"

The same thing happened with the treasurer, the cashier, the keeper of the royal seal and the royal swordsman. The princess found them all to be unworthy fools.

So the ministers decided to give up on the princess and find someone who could string the bow that only a thousand men can string. But again they could find no one. Similarly, they could find no one who knew the head of the royal square bed, or who could find the 16 treasures.

The ministers became more and more worried that they could not find a suitable king. So they consulted the royal family priest. He said to them, "Calm down, my friends. We will send out the royal festival carriage. The one it stops for will be able to rule over all India."

So they decorated the carriage and yoked the four most beautiful royal horses to it. The high priest sprinkled the carriage with holy water from a sacred golden pitcher. He proclaimed, "Now go forth, riderless carriage, and find the worthy one with enough merit to rule the kingdom."

The horses pulled the carriage around the palace and then down the main avenue of Mithilā. They were followed by the four armies – the elephants, chariots, cavalry and foot soldiers.

The most powerful politicians of the city expected the procession to stop in front of their houses. But instead it left the city by the eastern gate and went straight to the mango garden. Then it stopped in front of the sacred stone where Prince Fruitful was sleeping.

The chief priest said, "Let us test this sleeping man to see if he is worthy to be king. If he is the one, he will not be frightened by the noise of the drums and instruments of all four armies." So they made a great clanging noise, but the prince just turned over on his other side, remaining asleep. Then they made the noise again, even louder. Again the prince simply rolled over from side to side.

The head priest examined the soles of the feet of the sleeping one. He said, "This man can rule not only Mithilā, but the whole world in all four directions."[5] So he awakened the prince and said, "My lord, arise, we beg you to be our king."

Prince Fruitful replied, "What happened to your king?" "He died," said the priest. "Did he have any children?" asked the prince. "Only a daughter, Princess Sīvalī," answered the priest. Then Prince Fruitful agreed to be the new king.

The chief priest spread jewels on the sacred stone. After bathing, the prince sat among the jewels. He was sprinkled with perfumed water from the gold anointing bowl. Then he was crowned King Fruitful. The new king rode in the royal chariot, followed by a magnificent procession, back to the city of Mithilā and the palace.

Princess Sīvalī still wished to test the king. So she sent a man to tell him she wished him to come at once. But King Fruitful ignored him, simply continuing to inspect the palace with its furnishings and works of art.

The messenger told this to the princess and she sent him back two more times with the same results. He reported back to her, "This is a man who knows his own mind, not easily swayed. He paid as little attention to your words as we pay to the grass when we step on it!"

---

5   A universal monarch [*cakkavattin*] can be prognosticated by thirty-two auspicious marks that are on his body, such as webbed fingers and toes, eyebrows that are joined together, flat feet, and on the soles of his feet lines forming the image of a wheel complete with spokes and hub.

Soon the king arrived at the throne room, where the princess was waiting. He walked steadily up the royal staircase – not hurrying, not slowing down, but dignified like a strong young lion. The princess was so impressed by his attitude that she went to him, respectfully gave him her hand, and led him to the throne. He gracefully sat on the throne.

Then he asked the royal ministers, "Did the previous king leave behind any advice for testing the next king?" "Yes lord," they said, "'Whoever can satisfy my daughter Sīvalī.'" The king responded, "You have seen the princess give me her hand. Was there another test?"

They said, "'Whoever recognizes the head of the royal square bed.'" The king took a golden hairpin from his head and gave it to Princess Sīvalī, saying, "Put this away for me." Without thinking, she put it on the head of the bed. As if he had not heard it the first time, King Fruitful asked the ministers to repeat the question. When they did, he pointed to the golden hairpin.

"Was there another test?" asked the king. "Yes lord," replied the ministers, "'Whoever can string the bow that only a thousand men can string.'" When they brought the bow, the king strung it without even rising from the throne. He did it as easily as a woman bends the rod that untangles cotton for spinning.

"Are there any more tests?" the king asked. The ministers said, "'Whoever can find the 16 hidden treasures.' These are the last tests."

"What is the first on the list?" he asked. They said, "The first is the treasure of the rising sun." King Fruitful realized that there must be some trick to finding each treasure. He knew that a Silent Buddha [Pacceka-Buddha] is often compared to the glory of the sun. So he asked, "Where did the king go to meet and feed Silent Buddhas?" When they showed him the place, he had them dig up the first treasure.

The second was the treasure of the setting sun. King Fruitful realized this must be where the old king had said good-bye to Silent Buddhas. In the same manner he found all the hidden treasures.

The people were happy that he had passed all the tests. As his first official act, he had houses of charity built in the center of the city and at each of the four gates. He donated the entire 16 treasures to be given to the poor and needy.

Then he sent for his mother, queen of the dead King Badfruit, and also for the kind wise man of Campā. He gave them both the honor they deserved.

All the people of the kingdom came to Mithilā to celebrate the restoration of the royal line. They decorated the city with fragrant flower garlands and incense. They provided cushioned seats for visitors. There were fruits, sweets, drinks and cooked foods everywhere. The ministers and the wealthy brought musicians and dancing girls to entertain the king. There were beautiful poems recited by wise men, and blessings chanted by holy men.

The Enlightenment Being, King Fruitful, sat on the throne under the royal white umbrella. In the midst of the great celebration he seemed as majestic as the heavenly god, King Sakka. He remembered his great effort struggling in the ocean against all odds, when even the ocean goddess had abandoned him. Only because of that almost hopeless effort, he himself was now as magnificent as a god. This filled him with such joy that he spoke this rhyme –

"Things happen unexpectedly, and prayers may not come true:
But effort brings results that neither thoughts nor prayers can do."

After the wonderful celebration, King Fruitful ruled in Mithilā with perfect righteousness. And he humbly gave honor and alms food to Silent Buddhas – enlightened ones living in a time when their teachings could not be understood.

In the fullness of time Queen Sīvali gave birth to a son. Because the wise men of the court saw signs of a long and glorious life ahead of him, he was named Prince Longlife [Dīghāvukumāra]. When he grew up, the king made him second in command.

Chapter 3. Giving Up Power

This story happened very long ago, at a time when people lived much longer lives, even 10,000 years! After King Fruitful had ruled for about 7,000 years, it just so happened that the royal gardener brought him an especially wonderful collection of fruits and flowers. He liked them so much that he wanted to see the garden. So the gardener arranged and decorated the garden, and invited him to visit.

The king set out on a royal elephant, followed by the entire court and many of the ordinary people of Mithilā. When he entered through the garden gate he saw two beautiful mango trees. One was full of perfectly ripe mangos, while the other was completely without fruit. He took one of the fruits and enjoyed its delicious sweet taste. He decided to eat more of them on his return trip.

When the people saw that the king had eaten the first fruit, they knew it was all right for them to eat. In no time at all the mangos had been eaten. When the fruits were gone, some even broke the twigs and stripped the leaves looking for more.

When King Fruitful returned he saw that the tree was stripped bare and nearly destroyed. At the same time the fruitless tree remained as beautiful as before, its bright green leaves shining in the sunlight.

The king asked his ministers, "What has happened here?" They explained, "Since your majesty ate the first fruit, the people felt free to devour the rest. Searching for more fruits they even destroyed the leaves and twigs. The fruitless tree was spared and remains beautiful, since it has no fruit."

The king was saddened by this. He thought, "This fruitful tree was destroyed, but the fruitless one was spared. My kingship is like the fruitful tree – the more the power and possessions, the greater the fear of losing them. The holy life of a simple monk is like the fruitless tree – giving up power and possessions leads to freedom from fear."

So the Great Being decided to give up his wealth and power, to leave the glory of kingship behind, to abandon the constant task of protecting his position. Instead he decided to put all his effort into living the pure life of a simple monk. Only then could he discover lasting deep happiness, which would spread to others as well.

He returned to the city. Standing next to the palace gate, he called for the commander of the army. He said, "From now on, no one is to see my face except a servant bringing food and a servant bringing water and toothbrush. You and the ministers will rule according to the old law. I will live as a simple monk on the top floor of the palace."

After he had lived for a while in this way, the people began to wonder about the change in him. One day a crowd gathered in the palace courtyard. They said, "Our king is not as he was before. He no longer wants to see dancing or listen to singing or watch bullfights and elephant fights or go to his pleasure garden and see the swans on the ponds. Why does he not speak to us?" They asked the servants who brought the king his food and water, "Does he tell you anything?"

They said, "He is trying to keep his mind from thinking about desirable things, so it will be peaceful and wholesome like the minds of his old friends, the Silent Buddhas. He is trying to develop the purity of the ones who own nothing but good qualities. Once we even heard him say out loud, 'I can think only of the Silent Buddhas, free from chasing ordinary pleasures. Their freedom makes them truly happy – who will take me to where they live?'"

King Fruitful had been living on the top floor of the palace trying to be a simple monk for only about four months. At that point he realized there were too many distractions in the beautiful kingdom of Mithilā. He saw them as only an outer show keeping him from finding inner peace and Truth [Dhamma]. So he decided, once and for all, to give up everything and become a forest monk and go live in the Himalaya Mountains.

He had the yellow robes and begging bowl of a monk brought to him. He ordered the royal barber to shave his head and beard. Then early the next morning, he began walking down the royal staircase.

Meanwhile Queen Sīvalī had heard about his plans. She gathered together the 700 most beautiful queens of the royal harem and took them up the staircase. They passed King Fruitful coming down, but didn't recognize him dressed as a monk. When they got to the top floor, Queen Sīvalī found it empty, with only the king's shaven hair and beard still there. Instantly she realized the unknown monk must be her husband.

All 701 queens ran down the stairs to the palace courtyard. There they followed the king-turned-monk. As Queen Sīvalī had instructed them, they all let down their hair and tried to entice the king to stay. They cried and cried, pleading with him, "Why are you doing this?" Then all the people of the city became very upset and began following him. They were weeping as they cried out, "We have heard that our king has become a simple monk. How can we ever find such a good and fair ruler again?"

The 700 harem queens, wearing all their lovely veils and rich jewelry, crying and begging, did not change the mind of the Enlightenment Being. For he had made his decision and was determined to stick to it. He had given up the gold anointing bowl of state, which had passed the power of the royal family to him. Instead he now carried only the plain clay begging bowl of a humble monk, a seeker of Truth [Dhamma].

Finally Queen Sīvalī stopped crying. She saw that the beautiful queens from the harem had not stopped her husband. So she went to the commander of the army. She told him to set a fire among the slum houses and abandoned buildings that were in the king's path. She told him to set fires of brush and wet leaves in different areas of the city, to make a lot of smoke.

When this was done she fell to the ground at the king's feet and cried, "All Mithilā is burning, my lord! The beautiful buildings with their valuable art works, precious metals and jewels, and treasures are all being destroyed. Return, oh king, and save your riches before it is too late."

But the Enlightenment Being replied, "All these things belong to others. I own nothing. So I'm not afraid of losing anything. And losing things can't make me sad. My mind is at peace."

Then he left the city through the northern gate, still followed by all 701 queens. According to Queen Sīvalī's instructions, they showed him villages being robbed and destroyed. There were armed men attacking, while others seemed wounded and dead. But what looked like blood was really just red dye, and the dead were only pretending. The king knew it was a trick, since there were no actual robbers and plunderers in the kingdom in the first place.

After walking still farther, the king stopped and asked his ministers, "Whose kingdom is this?" "Yours, oh lord," they said. "Then punish any who cross this line," he ordered, as he drew a line across the road. No one, including Queen Sīvalī, dared to cross the line. But when she saw the king continuing on down the road, with his back to her, she was grief-stricken. Beating her breast she fell across the line. Once the line was crossed, the whole crowd lost its fear and followed her.

Queen Sīvalī kept the army with her as the entire crowd kept following King Fruitful. He continued for many miles, heading for the Himalayas in the north.

Meanwhile, there was a very advanced monk named Nārada, who lived in a golden cave in the Himalayas. He was a very wise man. By great mental effort he had gained supernatural powers that only the highest holy men are said to have. After meditating in a wonderful trance for a full week he suddenly shouted, "What happiness! Oh, what happiness!"

Then, using his special powers, he looked out over all India to see if there was anyone who was sincerely seeking that same happiness, free of all the distractions of the world. He saw only King Fruitful, the Bodhisatta who would someday become the Buddha. He saw that he had given up all his earthly power. And yet he was still blocked, still hindered by the obstacle of the crowd following him from his previous worldly life. In order to help and encourage him, he magically flew through the air and floated in front of the king.

He asked King Fruitful, "Oh monk, why is this crowd with all its noise following you?" The king replied, "I have given up the power of kingship and left the world for good. This is why my former subjects follow me, even though I leave them happily."

The holy monk said, "Don't be too confident, oh monk. You haven't succeeded in leaving the world quite yet. For there are still obstacles inside of you. These are the 'Five Hindrances' [*pañca-nīvaraṇa-s*] – the desire for ordinary pleasures of sight, sound and so forth; the desire to harm others; laziness; nervous worrying; and unreasonable doubts. Therefore, practice the Perfections [*pāramitā-s*], be patient, and don't think either too much or too little of yourself."

He finished by saying, "I give you my blessing – may goodness, knowledge and Truth [Saccaṁ] protect you on your way." Then he disappeared and reappeared back in his golden cave.

Due to this wise advice, King Fruitful became even less concerned with the crowd outside, realizing that the greatest obstacles, or hindrances, are the ones inside.

After Nārada had gone, another very advanced monk named Migājina, who had just arisen from a wonderful trance as well, saw King Fruitful, too. And he, too, flew through the air and floated in front of the king, and further encouraged him to be earnest in his resolve. He, too, then went back to his abode.

Meanwhile Queen Sīvalī fell at his feet once again. She pleaded, "Oh king, hear the wails of your subjects. Before leaving them for good, comfort them by crowning your son to rule in your place."

He replied, "I have already left my subjects, friends, relatives and my country behind. Have no fear, the nobles of Mithilā have trained Prince Longlife well, and they will protect and support you both."

She continued, "Oh king, by becoming a monk you are leaving me without a husband. What a shame! What am I to do?"

He said, "Only be careful to teach the prince no unwholesome thoughts, words or deeds. Otherwise you would bring painful results to yourself."

As the sun set, the queen made camp while the king went into the forest to sleep at the foot of a tree. The next day she continued to follow him, bringing the army with her. They approached a small city [Thūṇā].

It just so happened that a man in the city had bought a fine piece of meat from a butcher. After cooking it he placed it on a table to cool, when a stray dog grabbed it and ran off. The man followed the dog as far as the southern gate of the city. There he gave up because he was too tired to continue.

The escaping dog crossed the path of King Fruitful and Queen Sīvalī. Frightened by them, he dropped the meat on the road. The king saw that it was a good piece of meat and that the real owner was unknown. So he cleaned the meat, put it in his begging bowl, and ate it.

Queen Sīvalī, who was used to eating the delicacies of the palace, was disgusted. She said to him, "Even at the point of death a high-class person would not eat the leavings of a dog! Eating such disgusting food shows you are completely unworthy!" But he replied, "It is your own vanity that keeps you from seeing the value of this meat. If rightfully obtained, all food is pure and wholesome!"

As they continued to approach the city, King Fruitful thought, "Queen Sīvalī keeps following me. This is a bad thing for a monk. People say, 'He has given up his kingdom, but he can't get rid of his wife!' I must find a way to teach her she must go."

Just then they came upon some playing children. Among them was a girl with one bracelet on one wrist and two on the other. Thinking she was a wise child, the king asked her, "My child, why does your one arm make noise with every movement, while the other does not?"

The little girl replied, "Oh monk, it's because on one arm there are two bracelets, while on the other there is only one. Where there are two, it's the second that clangs against the first and makes noise. The arm with only one bracelet remains silent. So if you would be happy, you must learn to be contented when alone."

The Bodhisatta said to the queen, "Do you hear the wisdom of this child? As a monk I would be ashamed to let you stay with me in front of her. So you go your way and I'll go mine. We are husband and wife no more – good-bye!"

The queen agreed and they took separate paths. But she became grief-stricken again and returned to follow the king. They entered the city together, so he could collect alms food.

They came to the house of an arrow maker. They watched him wet the red-hot arrow, and straighten it while sighting down the shaft with only one eye open. The king asked him, "Friend, to make the arrow perfectly straight, why do you view it with one eye open and the other shut?"

The arrow maker answered, "With both eyes open, the wide view of the second eye is distracting. Only by concentrating my view in one eye can I truly see the straightness of the arrow. So if you would be happy, you must learn to be contented when alone."

The king collected alms food and then they left the city. He said to the queen, "Did you hear the same wisdom again from that craftsman? As a monk I would be ashamed to let you stay with me in front of him. So you go your way and I'll go mine. We are husband and wife no more – good-bye!" But still she followed him.

Then the Great Being cut a stalk of tall grass. He said to Queen Sīvalī, "Just as the two pieces of this stalk of grass cannot be joined again, so I will not join you again in the marriage bed! We two can never be joined together again. Like a full stalk of uncut grass, live on alone, my ex-wife Sīvalī."

On hearing this, the queen went crazy with shock and grief. She beat herself with both hands until she fell to the ground – completely unconscious. Realizing this, the Bodhisatta quickly left the roadway. He erased his footsteps and disappeared into the jungle.

First he had given up the power and wealth of a king. Now he had given up the power and desire of a husband. At last he was free to follow the path of a Truth-seeking wandering monk. He made his way to the Himalayas and in only one week he was able to develop special mental powers. Never again did he return to the ordinary world.

Meanwhile the royal ministers, who had been following at a distance, reached the fainted queen. They sprinkled water on her and revived her. She asked, "Where is my husband the king?" They said, "We don't know. Don't you know?" In a panic she ordered, "Search for him!" They looked and looked, but of course he was gone.

When Queen Sīvalī recovered from her fear and grief, she realized she felt no anger, jealousy or vengeance towards the monk Fruitful. Instead she admired him more than at any time since the first day they met, when she gave him her hand and led him to the throne.

She had monuments erected to honor the courageous King Fruitful on four sites: where he had spoken with the floating holy man Nārada, where he had eaten the good meat left by the dog, where he had questioned the little girl, and also the arrow maker.

Beside the two mango trees in the royal garden, she had Prince Longlife crowned as the new king. Together with the army and crowds of followers, they returned to the city of Mithilā.

In spite of herself, Queen Sīvalī had learned something by following, and finally losing, her husband King Fruitful. She too had tasted freedom!

The wise lady gave up her royal duties. She retired to meditate in the garden by the mango trees. With great effort, she gained a high mental state leading to rebirth in a heaven world.

* * *

After telling this Jātaka story, the Buddha identified the births in this way:

The ocean goddess Maṇimekhalā at that time was the Venerable Uppalavaṇṇā, the ascetic Migājina was the Venerable Moggallāna, the ascetic Nārada was the Venerable Sāriputta, the little girl was the Venerable Khemā, the arrow maker was the Venerable Ānanda, Queen

Sīvalī was the mother of the Venerable Rāhula, the parents were King Suddhodana and Queen Mahāmāyā, and I, myself, who have today become the Buddha, was King Fruitful."

The moral: "It's easier to gain power than to give it up."

53

A Gang of Drunkards
[Sobriety]
(Puṇṇapāti-Jātaka)

The Buddha told this story while living in Jetavana monastery about some drugged liquor.

A situation similar to that in this story happened to the millionaire Anāthapiṇḍika. Some drunkards who needed money to buy liquor thought of robbing the millionaire Anāthapiṇḍika of his rings and rich attire on his way from the palace by giving him drugged liquor. But Anāthapiṇḍika noticed that they were not drinking their own liquor, and challenged them to drink it themselves. Thereupon, the gang of drunkards fled.

Anāthapiṇḍika told this story to the Buddha. And the Buddha said, "These drunkards have tried the same trick in the past." And at Anāthapiṇḍika's request, the Buddha told this story:

Once upon a time, when Brahmadatta was king, the Enlightenment Being was born in a wealthy family. He became the richest man in Benares.

There also happened to be a gang of drunkards who roamed the streets. All they ever thought about was finding ways to get alcohol, the drug they thought they couldn't live without.

One day, when they had run out of money as usual, they came up with a scheme to rob the richest man in Benares. But they didn't realize that he was the reborn Bodhisatta, so he wouldn't be so easy to fool!

They decided to make a 'Mickey Finn', which is a drink of liquor with a sleeping drug secretly added to it. Their plan was to get the rich man to drink the Mickey Finn. Then when he fell asleep they would rob all his money, jewelry, and even the rich clothes he wore. So they set up a temporary little roadside bar. They put their last remaining liquor into a bottle, and mixed in some strong sleeping pills.

Later the rich man came by on his way to the palace. One of the alcoholics called out to him, "Honorable sir, why not start your day right – by having a drink with us? And the first one is on the house!" Then he poured a glass of the dishonest liquor.

But the Enlightenment Being did not drink any form of alcohol. Nevertheless, he wondered why these drunkards were being so generous with their favorite drug. It just wasn't like them.

He realized it must be some kind of trick. So he decided to teach them a lesson. He said, "It would be an insult to appear before the king in a drunken state, or with even the slightest smell of liquor on my breath. But please be so kind as to wait for me here. I'll see you again when I return from the palace."

The drunkards were disappointed. They would not be able to drink again as soon as they wanted. But they decided to be patient and wait.

Later that day the rich man came back to the little roadside bar. The alcoholics were getting desperate for a drink. They called him over and said, "Honorable sir, why not celebrate your visit to the king? Have a drink of this fine liquor. Remember, the first one is free!"

But the rich man just kept looking at the liquor bottle and glass. He said, "I don't trust you. That bottle and glass of liquor are exactly as they were this morning. If it were as good as you say it is, you would have tasted some yourselves by now. In fact, you couldn't help but drink it all! I'm no fool. You must have added another drug to the alcohol."

The richest man in Benares went on his way, and the gang of drunkards went back to their plotting and scheming.

The Buddha said:

"The drunkards today are the same as the drunkards before."

The moral: "Keep sober – and keep your common sense."

(54, 85)

The What-not Tree
[Prudence]
(Phala-Jātaka)

The Buddha told this story while living in Jetavana monastery about a gardener who was able to tell whether fruit on a tree was good to eat or not yet good to eat. The gardener could look up at a tree and see from the ground whether fruit was well ripened, not yet ripe, sweet, sour, bitter and so forth. The Buddha said, "This gardener is not the only one with such knowledge of fruit. Wise men in the past, as well, showed such knowledge." And at the request of the millionaire Anāthapiṇḍika, in the pleasure garden of whose mansion the Buddha and the monks had just had a meal [dāna], the Buddha told this story of the past:

* * *

Kiṁpakka-Jātaka

The Buddha told this story while living in Jetavana monastery with regard to a monk whose mind became consumed with lust after he saw a beautifully clad woman when on alms round in Sāvatthi.

When the Buddha heard of this, he summoned this monk and said to him, "Lust is like the beautiful fruit of the What-not Tree [*Kiṁpakka*-tree]. While fragrant and sweet to smell and taste, when eaten it racks the intestines with poison and leads to death. In the past, through ignorance of its nature, men were deceived by its beauty and eating it, they died. Just as those who ate the fruit of the What-not Tree died, so lust slays him who does not know its woes."

The monks then asked the enlightened one to tell the story of the past.

The Buddha told the story in this way:

* * *

Once upon a time there was a caravan leader. He went from country to country selling various goods. His caravans usually had at least 500 bullock carts.

On one of these trips his path led through a very thick forest. Before entering it, he called together all the members of the caravan. He warned them, "My friends, when you go through this forest be careful to avoid the poisonous trees, poisonous fruits, poisonous leaves, poisonous flowers and even poisonous honeycombs.

"Therefore, whatever you have not eaten before – whether a fruit, leaf, flower or anything else – must not be eaten without asking me first." They all said respectfully, "Yes, sir."

There was a village in the forest. Just outside the village stood a tree called a 'What-not Tree' [*Kiṁpakka*-tree]. Its trunk, branches, leaves, flowers and fruits look very similar to a mango tree. Even the color, shape, smell and taste are almost exactly the same as a mango tree. But unlike a mango, the What-not fruit is a deadly poison!

Some went ahead of the caravan and came upon the What-not Tree. They were all hungry, and the What-not fruits looked like delicious ripe mangos. Some started eating the fruits immediately, without thinking at all. They devoured them before anyone could say a word.

Others remembered the leader's warning, but they thought this was just a different variety of mango tree. They thought they were lucky to find ripe mangos right next to a village. So they decided to eat some of the fruits before they were all gone.

There were also some who were wiser than the rest. They decided it would be safer to obey the warning of the caravan leader. Although they didn't know it, he just happened to be the Enlightenment Being.

When the leader arrived at the tree, the ones who had been careful and not eaten asked, "Sir, what is this tree? Is it safe to eat these fruits?"

After investigating thoughtfully he replied, "No, no. This may look like a mango tree, but it isn't. It is a poisonous What-not Tree. Don't even touch it!"

The ones who had already eaten the What-not fruit were terrified. The caravan leader told them to make themselves vomit as soon as possible. They did this, and then were given four sweet foods to eat – raisins, cane sugar paste, sweet yogurt and bee's honey. In this way their taste buds were refreshed after throwing up the poisonous What-not fruit.

Unfortunately, the greediest and most foolish ones could not be saved. They were the ones who had started eating the poisonous fruits immediately, without thinking at all. It was too late for them. The poison had already started doing its work, and it killed them.

In the past, when caravans had come to the What-not Tree, the people had eaten its poisonous fruits and died in their sleep during the night. The next morning the local villagers had come to the campsite. They had grabbed the dead bodies by the legs, dragged them to a secret hiding place, and buried them. Then they had taken for themselves all the merchandise and bullock carts of the caravan.

They expected to do the same thing this time. At dawn the next morning the villagers ran towards the What-not Tree. They said to each other, "The bullocks will be mine!" "I want the carts and wagons!" "I will take the loads of merchandise!"

But when they got to the What-not Tree they saw that most of the people in the caravan were alive and well. In surprise, they asked them, "How did you know this was not a mango tree?" They answered, "We did not know, but our leader had warned us ahead of time, and when he saw it he knew."

Then the villagers asked the caravan leader, "Oh wise one, how did you know this was not a mango tree?"

He replied, "I knew it for two reasons. First, this tree is easy to climb. And second, it is right next to a village. If the fruits on such a tree remain unpicked, they cannot be safe to eat!"

Everyone was amazed that such lifesaving wisdom was based on such simple common sense. The caravan continued on its way safely.

* * *

The Buddha said:

"The members of the caravan are today the Buddha's followers. And the caravan leader was I who am today the Buddha."

The moral: "The wise are led by common sense. Fools follow only hunger."

(55)

Prince Five-Weapons and Sticky-Hair
[The Diamond Weapon]
(Pañcāvudha-Jātaka)

The Buddha told this story while he was living in Jetavana monastery with regard to a monk who was thinking of giving up his robes. The Buddha admonished him, "In the past, through perseverance in difficult situations, the wise and good gained a throne." And the Buddha told a story of the past:

Once upon a time, the Enlightenment Being was born as the son of the King and Queen of Benares. On the day of his naming, 800 fortunetellers were invited to the palace. As presents, they were given whatever they desired to make them happy for the moment. Then they were asked to tell the fortune of the newborn prince. This was so they could find a good name for him.

One of the fortunetellers was an expert in reading the marks on the body. He said, "My lord, this is a being of great merit. He will be king after you."

The fortunetellers were very clever. They told the king and queen whatever they wanted to hear. They said, "Your son will be skilled in five weapons. He will become famous as the greatest master of all five weapons throughout India." Based on this, the king and queen named their son 'Prince Five-Weapons' [Pañcāvudha].

When the prince turned 16, the king decided to send him to college. He said, "Go, my son, to the city of Takkasilā.[6] There you will find a world-famous teacher. Learn all you can from him. Give him this money as payment." He gave him a thousand gold coins and sent him on his way.

The prince went to the world-famous teacher of Takkasilā. He studied very hard and became his best pupil. When the teacher had taught him all he knew, he gave the prince a special graduation award. He gave him five weapons. Then he sent him back to Benares.

On his way home he came to a forest which was haunted by a monster. The local people warned Prince Five-Weapons, "Young man, don't go through the forest. There is a monstrous demon called Sticky-Hair [Silesaloma] living there. He kills everyone he sees!"

But the prince was self-confident and fearless like a young lion. So he pushed on into the forest, until he came to the dreadful monster. He was as tall as a tree, with a head as big as the roof of a house and eyes as big as dishes. He had two big yellow tusks sticking out of his gaping white mouth filled with ugly brown teeth. He had a huge belly covered with white spots, and his hands and feet were blue.

The monster roared and growled at the prince, "Where are you going in my forest, little man? You look like a tasty morsel to me. I'm going to gobble you up!"

The prince had just graduated from college and had won the highest award from his teacher. So he thought he knew just about everything, and that he could do just about anything. He replied, "Oh fierce demon, I am

---

6   Takkasilā, the capital of the kingdom of Gandhāra in the northwest of India, was a center of learning and trade in the Buddha's time. This was the city known as Taxila to Western classical writers.

Prince Five-Weapons, and I have come on purpose to find you. I dare you to attack me! I will kill you easily with my first two weapons – my bow and poison-tipped arrows."

Then he put a poison arrow in his bow and shot it straight at the monster. But the arrow just stuck fast to his hair, like glue, without hurting him at all. Then the prince shot, one after another, all the rest of his 50 poison-tipped arrows. But they also stuck fast to the hair of the one called Sticky-Hair.

Then the beast shook his body, from ugly rooftop-sized head to blue-colored feet. And all the arrows fell harmlessly to the ground.

Prince Five-Weapons drew his third weapon, a 33-inch-long sword. He plunged it into his enemy. But it just stuck fast in the thick coat of sticky hair.

He threw his fourth weapon, his spear, at the monster. But this too just stuck to his hair.

Next he attacked with the last of his five weapons, his club. This also stuck fast onto Sticky-Hair.

Then the prince yelled at him, "Hey you, monster – haven't you ever heard of me, Prince Five-Weapons? I have more than just my five weapons. I have the strength of my young man's body. I will break you in pieces!"

He hit Sticky-Hair with his right fist, just like a boxer. But his hand just stuck to the hairy coat, and he couldn't remove it. He hit him with his left fist, but this too just stuck fast to the gooey mess of hair. He kicked him with his right foot and then his left, just like a martial arts master. But they both stuck onto him like his fists. Finally he butted him as hard as he could with his head, just like a wrestler. But, lo and behold, his head got stuck as well.

Even while sticking to the hairy monster in five places, hanging down from his coat, the prince had no fear.

Sticky-Hair thought, "This is very strange indeed. He is more like a lion than a man. Even while in the grasp of a ferocious monster like me, he does not tremble with fear. In all the time I've been killing people in this forest, I've never met anyone as great as this prince. Why isn't he afraid of me?"

Since Prince Five-Weapons was not like ordinary men, Sticky-Hair was afraid to eat him right away. Instead he asked him, "Young man, why aren't you afraid of death?"

The prince replied, "Why should I be afraid of death? There is no doubt that anyone who is born will definitely die!"

Then the Enlightenment Being thought, "The five weapons given to me by the world-famous teacher have been useless. Even the lion-like strength of my young man's body has been useless. I must go beyond my teacher, beyond my body, to the weapon inside my mind – the only weapon I need."

The prince continued speaking to Sticky-Hair, "There's one small detail, oh monstrous one, I haven't told you about yet. In my belly is my secret weapon, a diamond weapon you cannot digest. It will cut your intestines into pieces if you are foolish enough to swallow me. So if I die – you die! That's why I'm not afraid of you."

In this way the prince used his greatest inner strength in a way that Sticky-Hair could easily understand. He knew this greatest of all weapons, the one inside his mind, was the precious diamond gem of his own intelligence.

Sticky-Hair thought, "No doubt this fearless man is telling the truth. Even if I eat as much as a pea-sized tidbit of such a hero, I won't be able to digest it. So I will let him go." Fearing his own death, he set Prince Five-Weapons free.

He said, "You are a great man. I will not eat your flesh. I let you go free, just like the moon that reappears after an eclipse, so you may shine pleasantly on all your friends and relatives."

The Enlightenment Being had learned from this battle with the monster Sticky-Hair. He had learned the only worthwhile weapon is the intelligence inside, not the weapons of the world outside. And with this diamond weapon he also knew that destroying life brings only suffering to the killer.

In gratitude, he taught the unfortunate demon. He said, "Oh Sticky-Hair, you have been born as a murderous blood- sucking flesh-eating demon because of unwholesome deeds in your past. If you continue killing in this way, it will lead only to suffering for you – both in this life and beyond. You can only go from darkness to darkness.

"Now that you have spared me, you won't be able to kill so easily. Hear this – destroying life leads to misery in this world, and then rebirth in a hell world, or as an animal or a hungry ghost. Even if you were lucky enough to be reborn as a human being, you would have only a short life!"

Prince Five-Weapons continued to teach Sticky-Hair. Eventually the monster agreed to follow the Five Training Steps [*pañca-sīla-s*, the first five *sikkhā-pada-s*]. In this way he transformed him from a monster into a friendly forest fairy. And when he left the forest, the prince told the local people about the change in the one-time demon. From then on they fed him regularly and lived in peace.

Prince Five-Weapons returned to Benares. Later he became king. Finally he died and was reborn as he deserved.

The Buddha then identified the births:

"The demon Sticky-Hair is now the Venerable Aṅgulimāla.[7] And I, myself, was Prince Five-Weapons."

The moral: "The only weapon you need is hidden inside you."

7   Aṅgulimāla was a bandit whom the Buddha converted, and who became a saint [Arahant].

56

A Huge Lump of Gold
[Moderation]
(Kañcanakkhandha-Jātaka)

The Buddha told this story while in Sāvatthi with regard to a certain monk who was overwhelmed by his teacher's instructions.

There was a young layman who was pleased by the Buddha's teachings and who decided to become a monk. But on hearing all the details of the various precepts on morality [sīla], he became overwhelmed and decided that he would not be able to observe them all. So he decided to go back to his wife and children. The Buddha heard of this, and summoned him. The Buddha told him that the rules of morality were very difficult to follow. But if he were only to follow three rules, to guard his voice, body and mind, and not to do evil whether in word, thought or deed, he would be successful in his meditation. Shortly thereafter, the monk gained sainthood [Arahant-ship].

The monks were talking about this in the preaching hall one day, when the Buddha entered. On hearing what they were discussing, the Buddha said, "Even a heavy burden becomes light, if taken bit by bit. So it was, as well, with the wise and good in past times." And on the invitation of the monks, the

Buddha told this story of the past:

Once upon a time there was a rich village. The wealthiest of the villagers decided to hide a huge lump of gold to protect it from bandits and robbers. So he buried it in a nearby rice field.

Many years later, the village was no longer rich, and the rice field was abandoned and unused. A poor farmer decided to plow the field. After some time plowing, it just so happened that his plow struck the long-forgotten buried treasure.

At first he thought it must be a very hard tree root. But when he uncovered it, he saw that it was beautiful shining gold. Since it was daytime he was afraid to try and take it with him. So he covered it up again and waited for nightfall.

The poor farmer returned in the middle of the night. Again he uncovered the golden treasure. He tried to lift it, but it was far too heavy. He tied ropes around it and tried to drag it. But it was so huge he couldn't budge it an inch. He became frustrated, thinking he was lucky to find a treasure, and unlucky to not be able to take it with him. He even tried kicking the huge lump of gold. But again it wouldn't budge an inch!

Then he sat down and began to consider the situation. He decided the only thing to do was to break the lump of gold into four smaller lumps. Then he could carry home one piece at a time.

He thought, "One lump I will use for ordinary day-to-day living. The second lump I will save for a rainy day. The third lump I will invest in my farming business. And I will gain merit with the fourth lump by giving it to the poor and needy and for other good works."

With a calm mind he divided the huge lump of gold into these four smaller lumps. Then it was easy to carry them home on four separate trips.

Afterwards he lived happily.

The Buddha then identified the birth:

"The poor farmer in the past was I who am today the Buddha."

The moral: "'Don't bite off more than you can chew.'"

Mr. Monkey and Sir Crocodile
[Good Manners]
(Vānarinda-Jātaka)

The Buddha told this story while dwelling in the Bamboo Grove temple with regard to Devadatta's attempts to kill him.

The Buddha said, "Not only today, but also in the past, Devadatta tried to kill me. But as today, he failed then, too."

And the Buddha then told this story of the past:

Once upon a time, Mr. Monkey was living by himself near a riverbank. He was very strong, and he was a great jumper.

In the middle of the river there was a beautiful island covered with mango, jackfruit and other fruit trees. There happened to be a rock sticking out of the water halfway between the bank and the island. Although it looked impossible, Mr. Monkey was used to jumping from the riverbank to the rock, and from the rock to the island. He would eat fruits all day and then return home by the same route each evening.

A high-class couple was living next to the same river – Sir Crocodile and Lady Crocodile. They were expecting their first brood of baby crocks. Because she was pregnant, Lady Crocodile sometimes wished for strange things to eat. So she made unusual demands on her faithful husband.

Lady Crocodile had been amazed, just like the other animals, by the way Mr. Monkey jumped back and forth to the island. One day she developed a sudden craving to eat the heart of Mr. Monkey! She told Sir Crocodile about her desire. To please her, he promised to get Mr. Monkey's heart for her in time for dinner.

Sir Crocodile went and laid himself down on the rock between the riverbank and the island. He waited for Mr. Monkey to return that evening, planning to catch him.

As usual, Mr. Monkey spent the rest of the day on the island. When it was time to return to his home on the riverbank, he noticed that the rock seemed to have grown. It was higher above water than he remembered it. He investigated and saw that the river level was the same as in the morning, yet the rock was definitely higher. Immediately he suspected the cunning Sir Crocodile.

To find out for sure, he called out in the direction of the rock, "Hi there, Mr. Rock! How are you?" He yelled this three times. Then he shouted, "You used to answer me when I spoke to you. But today you say nothing. What's wrong with you, Mr. Rock?"

Sir Crocodile thought, "No doubt on other days this rock used to talk to the monkey. I can't wait any longer for this dumb rock to speak! I will just have to speak for the rock, and trick the monkey." So he shouted, "I'm fine, Mr. Monkey. What do you want?"

Mr. Monkey asked, "Who are you?"

Without thinking, the crocodile replied, "I'm Sir Crocodile."

"Why are you lying there?" asked the monkey.

Sir Crocodile said, "I'm expecting to take your heart! There's no escape for you, Mr. Monkey."

The clever monkey thought, "Aha! He's right – there's no other way back to the riverbank. So I will have to trick him."

Then he yelled, "Sir Crocodile my friend, it looks like you've got me. So I'll give you my heart. Open your mouth and take it when I come your way."

When Sir Crocodile opened his mouth, he opened it so wide that his eyes were squeezed shut. When Mr. Monkey saw this, he immediately jumped onto the top of Sir Crocodile's head, and then instantly to the riverbank.

When Sir Crocodile realized he'd been outsmarted, he admired Mr. Monkey's victory. Like a good sport in a contest, he praised the winner. He said, "Mr. Monkey, my intention towards you was unwholesome – I wanted to kill you and take your heart just to please my wife. But you wanted only to save yourself and harm no one. I congratulate you!"

Then Sir Crocodile returned to Lady Crocodile. At first she was displeased with him, but when the little ones came they forgot their troubles for a time.

The Buddha said:

"Sir Crocodile is today the Venerable Devadatta. And Mr. Monkey was I who am today the Buddha."

The moral: "The bad intentions of foolish people can be easily
overcome by the wile of noble ones."
Also,
"A good loser is a true gentleman."

A Prince of Monkeys
[Carefulness]
(*Tayodhamma-Jātaka*)

The Buddha told this story while at the Bamboo Grove temple also with regard to Devadatta's attempts to kill him. The monks requested that the Buddha tell them this story of the past. The Buddha told it in this way:

Once upon a time there was a cruel monkey king who ruled in the Himalayas. All the monkeys in his band were his own wives and children. He was afraid that one of his sons might grow up and take over as king. So it was his policy to bite each son just after he was born. This altered him so he would be too weak to ever challenge his father.

A certain wife of the monkey king was pregnant. Just in case the unborn one was a son, she wanted to protect him from the cruel policy of her husband. So she ran away to a forest at the foot of a distant mountain. There she soon gave birth to a bright little baby boy monkey.

Before long this baby grew up to be big and strong. One day he asked his mother, "Where is my father?" She told him, "He is king of a band of monkeys living at the foot of a far-off mountain. That makes you a prince!"

The prince of monkeys said, "Kindly take me to my father." His mother said, "No my son, I am afraid to do so. Your father bites all his sons in order to weaken them for life. He is afraid one of his sons will replace him as king." The prince said, "Don't be afraid for me, mother. I can take care of myself." This gave her confidence, so she agreed and took him to his father.

When the cruel old king saw his strong young son, he thought, "I have no doubt that when this my son grows stronger he will steal my kingdom from me. Therefore I must kill him while I still can! I will hug him, pretending it is out of love for him. But really I will squeeze him to death!"

The king welcomed his son, saying, "Ah, my long-lost son! Where have you been all this time? I have missed you dearly." Then he took him in his arms and hugged him. He kept squeezing harder and harder, trying to squeeze the life out of him! But the prince of monkeys was as strong as an elephant. He hugged his father right back. He squeezed him tighter and tighter, until he could feel the old king's rib bones starting to crack!

After this terrible greeting, the monkey king was even more terrified that one day his son would kill him. He thought, "Nearby there is a pond possessed by a water demon. It would be easy to get him to eat my son. Then my problems would be over!"

The monkey king said, "Oh my dear son, now is the perfect time for you to come home. For I am old and I would like to hand over my band of monkeys to you. But I need flowers for the coronation ceremony. Go to the nearby pond and bring back two kinds of white water lilies, three kinds of blue water lilies and five types of lotuses."

The prince of monkeys said, "Yes my father, I will go and get them."

When he arrived at the pond, he saw that there were many kinds of water lilies and lotuses growing all over it. But instead of jumping right in and picking them, he investigated carefully. He walked slowly along the bank. He noticed there were footprints going into the pond, but none coming out! After considering, he realized this was a sure sign the pond was possessed by a water demon. He also realized his father must have sent him there to be killed.

He investigated further, until he found a narrow part of the pond. There, with great effort, he was able to jump from one side clear across to the other. In the midst of his leap he reached down and picked flowers, without actually getting into the water. Then he jumped back again, picking more flowers. He continued jumping back and forth, collecting lots of flowers.

Suddenly the water demon stuck his head up above the water. He exclaimed, "In all the time I've lived here, I have never seen anyone, man or beast, as wise as this monkey! He has picked all the flowers he wanted, without ever coming within the grasp of my power, here in my kingdom of water."

Then the ferocious demon made a path for himself through the water and came up onto the bank. He said, "My lord, king of monkeys, there are three qualities [*tayo-dhamma*-s] that make a person unbeatable by his enemies. It appears that you have all three – skill, courage and wisdom. You must be truly invincible! Tell me, mighty one, why have you collected all those flowers?"

The prince of monkeys replied, "My father wants to make me king in his place. He sent me to gather these flowers for the coronation ceremony."

The water demon said, "You are too noble to be burdened by carrying these flowers. Let me carry them for you." He picked up all the flowers and followed him.

From a distance, the monkey king saw the water demon carrying the flowers and following the prince. He thought, "I sent him to get flowers, thinking he would be eaten by the demon. But instead he has made the water demon his servant. I am lost!"

The monkey king was afraid all his unwholesome deeds had caught up with him. He went into a sudden panic, which caused his heart to break into seven pieces. Of course this killed him on the spot!

The monkey band voted to make the strong young prince the new king.

The Buddha said:

"The monkey king was the Venerable Devadatta. And I who am today the Buddha was his son."

The moral: "It pays to be careful."

Two Ways of Beating a Drum
[Excess]
(Bherivāda-Jātaka)

The Buddha told this story while living in Jetavana monastery about a disobedient monk. The Buddha said, "This is not the first time that you are disobedient. You were just so in the past, too." And the monks present asked the Buddha to tell the story of the past.

This is how it was:

Once upon a time there was a drummer living in a small country village. He heard there was going to be a fair in the city of Benares. So he decided to go there and earn some money by playing his drums. He took his son along to accompany him when playing music written for two sets of drums.

The two drummers, father and son, went to the Benares Fair. They were very successful. Everyone liked their drum playing and gave generously to them. When the fair was over they began the trip home to their little village.

On the way they had to go through a dark forest. It was very dangerous because of muggers who robbed the travelers.

The drummer boy wanted to protect his father and himself from the muggers. So he beat his drums as loudly as he could, without stopping. "The more noise, the better!" he thought.

The drummer man took his son aside. He explained to him that when large groups passed by, especially royal processions, they were in the habit of beating drums. They did this at regular intervals, in a very dignified manner, as if they feared no one. They would beat a drum roll, remain silent, then beat again with a flourish, and so on. He told his son to do likewise, to fool the muggers into thinking there was a powerful lord passing by.

But the boy ignored his father's advice. He thought he knew best. "The more noise, the better!" he thought.

Meanwhile, a gang of muggers heard the boy's drumming. At first they thought it must be a powerful rich man approaching, with heavy security. But then they heard the drumming continue in a wild fashion without stopping. They realized that it sounded frantic, like a frightened little dog barking at a calm big dog.

So they went to investigate and found only the father and son. They beat them up, robbed all their hard-earned money, and escaped into the forest.

The Buddha then identified the births in this way:

"The drummer is today this disobedient monk. And I who am today the Buddha was his father."

* * *

60. *Saṅkhadhamana-Jātaka*

The Buddha told this story also while living in Jetavana monastery about another disobedient monk. The story is the same as just before, except here the father and son are conch-blowers. And here it is the father who keeps blowing his conch as they pass through a dark forest, and the son who admonishes his father not to do so.

The Buddha identified the births in this way:

"The conch-blowing father is today this disobedient monk. And I who am today the Buddha was his son."

* * *

The moral: "Overdoing leads to a downfall."

61

Two Mothers
[Renunciation]
(Asātamanta-Jātaka)

The Buddha told this story while living in Jetavana temple with regard to a monk who was love-stricken by a woman. The Buddha told him, "Oh monk, women will cause you misery. Why be love-stricken if it will lead to unhappiness?" And the Buddha told this story of the past:

Once upon a time there was a very well-known teacher in the city of Takkasilā, in northern India. He taught religion, as well as all other subjects. His knowledge was enormous and his teaching ability made him world-famous.

At that time a son was born to a rich family in Benares. The family kept a holy fire burning constantly from that day on. When the son turned 16, they gave him a choice. They said, "This holy fire has been burning since your birth. If you wish to be reborn in a high heaven world, take it into the forest and worship the fire god.

"However, if you wish to live the home life of a family man, you must learn how to manage the wealth of our family in the affairs of the world. If that is the life you choose, go and study under the world-famous teacher of Takkasilā."

The young man said, "I don't want to be a holy man. I would much rather be a family man. Then I will be happy for the rest of my life." So his parents sent him to the world- famous teacher. They gave him a thousand gold coins to pay for his lessons.

After several years the man graduated with honors and returned home to Benares.

Meanwhile, his parents had come to wish more and more that he would become a holy man in the forest. This was just as they had wished on the day he was born. His mother wanted the best life possible for her son. She thought, "My son wants to marry and raise a family. He does not realize how dangerous a wicked woman can be to a man. I must find a way to get his teacher to teach him this."

So the wise woman asked her son, "Did you earn only the Ordinary Degree without also obtaining the higher Unhappiness Degree?" Her son replied, "I have earned only the Ordinary Degree."

His mother said, "How can you be called educated in the ways of the world if you have learned nothing about unhappiness? Return to the great teacher and ask for the Unhappiness Degree." The son dutifully followed his good mother's advice and returned to Takkasilā.

It just so happened that the world-famous teacher had a mother who was 120 years old. She was blind and very weak. The teacher bathed and fed and cared for her with his own hands. Since it took more and more of his time, he was forced to give up teaching. He and his mother moved into a forest hut, where he looked after her, night and day.

When the young student arrived from Benares he found that his old teacher was no longer at the college. Hearing that he had retired to the forest, he went and found him there.

After greeting each other, the teacher asked him, "Why have you come back so soon?" He replied, "Honorable professor, you did not give me the Unhappiness Degree." "Who told you about that degree?" asked the teacher. "My mother, sir," he said.

The teacher thought, "I've never heard of such a degree! No doubt his wise mother wanted me to teach him how wicked some women can be. For they bring great unhappiness to men."

He said, "All right, I will teach you so you can earn this high degree. The course is a work-study program. Your lessons will consist of taking care of my old mother for me. You will bathe, feed and care for her tenderly with your own hands.

"While you are washing and massaging her body, you must say, 'Dear lady, even in your old age your skin remains fair and beautiful.' You must constantly exaggerate her beauty in this way, saying, 'When you were young, you must have been even more beautiful!' And if she says anything to you, you must tell me without shame, whatever it is, hiding nothing.

"If you do these things correctly, you will earn the Unhappiness Degree. Then your mother will be proud of you."

The student agreed and began tending to the 120-year-old lady. He bathed and fed her with his own hands. He massaged her arms, legs, back and head. While doing this he said, "Madam, it is marvelous indeed! Even in such great old age, your arms and legs are so very beautiful! I can guess how beautiful you were in your youth!" In this way he exaggerated her beauty again and again, for many days.

Gradually, desire began to arise in the old lady's mind. Even though she knew she was blind and her body was rotten from old age, she thought, "No doubt this young man would like to live with me like a husband." So she asked him, "Do you want to be with me, just like a husband and wife?"

The man replied, "Oh yes of course, madam. I want to very much. But how can I? Your son is my teacher and he is very respectable. It would cause such a scandal! I will not dishonor my teacher."

Then the teacher's mother said, "Well in that case, if you really want to be with me, then kill my son!"

The student said, "How can I kill him when I have been studying with him for so long? How can I kill him just because of this desire for you?" Then she said, "If you will stay with me and not desert me, I will kill him myself!"

As he had agreed, the student went to the world-famous teacher and told him all that had taken place. Amazingly, the teacher did not seem surprised. He said, "You have done well to tell me this, my pupil. I appreciate your good work."

Then he examined his mother's horoscope and discovered that this was to be the day of her death. He said, "I will arrange a test for her."

The teacher carved a statue from the soft wood of a tree limb. He made it look exactly like himself, life-size. He laid it in his own bed and pulled the sheet up over it. He attached a long string to it and gave it to his pupil. He told him, "Now take this string and ax to my mother. Tell her it is time to do the killing."

Obediently the student returned to the blind old lady. He said, "Madam, my master is sleeping in his bed. If you follow this string it will lead you to him. Then kill him with this ax, if you really can do such a thing!"

She replied, "If you do not abandon me, I will do it." He said, "Why should I abandon you?"

Then she took the ax in her hands. She trembled as she stood up. Slowly she followed the string to her son's bed. She felt the statue and thought she recognized her son. She pulled down the sheet from the head and raised the ax. Thinking to kill him with one blow, she struck the neck as hard as she could with the ax. But it made a thumping sound, so she knew it had struck wood.

The teacher asked, "What are you doing, my mother?" Suddenly she realized she had been deceived and discovered. The shock was so overwhelming that she dropped dead on the spot! This time the horoscope had been correct.

The world-famous teacher respectfully burned his mother's body and offered flowers on her ashes.

Then he said to his pupil, "My son, there really is no such thing as the 'Unhappiness Degree'. Wicked women cause unhappiness. You are fortunate to have such a good and wise mother. By sending you here to earn the Unhappiness Degree, she wanted you to learn how evil some women can be.

"You have seen with your own eyes how my mother was filled with craving and vanity. She has taught you this lesson. Now return to your wise mother, who cares so much for your well-being."

When he arrived home his mother asked, "My dear son, have you finally earned the high degree in the subject of Unhappiness?" He replied, "Yes mother."

Then she said, "I ask you again, my son, do you wish to leave the worldly life and go into the forest to worship the fire god? Or do you wish to marry and lead the family life?"

Her son replied, "I do not wish to lead the family life. I have seen with my own eyes how evil some women can be. There is no limit to their craving and vanity. Therefore I want nothing to do with family life. I will seek peace as a forest monk."

He respectfully took leave of his parents. After many years of peaceful meditation in the forest, he eventually died and was reborn in a high heaven world.

The Buddha then identified the births in this way:

"The nun Kāpilāni was the young student's mother. His father was the Venerable Mahā Kassapa. The Venerable Ānanda was the student. And I, myself, who have become the Buddha was the world-famous teacher.

The moral: "Wickedness between women and men brings unhappiness to both."

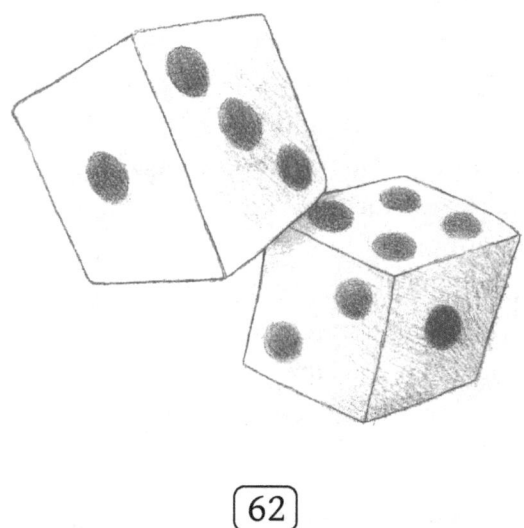

(62)

The Priest Who Gambled With a Life
[Misguided Morality]
(Aṇḍabhūta-Jātaka, Andhabhūta-Jātaka)

The Buddha told this story while living in Jetavana monastery with regard to a monk whose discipline was distracted by a woman and who wanted to give up his monkhood.

Once upon a time, there was a king [Brahmadatta] who loved to gamble with his royal priest. When he threw the dice, he always recited this lucky charm:

"If tempted any woman will, for sure,
Give up her faithfulness and act impure."

Amazing as it may seem, by using this charm the king always won! Before long, the royal priest lost almost every penny he owned.

He thought, "I have lost almost all my wealth to the king. It must be because of his lucky charm. I need to find a way to break the spell and win back my money. I must find a pure woman who has never had anything to do with a man. Then I will lock her up in my mansion and force her to remain faithful to me!"

This seemed like a good plan to him. But then he started having doubts. He thought, "It would be nearly impossible to keep a woman pure after she had already become accustomed to men. Therefore I must find the purest woman possible – one who has never even seen a man!"

Just then he happened to see a poor woman passing by. She was pregnant. The royal priest was an expert in reading the meaning of marks on the body. So he could tell that the unborn baby was a girl. And the thought occurred to him, "Aha! Only an unborn baby girl has never seen a man!"

The royal priest was willing to do anything to beat the king at dice. So he paid the poor woman to stay in his house and have her baby there. When the wonderful little girl was born, the priest bought her from her mother. Then he made sure she was raised only by women. She never saw a man – except of course the royal priest himself. When she grew up, he still kept her completely under his control. It was just as if he owned the poor girl!

The cruel priest did all this only because of his gambling habit. While the girl was growing up, he had avoided playing dice with the king. Now that she was of age, and still his prisoner, he challenged the king to a game of dice once again.

The king agreed. After they had made their bets, the king shook the dice and repeated his favorite lucky charm:

"If tempted any woman will, for sure,
Give up her faithfulness and act impure."

But just before he threw down the dice, the priest added:

"Except my woman – faithful evermore!"

Lo and behold, the king's charm didn't work. He lost that bet, and from then on the priest won every throw of the dice.

The king was puzzled by this turn of events. After considering, he thought, "This priest must have a pure woman locked up at home, one who is forced to be faithful to him alone. That's why my lucky charm doesn't work anymore."

He investigated and discovered what the cruel priest had done. So he sent for a well-known playboy character. He asked him if he could cause the lady's downfall. He replied, "No problem, my lord!" The king paid him handsomely and told him to do the job quickly.

The man bought a supply of the finest perfumes and cosmetics. He set up a shop just outside the royal priest's mansion. This mansion was seven stories high, with seven entrance gates – one on each floor. Each gate was guarded by women, and no man except the priest was allowed to enter.

The priest's lady was waited on by only one servant. She carried everything in and out, including perfumes and cosmetics. The priest gave her money for her purchases.

The playboy saw the servant going in and out of the priest's mansion. Soon he realized she was the one who could get him inside. So he devised a plan and hired some cronies to help him.

The next morning, when the serving lady went out to do her shopping, the playboy dramatically fell to the ground before her. Grabbing her knees he tearfully cried, "Oh my dear mother, it's so wonderful to see you again after such a long time!"

Then his cronies chimed in, "Yes, yes, this must be she! She looks the same – her hands and feet and face and type of dress. Yes, yes, this must be she!" They all kept saying how amazing it was that her looks had changed so little in all that time.

The poor woman must have had a long-lost son, for soon she was convinced this must be he. She hugged the king's clever playboy, and both sobbed tears of joy over their miraculous reunion.

In between bouts of sobbing, the man was able to ask her, "Oh dear, dear mother, where are you living now?" "I live next door," she said, "in the royal priest's mansion. Night and day I serve his young woman. Her beauty is without equal, like the mermaids sailors love to praise."

He asked, "Where are you going now, mother?" "I'm going shopping for her perfumes and cosmetics, my son." "There's no need, mother," he said, "from now on I will give you the best perfumes and cosmetics free of charge!" So he gave them to her, along with a bouquet of lovely flowers.

When the priest's lady saw all these, much better quality than usual, she asked why the priest was so happy with her. "No, no," said the serving woman, "these are not from the priest. I got them at my son's shop." From then on she got perfumes and cosmetics from the playboy's shop, and kept the priest's money.

After a while the playboy began the next part of his plan. He pretended to be sick and stayed in bed.

When the servant came to the shop she asked, "Where is my son?" She was told he was too sick to work, and was taken to see him. She began massaging his back and asked, "What happened to you, my son?" He replied, "Even if I were about to die, I couldn't tell you, my mother."

She continued, "If you can't tell me, whom can you tell?" Then, according to his plan, he broke down and admitted to her, "I was fine until you told me about your beautiful mistress – 'like the mermaids sailors love to praise'. Because of your description, I have fallen in love with her. I must have her. I can't live without her. I'm so depressed, without her I'll surely die!"

Then the woman said, "Don't worry, my son, leave it up to me." She took even more perfumes and cosmetics to the priest's lady. She said to her, "My lady, after my son heard from me about your beauty, he fell madly in love with you! I don't know what to do next!"

Since the priest was the only man she had ever seen, the lady was curious. And of course she resented being locked up by force. So she said, "If you can sneak him into my room, it's all right with me!"

Everything the servant took in and out was searched by the women guards at the seven gates. So she had to have a plan. She swept up all the dust and dirt she could find in the whole mansion. Then she began taking some of it out each day in a large covered flower basket. Whenever she was searched, she made sure some of the dust and dirt got on the guard women's faces. This made them sneeze and cough. Pretty soon they stopped searching her when she went in and out.

Finally one day she hid the playboy in her covered flower basket. He was trim and fit, not heavy at all. She was able to sneak him past all seven guarded gates, and into the priest's lady's private chamber. The two lovers stayed together for several days and nights. So the playboy was able to destroy her perfect faithfulness, which had been forced on her by the cold-hearted priest.

Eventually she told him it was time to go. He said, "I will go. But first, since the old priest has been so mean to you, let me give him one good blow to the head!" She agreed and hid him in a closet. This too was part of his secret plan.

When the priest arrived, his lady said, "My lord and master, I'm so happy today! I'd like to dance while you play the guitar."

The priest said, "Of course, my beauty." "But I'm too shy to dance in front of you," she added, "so please wear this blindfold while I dance." Again he agreed to her request and she put a blindfold over his eyes.[8]

The priest played a pretty tune on his complicated Indian guitar, while his lady danced. After a bit she said, "As part of my dance, won't you let me give you a tap on the head?" "As you wish, my dear," he said.

Then she motioned to the playboy, who came out of the closet, snuck up from behind, and hit the old priest on the head! His eyes nearly popped out, and a bump began rising from the blow. He cried out and the lady put her hand in his. He said, "Such a soft hand sure can deliver a wallop, my dear!"

---

8   There is here a visual and verbal pun on the state of mental blindness that the minister imposed on the young girl, "*andha-bhūta*" of one of the alternate titles of this story referring both to this state and to being blindfolded.

The playboy returned to the closet. The lady removed the priest's blindfold and put some ointment on his bump. When he had left, the serving woman hid the playboy in her flower basket and smuggled him out of the mansion. He went immediately to the king and told him the whole story, in a very boastful way of course.

The next day the royal priest went to the palace as usual. The king said, "Shall we gamble on the throw of the dice?" The priest, expecting to win once more, agreed. Just as before, the king recited his lucky charm:

"If tempted any woman will, for sure,
Give up her faithfulness and act impure."

As usual the priest added:

"Except my woman – faithful evermore!"

But lo and behold the dice fell in the king's favor and he took the priest's money.

The king said, "Oh priest, your woman is no exception! True faithfulness cannot be forced! Your plan was to snatch a newborn baby girl, lock her up behind seven gates guarded by seven guards, and force her to be good. But you have failed. Any prisoner's greatest wish is freedom!

"She blindfolded you and then her playboy lover gave you that bump on your old bald head – which proves your gates and guards were useless!"

The priest returned home and accused his lady. But in the meantime, she had come up with a plan of her own. She said, "No, no, my lord, I have been completely faithful to you. No man has ever touched me except you! And I will prove it in a trial by fire. I will walk on fire without being burned to prove I speak the truth."

She ordered the old servant woman to fetch her son, the playboy. She was to tell him to take the lady by the hand and prevent her from stepping in the flames. This the woman did.

On the day of the trial by fire, the priest's lady said to the crowd of onlookers, "I have never been touched by any man except this priest, my master. By this truth, may the fire have no power over me."

Then, just as she was about to step into the fire, the playboy leaped from the crowd and grabbed her hand. He shouted, "Stop! Stop! How can this priest be so cruel as to force this tender young lady into a raging fire!"

She shook her hand free and said to the priest, "My lord, since this man has touched my hand, the trial by fire is useless. But you can see my good intention!"

The priest realized he had been tricked. He beat her as he drove her away forever. At last she was free of him, and mistress of her own fate.

The Buddha said:

"The king in those days was I who have become the Buddha."

The moral: "You can't force someone to be good."

The Wicked Lady and the Buttermilk Wise Man
[Seduction]
(Takka-Jātaka, Takkāriya-Jātaka)

This story was also told while the Buddha was dwelling in Jetavana temple with regard to another monk who was enamored with a woman and who wanted to disrobe.

Once upon a time, a very rich man was living in Benares, in northern India. He had a daughter who was one of the most beautiful women in the city. Her skin was as soft as rose petals, her complexion was like lotus blossoms, and her hair was as black as midnight. But unfortunately her beauty was only skin deep. For, on the inside, she was very cruel. She insulted her servants and even enjoyed beating them. She became known as the 'Wicked Lady' [Duṭṭhakumārī].

One day she went down to the river for her bath. While she bathed, her servant girls played and splashed in the water. Suddenly it became dark and a heavy rainstorm came upon them. Most of the attendants and guards ran away. The servant girls said to each other, "This would be a perfect time to get rid of the Wicked Lady once and for all!" So they deserted her there, still bathing in midstream. The storm became more and more terrible as the sun set.

When the servant girls arrived home without the Wicked Lady, the rich man asked them, "Where is my precious daughter?" They replied, "We saw her coming out of the river, but since then we haven't seen her. We don't know where she went." The rich man sent out relatives to search for her, but she was nowhere to be found. Meanwhile the Wicked Lady had been swept downstream by the ferocious flooded river.

There just so happened to be a holy man living in the forest next to the river. In this peaceful area he had been meditating for a long time, until he had come to enjoy the inner happiness of a high mental state. Because of this happiness, he was quite sure he had left the ordinary desires of the world behind.

At about midnight the Wicked Lady was carried past the holy man's hut by the raging river. She was crying out and screaming for help. When he heard her, the holy man realized a woman was in danger. So he took a torch down to the river and saw her being swept along. He dived in and saved her. He comforted her, saying, "Don't worry, I'll look after you."

He carried her into his hut and made a fire to dry her off and warm her up. He gave her fruits to eat. When she had eaten her fill, he asked, "Where do you live? How did you fall in the river?" She told him about the storm and how she was deserted by her servants. He took pity on her and let her sleep in his hut for the next couple nights. He himself slept under the stars.

When she had recovered her strength, he told her it was time to return home. But she knew that he was the type of holy man who promised never to live with a woman, as husband and wife. That was why he had slept outside while she had slept in the hut.

Just to prove her own power and superiority over him, she decided to seduce him into breaking his religious promise. She refused to leave until she had tricked him into falling in love with her.

The Wicked Lady used the poses and tricks and flatteries that women learn. The holy man was not yet strong enough to resist her tempting ways. After a few days she succeeded in seducing him into breaking his promise. They began living together in the quiet forest as if they were husband and wife. He lost the inner happiness he had gained by years of meditating.

But soon the Wicked Lady grew bored with forest life. She missed the noise and excitement of crowded city life. So she cooed and coaxed until she got her way, and they moved to a nearby village.

In the beginning, the holy man supported her by selling buttermilk.[9] Later on, the villagers came and asked him for advice. They soon realized that listening to him brought good fortune. So they started calling him 'the Buttermilk Wise Man' [Takkapaṇḍita], and gave him a hut to live in.

Then one day a gang of bandits attacked the village. They robbed all the valuables and kidnaped some of the villagers, including the Wicked Lady. When they got to their forest hideout they divided up the loot. When they began dividing up the prisoners, the bandit chief was attracted by the Wicked Lady's great beauty. So he took her for himself as a wife.

All the other prisoners were soon released. When they returned to the village, the Buttermilk Wise Man asked what happened to his wife. They told him she had been kept as wife by the bandit chief. He thought, "She will never be able to live without me. She will find a way to escape and come back to me." Deciding the village was now unlucky, all the others left it. But the Buttermilk Wise Man remained in his hut, convinced that his wife would return.

---

9   There is an ambiguity here. The word "*takka*" can mean either 'buttermilk' or 'dates'.

Lo and behold, the Wicked Lady enjoyed the exciting life of bandits. But she worried that her husband would come and take her back. She thought, "Then I would lose all my newfound luxuries. I would be safer if I got rid of him. Therefore, I will send him a letter, pretending to be deeply in love with him. Just as before I will use my power of seduction to cause his downfall. But this time he will meet his death, and I will remain the bandit queen!"

When the Buttermilk Wise Man received the letter, he believed every word. He rushed into the forest and ran to the gang's hideout. When he called out to her, the Wicked Lady came out and said, "Oh my lord and master, I'm so happy to see you. I can hardly wait to escape with you. But now is not a good time. The bandit chief could easily follow us and kill us both. So let us wait until nightfall." She took him inside, fed him, and hid him in a closet.

When the chief returned in the evening he was drunk. The Wicked Lady asked him, "My lord and chief, if you saw my former husband now, what would you do?" "I would beat him up and kick him from one side of the room to the other!" he bragged, "Where is he now?" "He is much closer than you think," she said, "In fact, he is right here in this closet!"

He opened the door and dragged out the Buttermilk Wise Man. He proceeded to beat him up and kick him around the room, just as he had boasted. His poor victim did not cry out. He only muttered –

"Ungrateful hater,
Lying traitor."

That was all he said. It seemed he was finally learning a lesson – but so painfully!

Eventually the drunken bandit got tired of beating him. He tied him up, ate dinner, and passed out into a drunken sleep.

The next morning, after sleeping off his drunkenness, the bandit chief woke up sober. He began beating and kicking his tied up victim again. Still the Buttermilk Wise Man did not cry out, but kept on muttering –

"Ungrateful hater,
Lying traitor."

The bandit thought, "While I keep punishing this man, why does he keep saying the same thing over and over?" Seeing that his wife was still fast asleep, he asked him what he meant.

The Buttermilk Wise Man replied, "Listen and I will tell. I was a forest holy man, peacefully enjoying a high state of mind. One night I heard this woman crying out as she was being swept down river in a storm. I saved her life and brought her back to health. Meanwhile she seduced me and I lost all my inner calm and happiness. We went to live in a village and I led a very ordinary life. Then you kidnaped her. She sent me a letter saying she suffered living with you, and begged me to rescue her. So you see – she enticed me into this disaster. She put me at your mercy. That is why I say –

'Ungrateful hater,
Lying traitor.'"

The bandit chief was not stupid. He thought, "This man was such a good provider, and yet she has put him in this plight. What would she be capable of doing to me? It would be better to finish her off!"

He untied the Buttermilk Wise Man and comforted him, saying, "Don't worry, I'll look after you." He awakened the Wicked Lady and said, "My darling, let us kill this man right next to his own village." He took them to the boundary of the deserted village. He told her to hold her former husband. Then he raised his mighty sword and came down with it. But at the last instant he sliced the Wicked Lady in half!

Even someone as wicked as this murderous bandit can change his ways. He began by nursing his former rival back to health. After a few days of rest he asked, "What are you going to do now?"

The wise man replied, "I don't want to live as a householder anymore. I want to return to my old forest and meditate."

The bandit said, "I, too, would like to be ordained and learn to meditate in the forest." After giving up all his stolen goods, he went and lived in the forest with the Buttermilk Wise Man as his teacher. After much effort, they both attained a high state of inner happiness.

The Buddha then finalized this story, saying:

"The bandit chief is today Ānanda. And I, myself, was the holy man."

The moral: "Seduction can be dangerous to men and women both."

Country Man and City Wife
[Adultery]
(Durājāna-Jātaka)

The Buddha told this story while he was living in Jetavana monastery with regard to a layman of Sāvatthi whose wife changed her character unpredictably. Her husband could not figure her out. She upset him so much, that he neglected going to visit the Buddha. One day when he finally went to see the Buddha, with perfumes and flowers in his hands, the Buddha questioned him as to why he was absent for so long. On telling the Buddha the situation with his wife, the Buddha told him that he had already been told in the past that women were hard to figure out. But on account of re-becoming, this had become clouded over in his mind. And on so saying, the Buddha told this story of the past:

* * *

(Anabhīrati-Jātaka)

The Buddha told this story while he was living in Jetavana temple about another layman who, when he discovered that his wife was unfaithful to him, became so upset that he also neglected going to see the Buddha. When he finally went to see the Buddha, and was asked why he had been absent for so long, he told the Buddha the reason. The Buddha said, "Long ago, a wise person told you not to become upset by the naughtiness of women, but to preserve your equanimity. But on account of re-becoming, this has been forgotten by you." And at the layman's request, the Buddha told the story of the past:

* * *

Once upon a time, there was a well-known teacher who taught in and around Benares. He had over 500 students. One of these was from the distant countryside. Knowing little about the ways of city folks, he fell in love with a Benares girl and married her. After the marriage he resumed his studies with the famous teacher. But he started missing classes, sometimes staying away for two or three days at a time.

His wife was used to doing whatever she wanted. Even though she was married to the student, she was not loyal and faithful. She still had secret boyfriends.

It just so happened that after she had been with a boyfriend, she acted very humble with her husband. She spoke softly and tried very hard to please him. But on other days, when she had done nothing wrong, she was rude and domineering. She yelled at her husband and nagged him. This drove the man crazy. He was completely confused by how differently she acted from one day to the next.

The country man was so disturbed that he stayed away from his classes. And while he remained home he discovered that his city wife was unfaithful. He was so upset that he missed school for seven or eight days.

When he finally showed up, the famous teacher asked, "Young man, you have been away so long. What was the matter?" He replied, "Sir, my wife is cheating on me. She is a big problem to me. On some days she likes me very much, and acts as humble as a servant. But on other days she is arrogant and domineering, rough and rude. I can't figure her out. I don't know what to do or where to go for help. That's why I couldn't attend your classes."

The teacher said, "Young man, don't worry. Rivers can be bathed in by anyone, rich or poor. Highways too are open to all. Generous people build roadside rest houses to gain merit, and anyone can sleep there. Likewise, all are welcome to take water from the village well.

"So, too, there are some women who won't be faithful to one man. They love to keep their secret boyfriends. That's just the way some people are. It's hard to understand why they act the way they do. But why get angry about what you cannot change?

"On the days when your wife has been with a boyfriend, those are the days she acts meek and mild. But on the days when she has done nothing wrong, those are the days she acts rough and rude. That's just the way some people are. So why get angry about what you cannot change?

"Accept her the way she is. Treat her in the same understanding way, whether she is kind or mean to you. Why get angry about what you cannot change?"

The student from the countryside followed the famous teacher's advice. He no longer got upset by his city wife's behavior. And when she realized that her actions were no longer secret, she gave up her boyfriends and changed her ways.

* * *

"The husband and wife in the past are the same as the husband and wife today. And I who have become the Buddha was the teacher."

The moral: "Understanding relieves anger."

The Wisdom of Queen Tenderhearted
[Lust]
(Mudulakkhaṇa-Jātaka)

The Buddha told this story while living in Jetavana monastery with regard to a monk who, during alms round, saw a beautiful woman wearing beautiful clothing and because of this, his mind lost its equilibrium and he became consumed with desire. When the Buddha became aware of this, he said to this monk, "Such a situation is natural. It has happened before to many people of pure mind." And the Buddha told this story of the past:

Once upon a time, the Enlightenment Being [Mudulakkhaṇa] was born into a rich high-class family in Kāsi, in northern India. He grew to young manhood and completed his education. Then he gave up ordinary desires and left the everyday world. He became a holy man and went to live by himself in the Himalayan forests. He meditated for a long time, developed high mental powers, and was filled with inner happiness.

Having run out of salt, one day he came down to the city of Benares. He spent the night in the royal garden. In the morning he washed himself, tied his tangled hair in a knot on top of his head, and dressed in a black antelope skin. He folded up the robe made of red bark which he usually wore. Then he went into the city to collect alms food.

When he arrived at the palace gate, King Brahmadatta was walking back and forth on his terrace. When he saw the humble looking holy man he thought, "If there is such a thing as perfect calm, this man must have found it!" He had his servants bring him into the palace.

The holy man was seated on a luxurious couch and was fed the very best foods. He thanked the king. The king said, "You are welcome to live in my royal garden permanently. I will provide the 'Four Necessities' [*catu-paccaya*-s] – food, clothing, shelter and medicine. In so doing I may gain merit leading to rebirth in a heaven world."

The holy man accepted this kind offer. He spent the next 16 years living in the royal garden of Benares. During that time he taught all in the king's family, and received the Four Necessities from the king.

One day King Brahmadatta decided he must go to a frontier area and put down a revolt. Before leaving he ordered his queen to care for the needs of the holy man. Her name was Queen Tenderhearted [Mudulakkhaṇā].

She prepared food every day for the holy man. Then one day he was late in arriving for his meal. While waiting, Queen Tenderhearted refreshed herself in a perfumed bath, dressed in fine clothes and jewelry, and lay down on a little couch.

Meanwhile the Enlightenment Being had been meditating in a particularly joyful mental state. When he realized what time it was, he used the power of his mental purity to fly through the air to the palace.

When Queen Tenderhearted heard the rustling sound made by his bark robe, she rose up suddenly from her couch. In so doing, her blouse accidentally slipped down for just a moment – and the holy man glimpsed her from the window as he entered. He was surprised by the unusual sight of the queen's great beauty.

Desire, which had been subdued but not erased, rose within him. It was just like a cobra rises, spreading his hood, from the basket in which it is kept. His desire gained force, his perfect calm disappeared, and his mind lost its purity. He was wounded, like a crow with a broken wing.

The holy man could not eat his food. He took it back to his temple dwelling in the royal garden, and put it under his bed. His mind was enslaved by the sight of the beauty of Queen Tenderhearted. His heart was burning with desire. He remained on his bed, without eating or drinking, for the next seven days.

Finally the king arrived home again. He circled the city and then went directly to see the holy man in the garden temple. Seeing him lying in bed, he thought he was sick. He cleaned out the temple and sat down next to him. He began massaging his feet, and asked, "Reverend sir, what has happened to you? Are you sick?"

The holy man replied, "Oh great king, my only sickness is that I am caught in the chains of desire." "What is it you desire?" asked the king. "Queen Tenderhearted, my lord." "Your reverence," said the king, "I will give Tenderhearted to you. Come with me."

When they arrived at the palace, King Brahmadatta had his queen dressed in her finest clothing and jewelry. Then he secretly told her to help the unfortunate holy man regain his purity. She replied, "I know what to do, my lord, I will save him." Then the king gave her away and she left the palace with the holy man.

After they passed through the main gate she said, "We must have a house to live in. Go back and ask the king for one." He returned and asked the king for a house. The king gave them a tiny run-down hut that people had been using as an outhouse.

The holy man took the queen to their new home, but she refused to go inside. He asked why. She said, "Because it's filthy! Go back to the king and get a shovel and basket." He obeyed and when he returned she ordered him to do all the cleaning. He even had to plaster the walls and floor with fresh cow dung!

Then she commanded him to go to the palace and get her a bed. Then a chair. Then a lamp, bed linen, a cooking pot, a water pot. She ordered him to get all these things one at a time, and he obeyed dutifully. She sent him to get water for her bath and many other things. He set out the water for her bath and then made up the bed.

Finally they sat down next to each other on the bed. Suddenly she grabbed him by the whiskers, shook him back and forth, pulled him towards her and said, "Don't you remember that you are a holy man and a priest?"

Only then was he shocked out of his mad infatuation and made to realize who he was. Having regained his self-awareness, he thought, "Oh what a pitiful state I have fallen into. I have been blinded by my desire into becoming a slave. Beginning with only the sight of a woman, this mad craving could lead me into a hell world. My body was burning, as if I'd been shot in the heart with an arrow of desire. But there was no bleeding wound! Not seeing her body as it really was, my own foolishness caused all my suffering!"

Then he spoke out loudly, "On this very day I will return the wise Queen Tenderhearted to the noble King Brahmadatta. Then I will fly back to my forest home!"

After taking her back, he said to the king, "I don't want your queen anymore. Before I had her, she was my one desire. After I got her, one desire led to another endlessly, leading only to hell."

The wise Queen Tenderhearted, by using her intelligence and knowledge of life, had given a great gift to the holy man. Rather than taking advantage of his weakness, she had restored his purity.

In perfect calm the Enlightenment Being rose into the air, preached to the king, and then magically flew to the Himalayan forests. He never again returned to the ordinary world. After meditating for years in peace and joy, he died and was reborn in a high heaven world.

The Buddha then identified the births, saying:

"The king in those days is today the Venerable Ānanda. Queen Tenderhearted is today the nun Uppalavaṇṇā. And I, myself, was the holy man."

The moral: "Desire enslaves. Wisdom liberates."

A Wife and Mother Who Was a Sister First
[An Intelligent Woman]
(Ucchaṅga-Jātaka)

The Buddha told this story while living in Jetavana temple about a countrywoman who cried, as if in mourning. The Buddha said she did just so before. And he told this story of the past:

Once upon a time some bandits robbed a village. Then they escaped into a thick forest. Some men from the village chased them. They surrounded the forest and searched it for the robbers, but they could not find them.

When they came out of the forest they saw three farmers plowing in their field. They immediately captured them and said, "Aha! You bandits are pretending to be innocent farmers interested only in plowing! Come with us to the king, you thieves!" They tied them up and took them as prisoners to the king. He locked them in the palace dungeon.

Then a woman began coming to the palace courtyard. For several days she came and cried, as if in mourning.

One day the king heard her cries and asked her to come inside. He asked why she was crying. She said, "I have heard that my husband, son and brother are all your prisoners, my lord."

The king had the three men brought up from the dungeon. Being a generous ruler, he said to the woman, "I will give you one of these three. Which one do you choose?"

The woman asked, "Can't you give me all three, my lord?" The king replied, "No, I cannot."

After carefully considering, she said, "If you will not give me all three, then give me my brother, oh lord king."

The king was surprised by her choice. He said, "You should choose your husband or son. Why would you want your brother instead?"

The smart woman replied, "Oh my lord, when I go out onto the roadway, a new husband would be easy to find. And then I could easily have another son. A husband or a son is easy to come by in this world. But since my parents are dead, I could never get another brother!"

The king was impressed by the intelligence and thinking ability shown by this simple woman. Some of his own ministers were not nearly as smart! So he decided to reward her. He said, "I return all three to you – your brother, husband and son."

The Buddha said:

"The woman today is the same as the woman then. And the three men then were the same as three men today whose arrest was the cause for this woman's crying as if in mourning, today."

The moral: "It's a fortunate brother who has an intelligent sister."

3,000 Births
[Rebirth]
(*Sāketa-Jātaka*)

When the Buddha was staying in the garden named Añjanavana near Sāketa, this story was told to a Brahmin of that town.

One day, when the Buddha was going on alms round in the city of Sāketa, an old Brahmin fell at the Buddha's feet and said, "Son, why have you been gone for so long? It is the duty of children to take care of their parents in their old age? Come, your mother is waiting for you at home." The Brahmin then took the Buddha, together with the monks, to his house where his wife, too, greeted the Buddha saying, "Son, why have you been gone for so long? Is it not the duty of children to take care of their parents in their old age?" And the Buddha and the monks were shown hospitality [*dāna*]. The Buddha then recited the *Jarā Sutta*, the *sutta* concerning old age.[10] And the Brahmin and his wife attained the once-returner state of mind, becoming Sakadāgāmin-s. The Buddha and the monks then went back to Añjanavana.

The monks discussed this in the evening in the preaching hall. They said that the Buddha must be well aware that Suddhodana was his father,

10 The *Jarā Sutta* is the sixth *sutta* in the *Aṭṭhakavagga* of the *Sutta Nipāta*.

and Mahāmāyā his mother, yet the Buddha said nothing when this couple claimed him as their son. Hearing them talk, the Buddha said, "Oh monks, this old couple was correct in claiming me as their son." And saying this, he told a story of the past:

Once upon a time the Bodhisatta – the Enlightenment Being – was born into an ordinary family. It just so happened that he had the same father in his next 500 rebirths. The father was then reborn as the uncle in the next 500 rebirths, and the grandfather in the next 500.

In the next 500 rebirths he had the same mother, who was reborn as the aunt in the next 500, and finally the grandmother in the next 500.

Amazing as it may seem, after 3,000 rebirths, the man of 1,500 and the woman of 1,500 rebirths were reborn and became husband and wife. But the Bodhisatta was reborn with a different mother and father! However, he wisely respected everyone, not just the mother and father of his present rebirth.

The Buddha explained the connection in this way:

"This Brahmin and his wife were those relatives through all those lives. They were my parents in many births, and I who am today the Buddha was their son in many births."

The moral: "One way or another, we're all related."

(69)

The Strong-minded Snake
[Determination]
(Visavanta-Jātaka)

The Buddha delivered this Jātaka story when he was in Jetavana monastery with regard to the Venerable Sāriputta.

One day, villagers brought sweetcakes to the monks at the monastery, and most of these were eaten. It was suggested that what remained should be saved for those monks who were absent in the village. This was done, but one young monk who returned very late found that Sāriputta had eaten the sweetcakes set aside for him. Disappointed, he said, "Sāriputta must have a sweet tooth! After all, who does not like sweets?" This troubled Sāriputta a great deal, and he decided never again to eat sweetcakes.

This abstention became common knowledge among the monks. One day, the monks gathered in the evening in the preaching hall were talking about this, when the Buddha entered. The Buddha told them that Sāriputta, once he has given anything up, would never return to it even though his life might be at stake. And the Buddha told this story of the past:

Once upon a time there was a doctor who was an expert at treating snakebites. One day he was called for by the relatives of a man who had been bitten by a deadly poisonous snake.

The doctor told them, "There are two ways of treating this snakebite. One is by giving medicine. The other is by capturing the snake who bit him, and forcing him to suck out his own poison." The family said, "We would like to find the snake and make him suck the poison out."

After the snake was caught, the doctor asked him, "Did you bite this man?" "Yes, I did," said the snake. "Well then," said the doctor, "You must suck your own poison out of the wound." But the strong-willed snake replied, "Take back my own poison? Never! I have never done such a thing and I never will!"

Then the doctor started a wood fire and said to the snake, "If you don't suck that poison out, I'll throw you in this fire and burn you up!"

But the snake had made up his mind. He said, "I'd rather die!" And he began moving towards the fire.

In all his years, the snakebite expert doctor had never seen anything like this! He took pity on the courageous snake, and kept him from entering the flames. He used his medicines and magic spells to remove the poison from the suffering man.

The doctor admired the snake's single-minded determination. He knew that if he used his determination in a wholesome way he could improve himself. So he taught him the Five Training Steps [*pañca-sīla-s*, the first five *sikkhā-pada-s*] to avoid unwholesome actions. Then he set him free and said, "Go in peace and harm no one."

At the end of this story, the Buddha identified the births, saying:

"Sāriputta was the snake in those times. And I who have become the Buddha was the doctor."

The moral: "Determination wins respect."

The Shovel Wise Man
[Renunciation]
(Kuddāla-Jātaka)

The Buddha told this story while he was dwelling in Jetavanārāma with regard to the Venerable Cittahattha Sāriputta.

The Venerable Cittahattha Sāriputta, when he was living as a layman, used to till fields for people, for which he got paid. One day, he happened to go to the monastery, and there he was given very delicious food, much more tasty than the food he was used to eating. This made him think to himself that rather than exert great effort in tilling fields, he ought to become a monk. And he entered the monkhood [Saṅgha]. As he had difficulty in keeping his mind focused for meditation, though, after several weeks he disrobed. But then, his belly drew him back to the monkhood again. This happened six times. Then, the seventh time he came back to the order, through his chanting and meditation, he became an Arahant [saint]. Other monks chided him, and asked when he would be leaving them again. The Buddha told them, though, that this would not happen. And saying this, the Buddha told them a story of the past:

Once upon a time, the Enlightenment Being was born into a family of vegetable gardeners. After he grew up he cleared a patch of land with his shovel. He grew herbs, pumpkins, melons, cucumbers and other vegetables. These he sold to earn a humble living.

The shovel was his one and only possession in the whole world. He carried it with him everywhere. Some people thought he carried it in the same way a forest monk carries his walking staff. So he became known as the 'Shovel Wise Man' [Kuddālapaṇḍita].

One day he thought, "What good does it do me to live the ordinary everyday life of a gardener? I will give up this life and go meditate in the forest. Then I will be peaceful and happy." So the Shovel Wise Man hid his one possession, his shovel, and became a forest meditator.

Before too long, he started thinking about his only possession, his shovel. He was so attached to this shovel that he couldn't get it out of his mind, no matter how hard he tried! Trying to meditate seemed useless, so he gave it up. He returned to his shovel and his ordinary life as a vegetable gardener.

Lo and behold, in a little while the Shovel Wise Man again gave up the everyday life, hid his shovel and became a forest meditator. Again he could not get his shovel out of his mind, and returned to being a gardener. All in all, this happened six times!

The next time the Shovel Wise Man gave up his forest meditation, he finally realized it was because of his old worn out shovel that he had gone back and forth seven times! So he decided to throw it away, once and for all, in a deep river. Then he would return to the forest for good.

He took his shovel down to the riverbank. He thought, "Let me not see where this shovel enters the water. Otherwise it may tempt me again to give up my quest." So he closed his eyes, swung the shovel in a circle over his head three times, and let it fly into the midst of the river. Realizing that he would never be able to find the shovel again, he shouted, just like a lion roars, "I have conquered! I have conquered! I have conquered!"

It just so happened that the King of Benares [Brahmadatta] was riding by at that very moment. He was returning from putting down a revolt in a border village. He had bathed in the river, and had just seated himself on his magnificent royal elephant. He was riding back to Benares in a victory procession.

When he heard the triumphant shouts of the Enlightenment Being, he said to his ministers, "Listen. Who is shouting, just like a lion roars, 'I have conquered'? Whom has he conquered? Bring that man to me!"

When they brought the Shovel Wise Man to him, the king said,

"I am a conqueror because I have won a battle. You say that you have conquered. Whom did you conquer?"

The Enlightenment Being replied, "Your lordship, even if you conquer a hundred thousand armies, they are meaningless victories if you still have unwholesome thoughts and desires in your own mind! By conquering the craving in my mind, I know I have won the battle against unwholesome thoughts."

As he spoke he concentrated his mind on the water in the river, then on the idea of water itself, and reached a high mental state. In a sitting position he rose into the air. He preached these words of Truth [Dhamma] to the king: "Defeating an enemy who returns to fight you again and again is no real victory. But if you defeat the unwholesomeness in your own mind, no one can take that true victory from you!"

While the king was listening to these words, all unwholesome thoughts left his mind. It occurred to him to give up the ordinary world and seek real peace and happiness. He asked, "Where are you going now, wise one?" He answered, "I am going to the Himalayas, oh king, to practice meditation." The king said, "Please take me with you. I too wish to give up the common worldly life." Lo and behold, as the king turned northward with the Shovel Wise Man, so did the entire army and all the royal ministers and attendants.

Soon the news reached the people of Benares that the king and all those with him were leaving the ordinary world and following the Shovel Wise Man to the Himalayas. Then all the people in the entire city of Benares followed them towards the northern mountains. Benares was empty!

This great migration of people came to the attention of the god Sakka, King of the Heaven of 33. Never had he seen so many giving up worldly power. He ordered the architect of the gods [Vissakamma] to build a dwelling place in the Himalayan forests for all these people.

When they arrived in the Himalayas, the Shovel Wise Man was the first to announce that he had given up the ordinary world for good. Then all those with him did the same. Never was so much worldly power given up, or renounced, at the same time.

The Shovel Wise Man developed what holy men call the 'Four Heavenly States of Mind' [*cattāri-brahma-vihāra-s*]. First is loving-kindness [*mettā*], tender affection for all. Second is feeling sympathy and pity for all those who suffer [*karuṇā*]. Third is feeling happiness for all those who are joyful [*muditā*]. And the fourth state is balance and calm, even in the face of difficulties or troubles [*upekkhā*].

He taught the others advanced meditation. With great effort they all gained high mental states, leading to rebirth in heaven worlds.

The story having been told, the Buddha said:

"Ānanda was King Brahmadatta at that time. The Buddha's followers today were King Brahmadatta's followers. And the Shovel Wise Man was I who am today the fully enlightened one."

The moral: "Only one possession is enough to keep the mind from finding freedom."

[71]

The Green Wood Gatherer
[Laziness]
(*Varaṇa-Jātaka*)

When the Buddha was living in Jetavanārāma, this Jātaka story was told with regard to the Venerable Kuṭumbiyaputtatissa.

Kuṭumbiyaputtatissa once went to Jetavana temple with twenty-nine of his friends from Sāvatthi to make offerings to the Buddha. Hearing the Buddha preach, they all became monks. After staying there for five years with their teachers, they wished to go off into the forest to become ascetics and meditate. After asking the Buddha for topics for their meditation, they left Jetavanārāma. But Kuṭumbiyaputtatissa weakened in his determination, thinking of the hardships of ascetic life and the sweet food available at the temple. And he turned back.

When the rainy season was over the others, having all gained Arahant-ship [sainthood, through the eradication of defilement], returned to Jetavanārāma to see the Buddha. Kuṭumbiyaputtatissa heard the Buddha praise them, and set his mind on following their example. When they obtained permission to go back to the forest, he decided to return with them. That same night, though, filled with a yearning to begin his austerities at once, he slept in an upright posture. But in the middle of the night, he fell down and broke his thighbone. This accident delayed the departure of the other monks. The Buddha, hearing of this, blamed Kuṭumbiyaputtatissa for his unseasonable zeal. He said that this was not the first time that their departure was delayed because of Kuṭumbiyaputtatissa. And he told this story of the past:

Once upon a time there was a world-famous teacher and holy man in the city of Takkasilā. He had 500 students training under him.

One day these 500 young men went into the forest to gather firewood. One of them came upon a *Varaṇa*-tree with no leaves.[11] He thought, "How lucky I am! This tree must be dead and dry, perfect for firewood. So what's the hurry? I'll take a nap while the others are busy searching in the woods. When it's time to return, it will be easy to climb this tree and break off branches for firewood. So what's the hurry?" He spread his jacket on the ground, lay down on it, and fell fast asleep – snoring loudly.

After a while all the other students began carrying their bundles of firewood back to Takkasilā. On their way they passed the snoring sleeper. They kicked him to wake him up and said, "Wake up! Wake up! It's time to return to our teacher."

The lazy student woke up suddenly and rubbed his eyes. Still not fully awake, he climbed up the tree. He began breaking off branches and discovered that they were actually still green, not dry at all. While he was breaking one of them, it snapped back and poked him in the eye. From then on he had to hold his eye with one hand while he finished gathering

---

11 The bark of a *Varaṇa*-tree looks dry from the outside, but inside its wood is green.

his bundle of green wood. Then he carried it back to Takkasilā, running to catch up. He was the last one back, and threw his bundle on top of the rest.

Meanwhile an invitation arrived to a religious ceremony. It was to be held the next day at a remote village. The holy man told his 500 pupils, "This will be good training for you. You will have to eat an early breakfast tomorrow morning. Then go to the village for the religious service. When you return, bring back my share of the offerings as well as your own."

The students awoke early the next morning. They awakened the college cook and asked her to prepare their breakfast porridge. She went out in the dark to the woodpile. She picked up the top bundle of the lazy man's green wood. She brought it inside and tried to start her cooking fire. But even though she blew and blew on it, she couldn't get the fire going. The wood was too green and damp.

When the sun came up there was still no fire for cooking breakfast. The students said, "It's getting to be too late to go to the village." So off they went to their teacher.

The teacher asked them, "Why are you still here? Why haven't you left yet?" They told him, "A lazy good-for-nothing slept while we all worked. He climbed a tree and poked himself in the eye. He gathered only green wood and threw it on top of the woodpile. This was picked up by the college cook. Because it was green and damp, she couldn't get the breakfast fire started. And now it's too late to go to the village."

The world-famous teacher said, "A fool who is lazy causes trouble for everyone. When what should be done early is put off until later, it is soon regretted."

After telling this story, the Buddha identified the births in this way:

"The lazy student who hurt his eye in those days, is today Kuṭumbiyaputtatissa. The other students were the Buddha's followers today. And their world-famous teacher was I who have today become the Buddha."

The moral: "'Don't put off until tomorrow what you can do today.'"

The Elephant King Goodness
[Generosity and Ingratitude]
(Sīlavanāga-Jātaka)

The Buddha told this Jātaka story while he was living in the Bamboo Grove temple with regard to Devadatta's lack of gratitude, and his not recognizing the Buddha's virtues. At the request of the monks gathered in the preaching hall, who were discussing this topic, the Buddha told this story of the past:

Once upon a time the Enlightenment Being was born as an elephant. He was wonderfully white in color, glowing like polished silver. His feet were as smooth and bright as the finest lacquer. His mouth was as red as the most elegant red carpet. And his marvelous eyes were like precious jewels, sparkling in five colors – blue, yellow, red, white and crimson.

The splendid beauty of this magnificent elephant was the outer form of the Enlightenment Being. But this was only a pale reflection of his inner beauty – because during many previous lives he had filled himself with the Ten Perfections [dasa-pāramitā-s]: energy, determination, truthfulness, wholesomeness, giving up attachment to the ordinary world, evenmindedness, wisdom, patience, generosity, and of course – loving-kindness.

When he became an adult, all the other elephants in the Himalayan forests came to follow and serve him. Before long his kingdom contained a population of 80,000 elephants. Such a large nation was crowded and filled with distractions. In order to live more quietly, he separated himself from the rest and went to live alone in a secluded part of the forest. Because of his wholesomeness and purity, which were easily seen by everyone, he was known as the Elephant King Goodness [Sīlava].

In the meantime, a forester from Benares traveled into these Himalayan foothills. He was searching for things of value he could sell back in Benares. After a while he lost his sense of direction. He ran back and forth trying to find his way. Soon he became exhausted and scared to death! He began trembling and crying out loud from fear.

The Elephant King Goodness heard the sound of the poor lost man's frightened weeping. Immediately he was filled with pity and compassion. Wishing to help him in any way he could, he began walking through the forest towards him.

But the man was in such a big panic that, when he saw the gigantic elephant coming towards him, he started running away. When the wise elephant king saw this, he stopped moving. Seeing this, the forester also stopped. Then King Goodness began walking towards him again, the man started running, and once again stopped when the elephant stopped.

At that point the man thought, "This noble elephant! When I run, he stops. And when I stop, he walks towards me. No doubt he intends me no harm – he must want to help me instead!" Realizing this gave him the courage to stop and wait.

As the Elephant King Goodness slowly approached, he said, "My human friend, why are you wandering about, crying in panic?"

"Lord elephant," said the man, "I lost all sense of direction, became hopelessly lost, and was afraid I would die!"

Then the Enlightenment Being took the forester to his own secluded dwelling place. He comforted and soothed him by treating him to the finest fruits and nuts in all the Himalayas. After several days he said, "My friend, don't be afraid. I will take you to the land where people live. Sit on my back." Then he began carrying him towards the land of men.

While riding comfortably on this glorious being, the man thought, "Suppose people ask me where I was. I must be able to tell everything." So he made notes of all the landmarks, while being carried to safety by the kind elephant king.

When he came out of the thick forest near the highway to Benares, the Elephant King Goodness said, "My good friend, take this road to Benares. Please don't tell anyone where I live, whether they ask you or not." With these parting words, the gentle elephant turned around and went back to his safe and secret home.

The man had no trouble finding his way to Benares. Then one day, while walking in the bazaar, he came to the shops of the ivory carvers. They carved ivory into delicate and beautiful statues, scenes and shapes. The forester asked them, "Would you buy tusks that come from living elephants?"

The ivory carvers replied, "What a question! Everyone knows the tusks from a live elephant are much more valuable than from a dead one."[12] "Then I will bring you some live elephant tusks," said the forester.

Caring only for money, ignoring the safety of the elephant king, and without any gratitude towards the one who had saved his life – the man put a sharp saw in with his other provisions, and set out towards the home of King Goodness.

When he arrived the elephant king asked him, "Oh my dear human friend, what brings you back again?" Making up a story, the greedy man said, "My lord elephant, I am a poor man, living very humbly. As these times are very difficult for me, I have come to beg from you just a little piece of tusk. If you can give it to me, I will take it home and sell it. Then I will be able to provide for myself, and survive for a while longer."

Pitying the man, the Elephant King Goodness said, "Of course my friend, I will give you a big piece of tusk! Did you happen to bring a saw with you?" "Yes lord," said the forester, "I did bring a saw." "All right then," said the generous King Goodness, "cut from both my tusks!"

As he said this, the elephant bent down on his knees and offered up his spectacular silvery-white tusks. Without the slightest regret, the man sawed off big pieces of ivory from both tusks.

---

12 The ivory from a live elephant is not as dried out as the ivory from a dead elephant, and therefore is easier to carve.

The Enlightenment Being picked up both pieces with his trunk. He said, "Good friend, I am not giving you my lovely tusks because I dislike them and want to get rid of them. Nor is it because they are not valuable to me. But a thousand times, even a hundred thousand times more lovely and valuable are the tusks of all knowable wisdom, which leads to the realization of all Truth [Dhamma]."

Giving the wonderful tusks to the man, it was the elephant's wish that his perfect generosity would eventually lead him to the greatest wisdom.

The man went home and sold both pieces of ivory. But it didn't take long for him to spend all the money. So again he returned to the Elephant King Goodness. He begged him, "My lord, the money I got by selling your ivory was only enough to pay off my debts. I am still a poor man, living very humbly. Times are still hard in Benares, so please give me the rest of your tusks, oh generous one!"

Without hesitation, the elephant king offered what was left of his tusks. The man cut off all that he could see of them, right down to the sockets in the elephant's skull! He left without a word of thanks. The wonderful kind elephant meant no more to him than a bank account! He took the ivory back to Benares, sold it, and squandered the money as before.

Once again the forester returned to the Himalayan home of the Elephant King Goodness. And again he begged him, "Oh noble elephant king, it is so very hard to make a living in Benares. Have pity on me and let me have the rest of your ivory – the roots of your tusks."

Perfect generosity holds nothing back. So once again the elephant king bent down on his knees and offered his remaining stumps of ivory. The ungrateful betrayer did not care at all for the elephant. He stepped onto the magnificent trunk – like a thick silver chain. He climbed up and sat between the pure white temples, on top of the great head – like a snowy Himalayan dome. Then he roughly dug in with his heels, rubbing and tearing away the tender flesh from the stumps of the once-beautiful tusks. He used his dull worn-down saw to cut and hack the ivory roots out of the noble skull!

It is said there are many worlds – the hell world of torture, the worlds of hungry ghosts, of animals and of mankind, as well as many heaven worlds – from the lowest to the highest. In all these worlds there are millions of beings who, at one time or another, have been born and lived as elephants. And some who tell this story say, that although they knew not why, all those one-time elephants felt the pain of the Great Being – the Elephant King Goodness.

The forester departed carrying the bloody ivory stumps. Thinking there was no reason to see the elephant again, he didn't bother to show any sign of gratitude or respect.

The vast solid earth, which is strong enough to easily support great mountains, and is able to bear the worst filth and stench, could not bear and support this cruel man's enormous unwholesomeness. So, when he could no longer be seen by the suffering elephant, the mighty earth cracked open beneath him. Fire from the lowest hell world leaped up, engulfed him in bright red flames, and pulled him down to his doom![13]

This was witnessed by a tree-dwelling spirit that lived in the forest.[14]

---

13 The fire of the hell [*niraya*] Avīci burns, but it does not consume.
14 Snakes are often figured as tree-dwelling spirits, or tree fairies. Such an interpretation would be a pun on the Pāli title of this story, which could mean either "The Story of a Virtuous Elephant" or "The Story of a Virtuous Snake".

She made the forest echo with the words, "An ungrateful person will always be looked down on by everyone. Never do something good for an ungrateful person." The tree-dwelling spirit then taught this truth: "The more an ungrateful person gets, the more he wants. Nothing in the world can satisfy his appetite." The tree-dwelling spirit made the forest echo with such teachings.

As for the Elephant King Goodness, he lived out his life, passing on at last according to his wholesome deeds.

The Buddha identified the births in this way:

"The ungrateful forester was Devadatta. The tree-dwelling spirit that witnessed the events of this story was Sāriputta. And I who am today the Buddha was the Elephant King Goodness."

The moral: "The ungrateful stops at nothing, and digs his own grave."

73

Four on a Log
[Gratitude]
(*Saccaṁkira-Jātaka*)

The Buddha told this story while living at the Bamboo Grove temple with regard to Devadatta's attempts to kill him. The Buddha said, "Oh monks, just as nowadays Devadatta has attempted to kill me, but I have nevertheless survived, so it was also in the past." And the assembled monks requested the Buddha to tell the story of the past. The Buddha told it in this way:

Once upon a time, King Brahmadatta of Benares had a son. He grew up to be a mean and cruel he-man – the type that's always trying to prove he's tougher than everyone else. He was a bully who constantly pushed people around and picked fights. Whenever he spoke to people it was with a stream of obscenities – right out of the gutter. And he was always quick to anger – just like a hissing snake that's just been stepped on.

People inside and outside the palace ran from him as they would from a starving man-eating demon. They avoided him as they would a speck of dirt in the eye. Behind his back everyone called him the 'Evil Prince' [Duṭṭhakumāra]. In short – he was not a nice man!

One day the prince decided to go swimming. So he went down to the river with his servants and attendants. Suddenly it became almost as dark as night. A huge storm came up. Being so rough and tough, the prince was always trying to show he wasn't scared of anything. So he yelled at his servants, "Take me into the middle of the river and bathe me. Then bring me back to shore."

Following his orders, they took him out to midstream. Then they said, "Now is our chance! Whatever we do here, the king will never find out. So let's kill the Evil Prince. Into the flood you go, good-for-nothing!" With that they threw him into the stormy raging river.

When they returned to the bank, the others asked where the prince was. They replied, "We don't know. As the rain came up, he must have swum faster than us and gone back to Benares."

When they returned to the palace, the king asked, "Where is my son?" They said, "We don't know, your majesty. When the storm came up, we thought he went back ahead of us." King Brahmadatta collected a search party and began looking for the prince. They searched carefully, all the way to the riverside, but couldn't find him.

What had happened was this. In the darkness and wind and rain the prince had been swept down the flooding river. Luckily he was able to grab onto a floating dead tree trunk. Frantically he held on for dear life. As he was being swept along, the tough he-man was so afraid of drowning that he cried like a terrified helpless baby!

It just so happened that, not long before, a very rich man had died in Benares. He had buried his treasure hoard in the riverbank, along the same stretch of river. His fortune amounted to 40 million gold coins. Because of his miserly craving for riches, he was reborn as a lowly snake, slithering on his belly while still guarding his treasure.

At a nearby spot on the riverbank another rich miser had buried a treasure of 30 million gold coins. Likewise, due to his stingy clawing after wealth, he had been reborn as a water rat. He too remained to guard his buried treasure.

Lo and behold, when the storm came up, both the snake and the water rat were flooded out of their holes and washed into the raging river. In fear of drowning, they both happened to grab onto the same dead log carrying the frightened wailing prince. The snake climbed up on one end and the water rat on the other.

There also happened to be a tall cotton tree growing nearby. There was a young parrot roosting in it. When the storm-flooded river rose up, the cotton tree's roots were washed away and it fell into the water. When he tried to fly away, the wind and rain swept the little parrot onto the same dead log with the snake, the water rat and the Evil Prince.

Now there were four on the log, floating towards a bend in the river. Nearby a holy man was living humbly in a little hut. He just happened to

be the Bodhisatta – the Enlightenment Being. He had been born into a rich high-class family in Kāsi. When he had grown up, he had given up all his wealth and position, and had come to live by himself next to the river.

It was the middle of the night when the holy man heard the cries of panic coming from the Evil Prince. He thought, "That sounds like a frightened human being. My loving-kindness will not let me ignore him. I must save him."

He ran down to the river and shouted, "Don't be afraid! I will save you!" Then he jumped into the rushing torrent, grabbed the log, and used his great strength to pull it to shore.

He helped the prince step safely onto the riverbank. Noticing the snake, water rat and parrot, he took them and the man to his cozy little hut. He started up his cooking fire. Thinking of the weakness of the animals, he gently warmed them by the fire. When they were warm and dry he set them aside. Then he let the prince warm himself. The holy man brought out some fruits and nuts. Again he fed the more helpless animals first, followed by the waiting prince.

Not surprisingly this made the Evil Prince furious! He thought, "This stupid holy man doesn't care at all for me, a great royal prince. Instead he gives higher place to these three dumb animals!" Thinking this way, he built up a vengeful hatred against the gentle Bodhisatta.

The next day the holy man dried the deadwood log in the sun. Then he chopped it up and burned it, to cook their food and keep them warm. In a few days the four who had been rescued by that same log were strong and healthy.

The snake came to the holy man to say good-bye. He coiled his body on the ground, arched himself up, and bowed his head respectfully. He said, "Venerable one, you have done a great thing for me! I am grateful to you, and I am not a poor snake. In a certain place I have a buried treasure of 40 million gold coins. And I will gladly give it to you – for all life is priceless! Whenever you are in need of money, just come down to the riverbank and call out, 'Snake! Snake!'"

The water rat, too, came to the holy man to say good-bye. He stood up on his hind legs and bowed his head respectfully. He said, "Venerable one, you have done a great thing for me! I am grateful to you, and I am not a poor water rat. In a certain place I have a buried treasure of 30 million gold coins. And I will gladly give it to you – for all life is priceless! Whenever you are in need of money, just come down to the riverbank and call out, 'Rat! Rat!'"

Such grateful generosity from a snake and a water rat! A far cry from their previous stingy human lives!

Then came the parrot to say his good-bye to the holy man. He bowed his head respectfully and said, "Venerable one, you have done a great thing for me! I am grateful to you, but I possess no silver or gold. However, I am not a poor parrot. For if you are ever in need of the finest rice, just come down to the riverbank and call out, 'Parrot! Parrot!' Then I will gather together all my relatives from all the forests of the Himalayas and we will bring you many cartloads of the most precious scented red rice. For all life is priceless!"

Finally the Evil Prince came to the holy man. Because his mind was filled with the poison of vengeance, he thought only about killing him if he ever saw him again. However, what he said was, "Venerable one, when I become king, please come to me and I will provide you with the Four Necessities [*catu-paccaya*-s]." He returned to Benares and soon became the new king.

In a while the holy man decided to see if the gratitude of these four was for real. First he went down to the riverbank and called out, "Snake! Snake!" At the sound of the first word, the snake came out of his home under the ground. He bowed respectfully and said, "Holy one, under this very spot are buried 40 million gold coins. Dig them up and take them with you!" "Very well," said the holy man, "when I am in need I will come again."

Taking leave of the snake, he walked along the riverbank and called out, "Rat! Rat!" The water rat appeared and all went just as it had with the snake.

Next, he called out, "Parrot! Parrot!" The parrot flew down from his treetop home, bowed respectfully and said, "Holy one, do you need red rice? I will summon my relatives and we will bring you the best rice in all the Himalayas." The holy man replied, "Very well, when I am in need I will come again."

Finally he set out to see the king. He walked to the royal pleasure garden and slept there overnight. In the morning, in a very humble and dignified manner, he went to collect alms food in the city of Benares.

On that same morning the ungrateful king, seated on a magnificently adorned royal elephant, was leading a vast procession around the city. When he saw the Enlightenment Being coming from a distance he thought, "Aha! This lazy homeless bum is coming to sponge off me. Before he can brag to everyone how much he did for me, I must have him beheaded!"

Then he said to his servants, "This worthless beggar must be coming to ask for something. Don't let the good-for-nothing get near me. Arrest him immediately, tie his hands behind his back, and whip him at every street corner. Take him out of the city to the execution block and cut off his head. Then raise up his body on a sharpened stake and leave it for all to see. So much for lazy beggars!"

The king's men followed his cruel orders. They tied up the blameless Great Being [Bodhisatta] like a common criminal. They whipped him mercilessly at every street corner on the way to the execution block. But no matter how hard they whipped him, cutting into his flesh, he remained dignified. After each whipping he simply announced, for all to hear: "This proves the old saying is still true – 'There's more reward in pulling deadwood from a river, than in helping an ungrateful man!'"

Some of the bystanders began to wonder why he said only this at each street corner. They said to each other, "This poor man's pain must be caused by an ungrateful man." So they asked him, "Oh holy man, have you done some service to an ungrateful man?"

Then he told them the whole story. And in conclusion he said, "I rescued this king from a terrible flood, and in so doing I brought this pain upon myself. I did not follow the saying of the wise of old, that's why I said what I said."

Hearing this story, the people of Benares became enraged and said to each other, "This good man saved the king's life. But he is so cruel that he has no gratitude in him at all. How could such a king possibly benefit us? He can only be dangerous to us. Let's get him!"

Their rage turned the citizens of Benares into a mob. They pelted the king with arrows, knives, clubs and stones. He died while still sitting on the royal elephant. Then they threw the dead body of the one-time Evil Prince into a ditch by the side of the road.

Afterwards they made the holy man their new king. He ruled Benares well. Then one day he decided to go see his old friends. So he rode in a large procession down to the riverbank.

He called out, "Snake! Snake!" The snake came out, offered his respect and said, "My lord, if you wish it, you are welcome to my treasure." The king ordered his servants to dig up the 40 million gold coins.

He went to the water rat's home and called out, "Rat! Rat!" He too appeared, offered his respect and said, "My lord, if you wish it, you are welcome to my treasure." This time the king's servants dug up 30 million gold coins.

Then the king called out "Parrot! Parrot!" The parrot flew to the king, bowed respectfully and said, "If you wish, my lord, I will collect the most excellent red rice for you." But the holy man king said, "Not now my friend. When rice is needed I will request it of you. Now let us all return to the city."

After they arrived at the royal palace in Benares, the king had the 70 million gold coins put under guard in a safe place. He had a golden bowl made for the grateful snake's new home. He had a maze made of the finest crystals for the generous rat to live in. And the kind parrot moved into a golden cage, with a gate he could latch and unlatch from the inside.

Every day the king gave rice puffs and the sweetest bee's honey on golden plates to the snake and the parrot. And on another golden plate he gave the most aromatic scented rice to the water rat.

The king became famous for his generosity to the poor. He and his three animal friends lived together in perfect harmony for many years. When they died, they were all reborn as they deserved.

The Buddha then identified the births, saying:

"Devadatta was Duṭṭhakumāra in the past. Sāriputta was the snake. Moggallāna was the water rat. Ānanda was the parrot. And the holy man who became the righteous king was I, myself, who have become the Buddha."

The moral: "Gratitude is a reward, which is itself rewarded."

74

New Homes for the Tree Spirits
[Wise Advice]
(Rukkhadhamma-Jātaka)

The Buddha told this Jātaka story while at Jetavana monastery with regard to a quarrel between his Sakyā and Koliya relatives concerning the waters of the Rohiṇī River. The full details of this quarrel are given in the *Kuṇāla-Jātaka* [No. 536].[15]

At the time of this quarrel, the Buddha flew through the air and sat in the sky cross-legged emitting blue rays, startling his kinsfolk. He then alighted from mid-air, seated himself on the riverbank, and addressed his kinsmen on the advantages of concord and unity, saying that at one time, when a big storm came up, trees that stood alone, fell; whereas those in the forest, which were intertwined with one another withstood the wind. And at the request of his relatives, he told this Jātaka story.

This was told again at the request of the assembled monks in the preaching hall at Jetavanārāma.

Once upon a time, as happens to all beings, the King of the Tree Spirits died. King Sakka, ruler of the Heaven of 33, appointed a new King of the Tree Spirits. As his first official act, the new king [Vessavaṇa] sent out a proclamation that every tree spirit should choose a tree to live in. Likewise it was stated that every tree was to be pleased with its resident spirit.

There just so happened to be a very wise tree spirit who was the leader of a large clan. He advised his clan members not to live in freestanding trees. Instead it would be safer to live in the forest trees near him. The wise tree spirits settled down in the forest trees with their leader.

---

15 See the retelling of Jātaka No. 33, the *Sammodamāna-Jātaka*, for the details of this quarrel as in the *Kuṇāla-Jātaka*.

But there were also some foolish and arrogant tree spirits. They said to each other, "Why should we live in this crowd? Let us go to the villages, towns and cities inhabited by human beings. Tree spirits who live there receive the best offerings. And they are even worshipped by the superstitious people living in those places. What a life we will have!"

So they went to the villages, towns and cities, and moved into the big freestanding trees, looked after by people. Then one day a big storm came up. The wind blew strong and hard. The big heavy trees with old stiff branches did not do well in the storm. Branches fell down, trunks broke in two, and some were even uprooted. But the trees in the forest, which were intertwined with each other, were able to bend and support each other in the mighty wind. They did not break or fall!

The tree spirits in the villages, towns and cities had their tree homes destroyed. They gathered up their children and returned to the forest. They complained to the wise leader about their misfortune in the big lonely trees in the land of men. He said, "This is what happens to arrogant ones who ignore wise advice and go off by themselves."

When the Buddha finished telling this story, he connected the births in this way:

"The Buddha's followers today were tree spirits in those days. And the very wise tree spirit who was the leader of a large clan was I who am today the Buddha."

The moral: "Fools are deaf to wise words."

(75)

The Fish Who Worked a Miracle
[The Power of Truthfulness]
(*Maccha-Jātaka*)

The Buddha told this story while he was in Jetavana monastery with regard to his having made torrents of rain fall during a period of drought through his miraculous power.

There was a severe drought at one time in Kosala and everything, such as rice fields and banana trees, withered; and lakes, ponds and tanks dried up. Birds flew away, and fish and turtles buried themselves in the mud, where they became prey to crows and hawks. Even the tank at the gateway of Jetavanārāma dried up down to its bottom step.

Out of his compassion, the Buddha decided he had to do something to bring rain. So he determined to bathe in the tank at Jetavanārāma. At this point, the seat of the king of the gods Sakka grew hot, and he sought to find out the cause. Seeing that the Buddha wished to bathe, he summoned the rain god Pajjunna, and ordered him to make it rain. A great wind then blew up, and it rained torrents.

In the evening, the monks in the preaching hall were discussing this. When the Buddha entered, he asked them what they were discussing before he came. The monks told him, and the Buddha said, "Oh monks, this is not the first time I have made rain fall in an hour of need." And the monks asked the Buddha to tell the past story.

This is how it was:

Once upon a time, the Enlightenment Being was born as a fish in a pond in northern India. There were many kinds of fish, big and small, living in the pond with the Bodhisatta.

There came to be a time of severe draught. The rainy season did not come as usual. The crops of men died, and many ponds, lakes and rivers dried up.

The fish and turtles dug down and buried themselves in the mud, frantically trying to keep wet and save themselves. The crows were pleased by all this. They stuck their beaks down into the mud, pulled up the frightened little fish, and feasted on them.

The suffering of pain and death by the other fish touched the Enlightenment Being with sadness, and filled him with pity and compassion. He realized that he was the only one who could save them. But it would take a miracle.

The truth was that he had remained innocent, by never taking the life of anyone. He was determined to use the power of this wholesome truth to make rain fall from the sky, and release his relatives from their misery and death.[16]

---

16 In ancient India, it was believed that a person who fulfilled his function or duty in the cosmos perfectly could change the physical order of the world by what was termed an 'act of truth' [*sacca-kiriyā*]. For an Enlightenment Being, or Bodhisatta, such was observing perfectly the ethical principle of Ahiṁsā, not harming any life. The well-known Damayantī's declaration in the story of "Nala and Damayantī" in the third book of the *Mahābhārata* was based on her flawless chastity and devotion to her husband-to-be, Nala, which was complete, even in word and thought. For a prostitute mentioned in "The Questions of King Milinda" [*Milindapañha*] 4.1.47, her declaration was based on her being the perfect prostitute, perfectly fulfilling the prostitute's

He pulled himself up from under the black mud. He was a big fish, and as black from the mud as polished ebony. He opened his eyes, which sparkled like rubies, looked up to the sky, and called on the rain god Pajjunna. He exclaimed, "Oh my friend Pajjunna, god of rain, I am suffering for the sake of my relatives. Why do you withhold rain from me, who am perfectly wholesome, and make me suffer in sympathy with all these fish?

"I was born among fish, for whom it is customary to eat other fish – even our own kind, like cannibals! But since I was born, I myself have never eaten any fish, even one as tiny as a rice grain. In fact, I have never taken life from anyone. The truthfulness of this my innocence gives me the right to say to you: Make the rains fall! Relieve the suffering of my relatives!"

He said this the way one gives orders to a servant. And he continued, commanding the mighty rain god Pajjunna: "Make rain fall from the thunderclouds! Do not allow the crows their hidden treasures! Let the crows feel the sorrow of their unwholesome actions [akusala-kamma-s]. At the same time release me from my sorrow, who have lived in perfect wholesomeness."

After only a short pause, the sky opened up with a heavy downpour of rain, relieving many from the fear of death – fish, turtles and even humans. And when the great fish who had worked this miracle eventually died, he was reborn as he deserved.

The Buddha then said:

"The many fish then are today the Buddha's disciples. Ānanda was the rain god Pajjunna. And I, myself, was the fish who relieved his relatives' suffering."

The moral: "True innocence relieves the suffering of many."

---

duty, giving herself only for money, never denying anyone who would pay her price, and serving all alike. See also the 'act of truth' of the baby quail in Jātaka 35, the *Vaṭṭaka-Jātaka*, and of Prince Poorfruit in the beginning of Jātaka 52 (=539, the *Mahājanaka-Jātaka*) above.

76

The Meditating Security Guard
[Fearlessness]
(Asaṅkiya-Jātaka)

When the Buddha was living in Jetavana temple, this story was told with regard to a problem posed to the Buddha by a certain devout layman of Sāvatthi.

This layman once journeyed along with a caravan on some business or other. At night, when in the jungle, the caravan leader unyoked the bullocks, and made camp. The devout layman sat awake all night under a nearby tree. Because of this, he prevented the caravan from being robbed, robbers who had gathered around the caravan running away at the break of dawn when the man never fell asleep.

When the devout layman returned, he went to see the Buddha. He asked the Buddha, "Bhante, by guarding oneself, does one also guard others?" The Buddha responded, "Yes, lay brother. In guarding oneself, a man guards others. And in guarding others, he guards himself." And the devout layman told the Buddha what had happened on his journey. The Buddha then said, "In the past, too, the wise guarded others while guarding themselves." And at the layman's request, the Buddha told this story of the past:

Once upon a time, the Enlightenment Being was born into a rich and powerful family. When he grew up he became dissatisfied with going after the ordinary pleasures of the world. So he gave up his former lifestyle, including his wealth and position. He went to the foothills of the Himalayas and became a holy man.

It just so happened that one day he ran out of salt. So he decided to go and collect alms. He came upon a caravan and went with it part way on its journey. In the evening they stopped and made camp.

The holy man began walking at the foot of a big nearby tree. He concentrated until he entered a high mental state. He remained in that state throughout the night, while continuing to walk.

Meanwhile, 500 bandits surrounded the campsite. They waited until after supper, when all had settled down for the night. But before they could attack, they noticed the holy man. They said to each other, "That man must be on guard, for security. If he sees us, he'll warn the rest. So let's wait until he falls asleep, and then do our robbing and looting!"

What the bandits didn't know was that the holy man was so deep in meditation that he didn't notice them at all – or anything else for that matter! So they kept waiting for him to fall asleep. And he just kept walking and walking and walking – until the light of dawn finally began to appear. Only then was he finished meditating.

Having had no chance to rob the caravan, the bandits threw down their weapons in frustration. They shouted, "Hey, you in the caravan! If your security guard hadn't stayed up all night, walking under that tree, we would have robbed you all! You should reward him well!" With that they left in search of someone else to rob.

When it became light the people in the caravan saw the clubs and stones left behind by the bandits. Trembling with fear, they went over to the holy man. They greeted him respectfully and asked if he had seen the bandits. "Yes, this morning I did," he said.

"Weren't you scared?" they asked. "No," said the Enlightenment Being, "the sight of bandits is only frightening to the rich. But I'm not a rich man. I own nothing of any value to robbers. So why should I be afraid of them? I have no anxiety in a village, and no fear in the forest. Possessing only loving-kindness [*mettā*] and compassion [*karuṇā*], I follow the straight path leading to Truth [Dhamma]."

In this manner he preached the way of fearlessness to the lucky people of the caravan. His words made them feel peaceful, and they honored him.

After a long life developing the Four Heavenly States of Mind [*catu-brahma-vihāra-s*], he died and was reborn in a high heaven world.

The Buddha then said:

"The people in the caravan in those days are today the Buddha's followers. And the holy man was I who am today the Buddha."

The moral: "It pays to have a holy man around."

77

16 Dreams
(Mahāsupina-Jātaka)

The Buddha told this story while at Jetavana monastery with regard to 16 bad dreams that were had one night by King Pasenadi of Kosala. King Pasenadi's Brahmin advisers, on being consulted, said that they foretold harm either to his kingdom, his life or his wealth. And they prescribed all manners of sacrifices in order to avert the danger. Mallikā, the king's wife, heard of this and suggested that the Buddha should be consulted. The king followed her advice, and the Buddha explained the dreams.

After explaining the dreams, the Buddha told Pasenadi that he was not the first to have these dreams. They were had by kings in the past, as well. And just as today, the Brahmin priests found in them a pretext for sacrifices. But at the intervention of the good, the Enlightenment Being was consulted and the dreams were explained, just as today.

And saying this, at the king's request, the Buddha told the story of the past.

Chapter 1. Panic

Once upon a time there was a king called Brahmadatta who was ruling in Benares, in northern India. One night he had 16 frightening nightmare dreams. He awoke in the morning in a cold sweat, with his heart thumping loudly in his chest. The 16 dreams had scared him to death. He was sure they meant that something terrible was about to happen. In a panic, he called for his official priests, to ask their advice.

When the priests arrived at the royal bedchamber, they asked the king if he had slept well. He told them that it had been the worst night of his life, that he had been scared to death by 16 dreams, and that he was desperate to find out their meanings.

At this the priests' eyes lit up. They asked him, "What were these dreams, your majesty?" King Brahmadatta told them all 16 dreams. The priests pounded their foreheads and exclaimed, "Oh what horrors! It couldn't be worse, your majesty. Such dreams as these can mean only one thing – danger!"

The king asked them, "What danger, oh priests? You must tell me the meaning at once!" They replied, "It is certain, your majesty, these dreams show that one of three disasters will take place – terrible harm to the kingdom, to your life, or to the royal wealth."

The king had feared as much. He wrung his hands as the sweat kept pouring from his body. He was shaking all over with terror and panic. He asked, "Tell me, oh worthy royal priests, is there any way to avoid this disaster?" "Indeed, it is very dangerous," they said. "If you do nothing, the end is certain. But we can prevent it. If we couldn't, then all our training and learning would be useless. Trust us, lord."

The panic-stricken king cried out, "Just tell me what to do, priests. I'll do anything! What can you do to save me, my kingdom and my wealth?" "We must offer the greatest animal sacrifice that has ever been seen," they said. "We must kill, as sacrificial offerings, four of every type of animal that lives!"

Although he was usually a gentle, kind and merciful ruler, King Brahmadatta was so frightened that he couldn't think straight at all. Paralyzed with fear, he put all his hope and faith in his priests. He gave them permission to prepare the gigantic slaughter.

The priests said, "Have no fear, your majesty, we will take care of everything. We will prevent the coming doom!" They knew they would be paid well to perform the sacrifice. And the meat from the killed animals would be theirs as well. Their secret thoughts were, "This is a great way for us to get piles of money, and the best food and drink too!"

The priests got to work organizing the biggest sacrifice Benares had ever seen. Just outside of town they dug a huge pit. Into it they put the most perfect ones they could find of all the animals – land animals, birds and fish. From each kind they selected four to be killed in the ceremony. It became known as the 'Four-from-all' [Sabba-catukka] sacrifice.

Meanwhile, the king's senior teaching priest had a promising young pupil. He was gentle and compassionate, and very well educated. He wondered about all that was happening. So he asked the teacher priest, "Oh master, you have taught me well the wise teachings of old. Can you show me anywhere it says the killing of one will save the life of another?"

The priest answered, "What kind of question is that? Open your eyes and be realistic, my boy. Don't you see that this great sacrifice, the Four-from-all, will make us rich? You must be trying to help the king hold onto his riches!"

The idealistic and sincere pupil said, "You have not answered my question, master. If this sacrifice is to be your work, it shall be mine no longer!" With these words he departed and went to the royal pleasure garden to consider what he would do.

It just so happened that the Enlightenment Being had been born into a rich high-class family. For many generations the men in that family had been priests, just like the ones who were now preparing the Four-from-all sacrifice. But when the Bodhisatta grew up he abandoned the life of a rich priest. Instead he went to the Himalayas and lived as a humble forest monk. He concentrated his mind in meditation and entered high mental states [adhigama]. He gained the sweetest inner happiness, and even miraculous supernatural powers.

This forest monk loved all the animals. When he heard about what was happening in Benares he was filled with tenderness and compassion. He decided, "I must teach the ignorant people and release them from the chains of superstition. I will go to the city at once!" Then he used his supernatural power to fly through the air to Benares. In an instant he was seated on a rock in the king's pleasure garden. His gentle nature made him glow like a golden sunrise.

The idealistic young student approached and recognized him as a great holy man. He bowed respectfully and sat on the ground. The forest monk asked him, "Young man, do you have a good and just king reigning here in Benares?"

"Yes," said the student, "our king is kind and good. But he is being misled by the royal priests. He had 16 dreams which left him completely panic-stricken. The priests took advantage of this when he told them his dreams. They have convinced him to have a huge sacrifice and kill many animals. Oh holy one, please tell the king the true meanings of his dreams. Free the many helpless beings from fear and death."

The holy man said, "If he comes and asks me, I will tell him." "I will bring him, sir," said the young man. "Kindly wait here a short while until I return."

The student went to the king and told him there was a marvelous holy man seated on a rock in the royal pleasure garden. He told him he had said he could interpret the king's dreams. Hearing this, the king went with him to the garden. A crowd followed behind.

Chapter 2. Roaring Bulls With No Fight

King Brahmadatta knelt down before the holy man and then sat next to him. He asked, "Your reverence, can you tell me the meanings of my 16 dreams?"

"Of course I can," said the forest monk. "Tell them to me, beginning with the first eight."

The king replied, "These were the first eight dreams:

> roaring bulls with no fight,
> midget trees bearing fruit,
> cows sucking milk from calves,

> calves pulling carts with bulls trailing behind,
> a horse eating with two mouths,
> a jackal urinating in a golden bowl,
> a she-jackal eating a rope maker's rope,
> one overflowing pot with all the rest empty."

"Tell me more about your first dream," said the monk.

"Your reverence, I saw four pure black bulls who came from the four directions to fight in the palace courtyard. People came from miles around to see the bulls fight. But they only pretended to fight, roared at each other, and went back where they came from."

"Oh king," said the holy man, "this dream tells of things that will not happen in your lifetime or in mine. In the far-off future, kings will be unwholesome and stingy. The people too will be unwholesome. Goodness will be decreasing while evil increases. The seasons will be out of whack, with sunstroke on winter days and snowstorms on summer days. The skies will be dry, with poor clouds and little water. Harvests will be small and people will starve. Then dark clouds will come from the four directions, but even after much thunder and lightning, they will depart without letting rain fall – just like the roaring bulls who leave without fighting.

"But have no fear, there will be no harm to the people of today. The priests say this dream requires sacrifice, only because that is how they earn their money. Now tell me your second dream."

"Your reverence, I had a dream where tiny midget plants grew no more than one foot tall, and then flowered and gave fruit."

"Oh king," said the holy man, "the soil will be poor for growing crops, and humans will live short lives. The young will have strong desires, and even young girls will have babies – just like midget trees bearing fruit.

"But this will not happen until the distant future when the world is declining. What was your third dream, oh king?"

"Your reverence, I saw cows sucking milk from their own calves, born the same day," said the king, shuddering with fear.

"Be calm," said the monk, "this too will not happen in our lifetimes.

But someday people will no longer respect their mothers, fathers, mothers-in-law and fathers-in-law. People will give everything to their own children, taking over the savings of their elder parents and in-laws. Then, by whim alone, they may or may not feed and clothe their elders. So the elderly will be at the mercy of their own children – just like cows sucking milk from their day-old calves.

"But clearly it is not like that today, oh king, so you have nothing to fear. Now tell me your fourth dream."

Somewhat relieved, the king continued, "Your reverence, I dreamed I saw big strong full-grown bulls following behind bullock carts. They were being pulled by frail awkward calves. The calves stopped and stood still, unable to pull the heavily loaded carts. Caravans could no longer travel and goods could not be taken to market."

"There will be a time," said the holy man, "when unwholesome stingy kings will no longer respect wise experienced judges. Instead they will appoint young foolish judges, granting them the highest privileges. But they will not be able to make difficult decisions. They will become judges in name only, doing no real work – just like the calves who can't pull the carts. Meanwhile, the older wiser ones will offer no help, thinking it is no longer their concern – just like the bulls trailing behind.

"Again you have nothing to fear, oh king, from those far-off times when all the nations will be poorly run by the young and foolish. What was your fifth dream?"

"Your reverence, my fifth dream was very strange indeed. I saw a horse eating with two mouths, one on each side of his head!" Again the king trembled as he spoke.

The forest monk said, "This will happen in another far-off future time, when unwholesome foolish kings appoint unwholesome greedy judges. Not caring in the least about right and wrong, they will take bribes from both sides in the same case – just like a horse eating greedily with two mouths.

"Now tell me your sixth dream."

"Your reverence, I dreamed I saw a golden plate worth a hundred thousand pieces of money. People were holding it and coaxing an old skinny jackal to urinate in it. And that's just what he did!" said the king, making a face.

"Oh king, this too will come to pass in a far-off time when the kings will be outsiders, not born in the ruling families of the countries they rule. So they will not trust the experienced ministers from the native noble class. They will replace them with low-class ministers they can control more easily. Meanwhile the old nobles will depend on the new ruling class. So they will offer their high-class daughters in marriage to the low-class ministers – just like golden bowls urinated in by jackals.

"But this will not happen in your time, oh king. What was your seventh dream?"

"Your reverence, I dreamed I saw a man making a rope and letting it pile up under his chair. There a hungry female jackal was eating the rope as it fell, without the man knowing it."

"There will come a time," said the monk, "when women's cravings will increase. They will desire men, strong liquor, jewelry and all sorts of useless possessions. They will spend a lot of time window-shopping. Paying more attention to their lovers than to their husbands, they will ignore even the most important household activities. And they will waste all the money earned by their husbands – just like the jackal devouring the rope that is produced by the rope maker.

"But as you can see, oh king, these times are not upon us. Tell me about your eighth dream."

"Your reverence," said the king, "I saw one big pot full of water, and many small empty pots, in front of the palace gate. All the warriors, priests, merchants and farmers were bringing water from all directions. But they were pouring it only into the big pot. That one was overflowing and wasting the water, while all the little pots remained empty!" Again the king shook in fear as he spoke.

"Have no fear, oh king," said the holy man. "Way off in the future the world will be declining. The land will be less fertile, so crops will be harder to grow. The richest will have no more than 100,000 pieces of money – there will be no more millionaires! Even the kings will be poor and stingy.

"The kings and the wealthy will make all the rest work for them only. The poor will be forced to bring all their products, grains, vegetables and fruits to the warehouses of the rich and powerful. And the barns of the hard-working poor will remain empty – it will be like the big pot filled to overflowing, with all the little ones empty.

"So now you know the meanings of your first eight dreams. They have foretold:

thunderclouds with no rain,

young girls having babies,

the elderly at the mercy of their children,

young foolish judges with no help from the wise,

greedy judges taking bribes from both sides,

low-class ministers with high-class wives,

wives wasting the earnings of their husbands,

the rich taking from the poor leaving them nothing.

"So your mind may be at peace, oh king, regarding these first eight dreams. Clearly such times are not upon us, and these dangers are not to be feared in the present day."

Chapter 3. The Frightening Sound of 'Munch, Munch, Munch'

"Indeed," said King Brahmadatta to the humble forest monk, "you have set my mind to rest concerning my first eight dreams. But my last eight dreams are even more frightening. I must do something to prevent the doom they predict." Again the king began shaking uncontrollably with fear and panic.

"Calm down," said the holy man, "and tell me these dreams also, that I may relieve your distress."

The king replied, "These were my last eight dreams, the ninth to the 16th:

a pond that's muddy in the middle and clear by the shore,

rice cooking unevenly in a pot,

fine sandalwood traded for spoiled buttermilk,

empty pumpkins sinking in water,

solid rocks floating on water,

giant snakes gobbled up by tiny she-frogs,

royal golden swans waiting on a bad village crow,

the frightening sound of 'munch, munch, munch'."

"Please tell me the details of your ninth dream," said the monk.

"Your reverence, I dreamed I saw a pond which was deep in the middle and shallow by the shore. It was filled with all five kinds of lotuses,[17] and there were all kinds of animals – two-footed and four-

---

17 The five kinds of lotuses are red, white, blue, yellow, and purple.

footed – drinking near the shore. And yet the water remained clear by the shore, and got muddy only in the middle. How could this be? What does this mean?"

"Oh king," said the forest monk, "in the distant future there will be only unwholesome kings. They will rule based on their will power, along with their anger and fear. They will not care at all about wholesomeness and justice. They will be much more interested in becoming rich from all kinds of bribes, than in the well-being of the citizens. No longer will rulers have patience, loving-kindness and compassion towards the people they rule. Instead they will be rough and cruel, crushing the people to squeeze the last penny from them in taxes – just as the sweet juice is squeezed from sugar cane.

"Therefore the citizens, unable to pay the taxes and bribes, will flee to the borderlands. Soon there will be less people living in the corrupt central capitals, and the borderlands will be heavily populated by the humble – just like the pond that is muddy in the middle and clear by the shore.

"But obviously there is nothing in this for you to fear, oh good and wholesome king. What was your tenth dream?"

"Your reverence, I dreamed I saw rice cooking unevenly in a pot. Some was overcooked, some well-cooked, and some still raw."

"Don't worry about this either," said the holy man. "This dream foretells a time when all will be unwholesome, not like today! Kings will be unwholesome, and so will officials and ministers, priests and homemakers, city and country folks. Amazing as it may seem, this dream indicates a time when holy men will be unwholesome too! In addition, even the gods, tree spirits and fairies will be unwholesome and wicked!

"The winds will change quickly, sometimes blowing too hard and sometimes not at all. These winds will shake the heavenly homes of the sky gods. Therefore, in some places rains will cause floods, it will rain just right in some areas, and there will be terrible droughts in other places. It will be like rice in the cooking pot – some overcooked, some well-cooked, and some raw.

"Now tell me your 11th dream, oh king."

"Your reverence, I dreamed I saw the finest sandalwood, worth 100,000 pieces of money, being traded for spoiled buttermilk. What is the meaning of this?"

"This too indicates a far-off future time, when knowledge of Truth [Dhamma] is disappearing. There will be many greedy shameless preachers who distort the Four Necessities [catu-samuccaya-s]: food, clothing, shelter and medicine. They will make these into luxuries, far richer than they really need.

"They will teach the worthlessness of luxuries and the unwholesomeness of greed, by preaching the Truth of nonattachment [arahatta]. But in return for preaching, they will require money and luxuries. So they will cause an increase in craving, rather than showing the way towards Liberation from craving [virāga, dukkha-nirodha]. They will preach Truth [Dhamma] only so they can obtain worthless things – just like priceless sandalwood traded for spoiled buttermilk.

"Now let me hear your 12th dream."

"Your reverence, I saw, in a dream, empty pumpkins sinking to the bottom of the water."

"Oh king, this foretells a distant future when the world will be upside down. So once again, you have nothing to fear in this life. Unwholesome kings will grant high positions to the low class rather than the high class. The low-class will quickly become rich and the high-class poor. In all departments and functions, the ignorant words of the uneducated low-class officials will be greatly respected – just like empty pumpkins sinking to the depths of the water.

"Even among the religious, humble wholesome monks will lose respect, while the unwholesome teachings of shameless monks will be followed and adored – just like empty pumpkins sinking to the bottom.

"What was your 13th dream?"

"Your reverence, I dreamed I saw solid rocks floating on top of the water. How strange this seems. What does it mean, wise one?"

"This too indicates the future era when the world will be upside down. In all departments and functions, the wise words of the well-educated nobles will be ignored, due to their birth alone.

"Likewise among the religious, the words of Truth [Dhamma] spoken by humble wholesome monks will be ignored – just like solid rocks floating away on the surface of the water.

"What was your 14th dream?"

"Your reverence, it was a frightening dream in which I saw tiny female frogs chasing big long black snakes. When they caught up to them they cut them and broke them in pieces like water lily stumps, and then gobbled them up!"

"There is nothing for you to fear in this dream either, oh king. This represents a future time when the world will be declining. The wholesomeness in people's natures will decrease. Desires will increase in their minds until they are enslaved by their cravings. Because of this, men will be under the orders of their youngest prettiest wives. The servants, bulls, buffalos and all other household wealth will be managed by the youngest wives – due to the uncontrolled desires of their husbands.

"These wives will treat their husbands like slaves, keeping them under their thumbs. If the men ask about family affairs, their wives will say, 'There's no need for you to ask. Everything in my home belongs to me, not you!' It will be like big long snakes gobbled up by tiny she-frogs.

"Now tell me your 15th dream."

"Your reverence, I saw a crow, the kind that lives near villages. I knew he was filled with the 'Ten Bad Qualities'.[18] He was being followed and served by golden swans, the kind seen as kings by other birds."

---

18 The 'Ten Bad Qualities' [*dasa-akusala-dhamma*-s], or ten unwholesome actions [*dasa-akusala-kamma*-s], are destroying life; taking what is not given; doing wrong in sexual ways; speaking falsely; losing your mind from alcohol; eating at improper times; dancing, singing and playing music; wearing garlands and using unguents, perfumes and makeup; using luxurious chairs and beds; accepting jewelry and wearing jewelry so as to show off your wealth. All the *akusala-kamma*-s are based on greed, hatred and delusion, the three types of unwholesome thoughts [*akusala-citta*-s]. As crows are black, they are considered

"This too indicates a distant time when all kings will be weaklings. They will be no good at riding elephants or horses, or fighting battles. So you can easily see there is nothing for you to fear, mighty king.

"Those weakling kings will be so afraid of being overthrown that they will be afraid to give powerful positions to worthy well-educated nobles. Instead they will appoint foot servants, bath attendants, barbers and so forth. And the nobles will have to become the lowest servants of the untrained new officials – just like royal golden swans waiting on a bad village crow.

"At last we have reached your 16th dream, oh king. Describe it to me."

"Your reverence, I will tell you my last dream, the only one that still frightens me. Ordinarily, leopards chase and eat goats. But in my 16th dream, I saw goats chasing leopards! And when they caught them they ate them up, making the sound, 'munch, munch, munch!' All the other animals who heard this frightening sound and saw the meat-eating goats approaching, ran and hid in the forest. The memory of this dream still frightens me, holy one."

"Alas, even this dream applies only to the far-off time when the world will be ruled by unwholesome kings. The lowly, who are unaccustomed to power, will become closest to the kings. They will gain power while the nobles become poor and unknown.

"In the law courts, the newcomers will confiscate the inherited wealth from the nobles – all their lands, homes and possessions. And when the nobles go to the courts to protest, they will be told, 'How dare you argue with us! You do not understand the situation you are in. We will tell the king and have your hands and feet cut off!' The nobles will run away and hide in fear.

"Likewise, bad monks will injure good monks as much as they please. With no one to support and defend them, the good monks will leave the

to be filled with the 'ten bad qualities,' while things that are white are said to be wholesome.

cities and villages. They will live in the jungle in fear of the bad monks. It will be like all those who hear the sound of 'munch, munch, munch', and live in fear of meat-eating goats.

"Oh king, now you know the meanings of all 16 dreams. The last eight have foretold:

> over-taxed people fleeing to the borderlands,
> an unwholesome world with uneven rains,
> Truth being taught by preachers greedy for money,
> ignorant and unwholesome words gaining respect,
> wise words and Truth losing respect,
> husbands enslaved by desires for their youngest wives,
> educated nobles in the service of untrained newcomers,
> noble and good living in fear of powerful and bad."

Chapter 4. Teaching

King Brahmadatta bowed to the ground before the holy man and said, "Your wisdom has taken my fear and panic from me. Your compassion has kept me from doing terrible unwholesome things to many helpless beings. My gratitude is endless, oh holy monk."

The Enlightenment Being said to the king, "Now you must realize why your royal priests wanted to have a sacrifice ceremony. It was not because they understood the Truth [Saccaṁ], and it was not because they cared for you and your well-being. Instead it was due to greediness. They wanted only to get rich, eat fine food, and keep their jobs at your court.

"Your 16 dreams have indicated disasters in the distant future. What you do now will have no effect on them. Those things will happen when the world is declining, when the unreal is seen as real, when the unreasonable is thought to be reasonable, and when the nonexistent seems to exist. It will be a time when many will be unwholesome without shame, and few will be ashamed of their own wrongdoing.

"Therefore, to prevent these things by performing a sacrifice today is impossible!"

Remaining seated, the Bodhisatta miraculously rose into the air. Then he continued his teaching: "Oh king, it was fear that unbalanced your mind and brought you close to killing so many helpless ones. Real freedom from fear comes from a pure mind. And the way to begin purifying your mind is to climb the five steps of training [*pañca-sīla-s*, the first five *sikkhā-pada-s*]. You will benefit greatly from giving up the five unwholesome actions [*akusala-kamma-s*]. These are:

- destroying life, for this is not compassion;
- taking what is not given, for this is not generosity;
- doing wrong in sexual ways, for this is not loving-kindness;
- speaking falsely, for this is not Truth;
- losing your mind from alcohol, for this leads to falling down the first four steps.

"Oh king, from now on do not join with the priests in killing animals for sacrifice."

In this way the Great Being taught the Truth [Dhamma], freed many people from bondage to false beliefs, and released many animals from fear and death.

In an instant he returned through the air to his home in the Himalayas.

King Brahmadatta practiced the Five Training Steps. He gave alms and did many other good things. At the end of a long life he died and was reborn as he deserved.

* * *

The Buddha then identified the births, saying:

"Ānanda was the king in those days. Sāriputta was the idealistic and sincere pupil. And I who am today the Buddha was the humble forest monk."

The moral: "Beware of the panic-stricken man. What he can do is more dangerous than what scared him in the first place."

Illīsa the Cheap
[Miserliness]
(Illīsa-Jātaka)

The Buddha told this story while living in Jetavana monastery with regard to the miserly banker named Macchari Kosiya.

There was a very wealthy banker of the town of Sakkhara, which is near the city of Rājagaha. His real name was Kosiya; but because he was very miserly, he came to be called Macchari Kosiya, or Stingy Kosiya.[19] One day, when returning from the palace, he saw a half-starved urchin eating a sweetcake, which he was dipping in a sweet gruel. This made him hungry, but he feared spending money on such food. When he went to bed, he could not get this out of his mind. And he stayed in bed brooding. His wife, seeing this, asked him the reason for his misery. And finding out the reason, she said she would cook enough sweetcakes for the entire town. But Kosiya said that would be an extravagance, and persuaded his wife to cook just one cake, and to make it using broken grains of rice. Fearful that someone might ask for a piece of his cake, he retired with his wife to the seventh story of his mansion, and there had his wife start cooking after he had bolted all the doors.

The Buddha saw him with his divine eye [dibba-cakku], and sent the Venerable Moggallāna to him. Moggallāna stood poised in mid-air just outside Kosiya's window and indicated his wish to have something to eat. Kosiya, at first, refused to give him anything. But afterward, he asked his wife to cook a single small cake for Moggallāna. When she

---

19 The Kosiya clan in the usual course of events is a Brahmin clan that is noted for voluntarily helping others.

tried to do this, though, she was not able to cook a small cake. And the cakes she cooked kept getting bigger and bigger.

As she was cooking, she put the cakes in a basket. Finally, when she tried to take a single cake for Moggallāna, they all stuck together. So Kosiya, out of frustration, presented all the cakes and the basket itself to the elder.

Moggallāna then preached the importance of generosity [*dāna*], and transported Kosiya, his wife and the cakes to Jetavana monastery. There, the cakes were offered to the Buddha and to 500 monks. And even after they had all eaten, there were still cakes left. Those remaining cakes were thrown away at one of the gates of Jetavanārāma.

The Buddha then preached to Kosiya and his wife, and they entered the stream entrance state of mind [*sotāpatti*]. Afterward, Kosiya spent all his wealth in the service of the Buddha and his disciples.

One evening, the monks gathered in the preaching hall were talking about the Buddha being able to see what is happening with his divine eye, and how the Venerable Moggallāna had converted Kosiya, cleverly making a little thing miraculously become many. When the Buddha entered, he asked the monks what they were talking about. And on finding out, he said, "This is not the first time that this miserly billionaire was converted by the Venerable Moggallāna." And on the request of the monks, he told this story of the past:

Once upon a time, there was a billionaire in northern India. He was an adviser to a king. Although he was very rich, he was not at all good looking. He was lame due to crooked feet, and his hands were also deformed into crooked positions. His eyes were crooked too, that is to say, he was cross-eyed. And some would say he had a crooked mind as well, for he was without any religion whatsoever! You might think people would call him, 'Illīsa the Crooked', but that was not the case.

Illīsa also happened to be a miser, one who will not give anything to anybody. He would not even spend any of his wealth on his own enjoyment. Therefore, it was said that his home was like a pond possessed by demons, where no one could quench his thirst.

However, Illīsa's ancestors, going back seven generations, were the most generous of gift givers. They gave away the very best of their possessions. But when Illīsa inherited the family fortune, he abandoned that great family tradition.

The family had always maintained a charity dining-hall, where anyone could come for a free hot meal. Illīsa burned this free food kitchen to the ground, since he wanted to be rid of the expense. Then he pushed the poor and hungry from his door, hitting them as they went. He quickly earned a reputation for hoarding all his wealth and possessions. Soon people began calling him, 'Illīsa the Cheap'.

One day when he was returning home from advising the king, Illīsa saw a tired worn out villager by the side of the road. He had obviously walked a great distance. He was sitting on the ground pouring cheap wine into a cup. He was drinking it, along with some smelly dried fish.

Seeing this made Illīsa thirsty for a drink of liquor. Then he thought, "I would love to have a drink! But if I do, others may want to drink with me, and that could cost me money!" For that reason alone, he suppressed his craving for alcohol.

As time passed, his craving did not disappear. Instead, fighting it and worrying constantly made him look sick. His skin turned yellow, and he became thinner and thinner until the veins stuck out from his flesh. He fought a constant battle against his thirst for liquor. He slept face down, holding onto the bed tightly while he slept.

His wife began to notice the changes in him. One day, while massaging his back to comfort him, she asked, "Are you sick, my husband?" "No," said Illīsa. "Did the king get angry at you?" she asked. "No," said he. "Have our children or the servants done anything to upset you?" asked his wife. Again he said "No." "Do you have a strong craving for something?" she continued.

Illīsa the Cheap kept silent. He was afraid that if he told her it might end up costing him money! But his wife began pleading, "Tell me, please tell me." Finally, swallowing hard and clearing his throat, he answered,

"Yes, I do have a strong craving." "A craving for what?" she asked. "For a drink of alcoholic liquor," he admitted at last.

"Oh, is that all!" said his wife. "Why didn't you tell me this at first? You are not poor. You can easily afford to buy a drink for yourself and the whole city as well! Shall I brew a big batch of liquor for us all?"

Of course this was not what Illīsa the Cheap wanted to hear. He blurted out, "Why should we give liquor to others? Let them earn their own!" Then his wife asked, "Well then, what about just for us and our neighbors?" "I didn't know you had become so rich all of a sudden!" he shot back at her. "How about just our household?" she asked. "How generous you are with my money!" he replied. "All right then," she said, "I will brew just enough liquor for you and me, my husband." "Why should you be included? Women should not drink liquor!'"

"Now I understand you perfectly well!" said Illīsa's wife. "I will make only enough liquor for you alone." But Illīsa the Cheap always thought of even the slightest chance of spending money. He said, "If you prepare liquor here, people will notice and come ask for some. Even if I buy some in a liquor store and bring it here to drink, others will find out and want some. There will be no liquor given away in this house!"

So Illīsa decided to give the smallest coin he had to a servant boy, and sent him to the liquor store. When he returned, Illīsa took him down to the riverside. He took the small bottle of liquor from the boy, and set him to stand watch nearby. Then Illīsa the Cheap hid in the underbrush, poured some liquor into a cup, and secretly began drinking.

It just so happened that when Illīsa's father had died, he had been reborn as Sakka, King of the Heaven of 33. This was because of his lifelong generosity.

At this particular moment, Sakka was curious about whether his free food kitchen was still giving out food to all who wished it. He discovered that it no longer existed, that his son had given up the family tradition and had even kicked the hungry out onto the street! He saw his miserly son drinking by himself, hiding in the bushes, afraid he might have to share with others.

Sakka decided to change Illīsa's mind and teach him a lesson about the results of both good and bad actions. He decided to make him become generous, rather than cheap, so that he too might be reborn in a heaven world.

The King of the Heaven of 33 disguised himself so that he looked *exactly* like Illīsa the Cheap. He too had crooked feet, crooked hands and crooked eyes. He entered the city, went to the palace, and asked for an audience with the king. The king said, "Let my adviser Illīsa come in."

He asked, "Why have you come at this untimely moment?" "My lord," said Sakka, "I have come to give my billionaire's wealth to you to fill up the treasury." The king replied, "No, no. I have enough, much more than that." The disguised Sakka said, "Then if you do not want it my lord, kindly permit me to give it away as I wish." "Do as you say," said the king.

Sakka went to Illīsa's house. The servants greeted him as if he were indeed their master. He entered the house and sat down. He summoned the gatekeeper and said, "If anybody comes here who looks like me and says, 'This house is mine', don't let him in. Instead beat him on the back and kick him out!" Then he went upstairs and called for Illīsa's wife. Smiling at her he said, "My love, let us be generous!"

At first, Illīsa's wife, children and servants were surprised. They said to each other, "It was never in his mind to give anything to anybody before today. This must be because he's been drinking alcohol and has gotten a little soft in the head!"

Illīsa's wife said, "As you wish, my lord, give away as much as you like." "Call for the drummer," said Sakka, "and order him to go and beat his drum in the city. Have him announce that all who desire gold, silver, pearls, jewels, lapis lazuli, diamonds and coral, are to come to the home of Illīsa the billionaire." She did as he said.

Soon a big crowd began to arrive, carrying baskets, buckets and bags. Sakka opened up the storerooms of Illīsa's wealth. He said, "I give you all these riches. Take as much as you want and go." The people took it all outside and piled it up. They filled up their containers and carried them away.

One clever man from the countryside harnessed Illīsa the Cheap's bullocks to Illīsa the Cheap's bullock cart. Then he filled it to the brim with Illīsa the Cheap's seven treasures,[20] and rode out of the city by the main road.

Without knowing it, he passed by the bushes where the real Illīsa was still drinking liquor. He was so happy to be suddenly rich, that he shouted out as he went, "May Lord Illīsa the billionaire live a hundred years! Because of you I have struck the jackpot. I won't have to work another day in my life! These were your bullocks, your cart and your seven treasures. They were not given to me by my father and mother – but by you, Illīsa the generous!"

The hidden Illīsa was shocked to hear this. He thought, "This man is talking about me! Has the king taken my wealth and given it away?" Then he jumped out from the bushes and shouted, "Hey you, what are you doing with my bullock cart?" He grabbed the reins and stopped the cart.

The villager got down and said, "What's wrong with you? The billionaire Lord Illīsa is giving his wealth to all the people of the city. What do you think you're doing?" As he said this he struck Illīsa on the head as hard as a thunderclap and rode away on the cart filled with treasure.

---

20 The seven treasures, or kinds of wealth, are gold, silver, pearls, jewels (or, perhaps, crystal), lapis lazuli, diamonds, and coral.

Illīsa the Cheap bounced to his feet and chased after the cart. He grabbed the reins again. This time the villager held onto Illīsa by the hair, pulled his head down, and struck it hard with his elbow. He grabbed him by the neck, threw him to the ground, and then continued on his way.

All this rough treatment sobered up Illīsa. He ran home as fast as he could. He saw the crowds of people carrying off his precious riches. He grabbed hold of them to stop them, but they just pushed him out of the way and knocked him down. Nearly fainting from his bruises, he tried to get into his home. But the gatekeeper said, "Where do you think you're going?" Beating him with a cane, he grabbed him by the neck and threw him out.

Illīsa thought, "Now no one can help me but the king." So he ran to the palace and went straight inside. He said, "My lord, why do you want my house to be looted?" The king said, "This is not my doing. I myself heard you say that if I would not accept your wealth, you would give it to all the citizens. I applaud your generosity! And did you not send a drummer into the streets to announce you were giving your wealth to any and all?"

"My lord king must be joking!" said Illīsa. "I didn't do any such thing. People don't call me 'Illīsa the Cheap' for nothing! I don't give anything to anybody if I can help it! Please, lord king, summon whoever is giving my treasures away, and clear up this matter."

After being summoned by the king, Sakka came to the palace. Illīsa asked, "Who is the real billionaire, my lord king?" Neither the king nor his ministers could tell the difference between them.

The king said, "We cannot recognize which one it is. Do you know someone who can recognize you for sure?" "Yes, my lord, my wife can recognize me," said Illīsa. But when she was called for and asked to decide, she stood next to Sakka and said, "This is my husband." When Illīsa's children and servants were summoned, they too picked Sakka.

Illīsa thought, "I have a wart on my head, covered up by my hair. Only my barber knows this." So he said to the king, "Please summon my barber. He knows me very well."

The barber was called for and the king asked him, "Can you tell us which of these two men is Illīsa the billionaire?" "I must examine their heads," he said, "then I will determine who the real Illīsa is." "Do so," said the king.

Immediately Sakka, King of the Heaven of 33, made a wart appear on his head. When the barber examined them he found warts on both their heads. He said, "Oh lord king, I cannot recognize which of these is Illīsa. Both have crooked feet, both have crooked hands, both have crooked eyes, and both have warts on the same spots on their heads. I can't tell the difference!"

Hearing these words, Illīsa began trembling. His mind became so unbalanced from losing his last hope of regaining his wealth, that he fainted on the spot.

At that very moment, Sakka said, "I am not Illīsa. I am Sakka, King of the Gods of the Heaven of 33." As he said this, he used his super powers to rise into the air and remain suspended there.

Attendants splashed cold water on Illīsa's face and woke him from his fainting spell. He knelt down in respect before Sakka, King of Gods.

Then Sakka spoke: "This wealth came from me, Illīsa, not from you. I myself, when I was your father, did many meritorious deeds. I was glad to give to the poor and needy. That is why, when I died, I was reborn as Sakka, King of Gods.

"However, you have violated our family tradition. Being a non-giver, living the life of a miser, burning my charity dining-hall to the ground, and chasing the homeless beggars from your door – you have kept all the family wealth to yourself. You are so cheap that you cannot even use the wealth for your own enjoyment! It is utterly wasted and useless. The family fortune has become like a pond possessed by demons, where no one can quench his thirst. It would be better if you were dead!

"Illīsa, my former son, if you change your ways you will be the one to benefit most. If you rebuild my free food kitchen and give hot meals to all who ask, you will earn both merit and peace of mind. But if you refuse to be generous, I will make all your riches disappear. And I will split your crooked skull with my divine diamond dagger [*vajira*]!"

In fear of his own death, Illīsa the Cheap promised, "I will give generously from now on, oh King of Gods."

Sakka accepted his promise. Still floating in the air, he preached on the true value of giving [*dāna*]. He also convinced him to practice the Five Training Steps [*pañca-sīla*-s, the first five *sikkhā-pada*-s], for the benefit of himself and others. These are to give up entirely: destroying life, taking what is not given, sexual wrongdoing, speaking falsely, and losing one's mind from alcohol.

Then Sakka disappeared and returned to his heavenly home.

Illīsa did indeed change his ways. He gave alms generously, did many other good deeds, and became much happier. When he died he was reborn in a heaven world.

After finishing the telling of this Jātaka story, the Buddha identified the births in this way:

"The billionaire banker today was also the billionaire of the past. The good King Sakka then is today the Venerable Moggallāna. And the king then is today the Venerable Ānanda."

The moral: "Poor indeed is the rich man who won't part with a penny."

79

A Motherless Son
[Betrayal]
(*Kharassara-Jātaka*)

The Buddha told this Jātaka story while he was in Jetavana monastery with regard to a treacherous minister of the king of Kosala.

The Buddha said, "This man has done exactly the same treachery in the past, as well." And at the request of the king of Kosala, the Buddha told this story of the past:

Once upon a time, King Brahmadatta was ruling in Benares in northern India. He had a clever minister who pleased him very much. To show his appreciation he appointed him headman of a remote border village. His duty was to represent the king and collect the king's taxes from the villagers.

Before long the headman was completely accepted by the villagers. Since he had been sent by the just King Brahmadatta, they respected him highly. They came to trust him as much as if he had been born among them.

In addition to being clever, the headman was also very greedy. Collecting the king's taxes was not enough reward for him. After becoming friendly with a gang of bandits, he thought up a plan to make himself rich.

The headman said to his friends, the robbers, "I will find excuses and reasons to lead all the villagers into the jungle. This will be easy for me, since they trust me as one of their own. I will keep them busy in the jungle, while you invade the village and rob everything of value. Carry everything away before I bring the people home. In return for my help, you must give me half of all the loot!" The bandits agreed, and a date was set.

When the day arrived, the headman assembled all the villagers and led them into the jungle. According to the plan, the bandits entered the unprotected village. They stole everything of value they could find. They

also killed all the defenseless village cows, and cooked and ate the meat. At the end of the day the gang collected all their stolen goods and escaped.

It just so happened that on that very same day a traveling merchant came to the village to trade his goods. When he saw the bandits he stayed out of sight.

The headman brought all the villagers home in the evening. He ordered them to make a lot of noise by beating drums as they marched towards the village. If the bandits had still been there, they would have heard the villagers coming for sure.

The village people saw that they had been robbed and all their cows were dead and partly eaten. This made them very sad. The traveling merchant appeared and said to them, "This treacherous village headman has betrayed your trust in him. He must be a partner of the gang of bandits. Only after they left with all your valuables did he lead you home, beating drums as loudly as possible!

"This man pretends to know nothing about what has happened – as innocent as a newborn lamb! In truth, it's as if a son did something so shameful that his mother would say – 'I am not his mother. He is not my son. My son is dead!'"

Before long, news of the crime reached the king. He recalled the treacherous headman and punished him according to the law.

The Buddha then said:

"The treacherous minister of today was also the treacherous headman of the past. And the traveling merchant was I who am today the Buddha."

The moral: "No one defends a betrayer of trust."

80

Fear Maker and Little Archer
[Self-deception]
(Bhīmasena-Jātaka)

The Buddha told this Jātaka story while he was living in Jetavana temple about a monk who always bragged and exaggerated the truth.

This monk used to boast ceaselessly about his ancestry, deluding everyone as to his noble descent. But another monk, on inquiry, exposed his deceit.

One day, the monks gathered in the preaching hall were discussing this monk's lying boasts. When the Buddha entered and inquired as to the monks' topic of discussion, he said, "This is not the first time, oh monks, that this monk has gone about boasting. He did the same in the past, too." And at the invitation of the monks, the Buddha told this story of the past:

Some say that the world comes into being, disappears, and comes into being ... over and over, throughout time. In one of these previous worlds, countless years ago, Truth [Dhamma] was unknown and the Five Training Steps [pañca-sīla-s, the first five sikkhā-pada-s] were practiced by only a few. Even the Enlightenment Being – the Bodhisatta – did not know Truth, and had not yet discovered the Five Training Steps.

Once upon a time in that long ago world, there was a king named Brahmadatta. Like many other kings of that name, he ruled in the place known today as Benares.

The Bodhisatta was born in a rich high-class family in a market town, also in northern India. He happened to be a dwarf, bent over and partly hunchbacked. When he became a young man he remained short and stooped. Many people found him unpleasant to look at.

He studied under a very outstanding teacher. He learned all there was to know, at that time, about the two great branches of knowledge – religion [Veda] and science [Vedāṅga].[21] He also learned how to use a bow and arrow better than anyone else in India. For this reason his teacher called him 'Little Archer' [Culladhanuggaha].

Like most new graduates he was quite clever. He thought, "Many people judge by appearance alone. If I go to a king and ask for a job, he'll probably ask, 'Having such a short body, what can you possibly do for me?' Therefore it would be better if I can team up with a front man – someone who is handsome in appearance, tall and well-grown in body, and strong in personality. I will provide the brains, but remain out of sight behind his shadow. In this way we can earn a good living together."

One day he was walking in the district where the weavers live and work. He happened to see a big, strong looking man. He greeted him and asked his name. The weaver said, "Because of my appearance, people call me Fear Maker [Bhīmasena]."

"With such an impressive name," said Little Archer, "and being so big and strong looking, why do you have such a low paying job?" "Because life is hard," he replied.

"I have an idea," said the dwarf. "In all India there is no one as skilled with a bow and arrow as I am. But I don't look the part! If I asked a king for work he would either laugh or get angry at me. He would not believe that a hunchbacked little dwarf could be the greatest archer in India!

"But you look perfect. And your name helps too. Therefore, let us go together to the king. You will be the front man and do all the talking. The king will hire you immediately. Meanwhile I will remain as if hidden underneath your shadow. I will be the real archer and we will prosper and be happy. You just have to do whatever I tell you."

---

21 The Veda is the most sacred Hindu text, consisting principally of divinely inspired hymns and prayers. There are six Vedāṅga-s 'limbs of the Veda', or Vedic sciences. These are phonology, metre, grammar, etymology, astronomy, and ritual with the rules for ceremonial and sacrificial acts.

Thinking he had nothing to lose, Fear Maker agreed, saying, "It's a deal, my friend!"

The two partners went off to Benares to see the king. When they entered the throne room, they bowed respectfully to the king. He asked them, "Why have you come here?"

Fear Maker stood in front and did all the talking. He answered, "I am the great archer known as Fear Maker. There is no one in all India who understands the science of archery as well as I do. I wish to be in your service, your majesty."

The king was quite impressed. He asked, "What shall I pay you?" "I will serve you for 500 pieces of money per week, your majesty," he replied.

Nodding, the king noticed the silent dwarf stooping behind him, almost out of sight. "Who is this little man?" he asked. "What does he do for you?" "He's my little assistant," said Fear Maker. "Very well," said King Brahmadatta, "the job is yours."

In this way Fear Maker was accepted into the king's service, but it was Little Archer who did all the work.

Before long, news came to the palace that there was a ferocious tiger living in the jungle next to the king's highway. He ambushed travelers, and then killed and ate them. Many began to avoid the king's highway out of fear of the man-eater.

The king summoned Fear Maker and asked, "Can you capture this rampaging tiger, young man?" "Your majesty," he answered, "I am known as your best archer. Why wouldn't I be able to capture a tiger?" Hearing this, the king gave him an extra sum of money and sent him out to catch the tiger.

Fear Maker went home and told all this to his partner. "All right," said Little Archer, "be on your way!" "Aren't you coming too?" asked the surprised Fear Maker. "No, I won't go," he replied, "but I will give you a perfect plan. You must do exactly as I say." "I will, my little friend. Please tell me," said the big front man.

The clever little dwarf said to his friend, "Go to the district of the tiger, but don't rush straight to his home by yourself. Instead, gather together a thousand local villagers and give them all bows and arrows. Take them directly to the tiger's home. But then you must let them go on ahead while you hide in the underbrush.

"The local villagers will be very afraid of the tiger. When they see him they will surround him and beat him. Being so terrified, they won't stop beating him until he's dead!

"Meanwhile you must cut a piece of vine with your teeth. Then come out of hiding and approach the dead tiger, holding the vine in your hand. When you see the tiger's body, shout at the people, 'Hey! Who has killed the tiger? I was going to capture him with this vine and lead him like a bull to the king. That's why I've been searching in the jungle. Now tell me who has killed the tiger before I could get here with my vine.'

"The villagers will be easily frightened by this. They will say, 'Lord Fear Maker, please don't tell the king!' Then they will give you a big bribe to be quiet. Thinking you have killed the dangerous tiger, King Brahmadatta will also reward you greatly." This was the tricky plan of the clever Little Archer.

Fear Maker did exactly as he had been instructed. The man-eating tiger was killed, and fear was removed from that part of the king's highway. Followed by a big crowd he returned to the king and said, "Your majesty, I have killed the tiger and made the jungle safe for people again." The king was pleased and gave him a huge reward.

Before long there were similar complaints about a buffalo who threatened another royal road. Again the king sent Fear Maker. Following Little Archer's strategy he did exactly as before. He took credit for killing the buffalo and was greatly rewarded again by the grateful king.

By this time Fear Maker had become a very rich and powerful nobleman. All the wealth and praise, which he didn't really deserve, soon went to his head. He became intoxicated with his own conceit, and began thinking he was a 'big man' in his own right. He even looked down on

Little Archer and ignored his advice. He said to him, "You think this is all because of you. But I don't need you. I can do all this without you!" He had come to believe the appearance created by Little Archer's plan.

Then it happened that an enemy king attacked. He surrounded the city of Benares with his army. He sent a message to King Brahmadatta that he must either surrender his kingdom or wage war. The King of Benares ordered his greatest hero, Fear Maker, to go out and fight the enemy.

Fear Maker was dressed in full military armor. He mounted the mightiest armored war elephant. Little Archer knew that the ungrateful conceited braggart, called Fear Maker, was really scared to death underneath. So he too mounted the elephant and sat behind Fear Maker. The mighty elephant walked through the city gates towards the battlefield, followed by a big crowd.

When Fear Maker heard the huge noise made by the war drums, he began trembling with fear. To keep him from falling off the elephant and being killed, Little Archer tied a rope around him and held him with it.

When Fear Maker saw the field of battle he was overwhelmed by the terrible fear of death. So much so, that he couldn't help but release his bowels and urinate at the same time – all over the back of the poor brave war elephant!

The Enlightenment Being said, "Before, you bragged and spoke roughly like a *big man*. But now, the only *big* thing you do is make a filthy mess all over this elephant's back! Your present actions prove your past appearance was false."

Fear Maker had embarrassed himself. Little Archer had humbled him by speaking the truth. But he couldn't help feeling sympathy for him. He said, "Don't be afraid anymore, my friend. With me to protect you, your life is safe. Climb down from the elephant and go home and take a bath."

Alone atop the great elephant, the Enlightenment Being thought, "Now is the time to show what is in the heart of this hunchbacked little dwarf!" Shouting mightily as he rode, he charged into the field of battle. Without killing any men or animals, he crashed through the enemy's

defenses. He broke into the king's camp, captured him, and took him back as prisoner to the King of Benares.

King Brahmadatta was delighted with Little Archer's great victory. He rewarded him with wealth and fame. He became known throughout all India as 'Little Archer the Wise'. He sent his friend Fear Maker back to his home village and supported him with monthly payments.

Little Archer the Wise practiced generosity and other meritorious deeds. When he died he was reborn as he deserved.

The Buddha then identified the births, saying:

"Fear Maker was this boastful monk today who exaggerates. And Little Archer was I who am today the Buddha."

The moral: "'Appearances can be deceiving.'"

Forest Monks in a King's Pleasure Garden
[Pupils Without a Teacher]
(*Surāpāna-Jātaka*)

The Buddha told this story while he was living in Ghosita temple near Kosambī with regard to the elder Sāgata.

After spending the rainy season at Sāvatthi, the Buddha came near the town Bhaddavatikā. There, people warned him about a poisonous and deadly serpent that dwelt in that area. But the Buddha ignored their warning, and went on to Bhaddavatikā anyway.

While the Buddha was dwelling at Bhaddavatikā the elder Sāgata, a follower of the Buddha who had won supernatural powers [*iddhi*-s], went to where this serpent king dwelt and seating himself cross-legged on a prepared seat of leaves, overpowered the serpent through his miraculous powers and brought him into the Buddha's following. Sāgata thereupon went back to the Buddha, who then dwelt in Bhaddavatikā for as long as he pleased. The Buddha and his followers afterward went on to Kosambī.

The story of how Sāgata had converted the serpent king got bandied about. And the townsfolk of Kosambī, when they approached the Buddha, asked him and the elder Sāgata how they could please them. The Buddha remained silent. But the evil six Chabbaggiyā monks,[22] suggested that the townsfolk should offer Sāgata alcoholic *kāpotikā* spirits.[23]

---

22 The Chabbaggiyā monks are a group of six sinful monks contemporary with the Buddha who are taken to exemplify trespassing the rules of monastic discipline [*vinaya*] set out by the Buddha. Their names are Assaji, Punabbasu, Paṇḍuka, Lohitaka, Mettiya, and Bhummajaka.

23 *Kāpotikā* is to date an unidentified kind of alcoholic drink. Derivation of the term from *kapota* 'pigeon' is probably a folk etymology, and is doubtful. Cowell's Jātaka translation understands it as '*kāpotaka*' 'pigeon-colored, gray,

The next day when Sāgata went for alms, he was plied with intoxicating spirits. He got so drunk that on the way out of town, he fell prostrate at the town's gateway, babbling nonsense. On his way back from his meal in the town, the Buddha came on Sāgata lying in this condition, and asked the accompanying monks to carry Sāgata back to the temple. The monks then laid the elder down with his head toward the Buddha's feet. But he turned round, so that his feet lay towards the Buddha.[24]

The Buddha pointed out his condition to the monks, using it as an example of the evil effects of liquor. And the Buddha at this time set down a rule against the use of alcohol.

When the monks were later assembled in the preaching hall, they discussed the badness of drinking alcohol, pointing to the otherwise wise and gifted Sāgata's condition. When the Buddha entered and found out what they had been discussing before he came, he said, "Oh monks, this is not the first time that those who have renounced the world have lost their senses through drinking spirits. The very same thing happened in the past, as well." And the Buddha told this Jātaka story of the past:

Once upon a time, there was a high-class rich man who gave up his wealth and his easy life in the ordinary world. He went to the Himalayan forests and lived as a homeless holy man. By practicing meditation, he developed his mind and gained the highest knowledge [*abhiññā*]. Dwelling in high mental states [*brahma-vihāra*-s], he enjoyed great inner happiness and peace of mind. Before long, he had 500 pupils.

In a certain year, when the rainy season was beginning, the pupils said to their teacher, "Oh wise master, we would like to go to the places where most people live. We would like to get some salt and other seasonings and bring them back here."

---

of a dull white' and translates here 'white spirit.' The Pali Text Society's *Pali-English Dictionary* translates it as 'a kind of intoxicating drink of a reddish color (like pigeon's feet).'

24 Such is taken as a sign of disrespect. One's head ought to be near the feet of a person of higher status.

The teacher said, "You have my permission. It would be healthy for you to do so, and return when the rainy season is over. But I will stay here and meditate by myself." They knelt down and paid their farewell respects.

The 500 pupils went to Benares and began living in the royal pleasure garden. The next day they collected alms in the villages outside the city gates. They received generous gifts of food. On the following day they went inside the city. People gladly gave them food.

After a few days, people told the king [Brahmadatta], "Oh lord king, 500 forest monks have come from the Himalayas to live in your pleasure garden. They live in a simple way, without luxuries. They control their senses and are known to be very good indeed."

Hearing such good reports, the king went to visit them. He knelt down and paid his respects. He invited them to stay in the garden during the whole four months of the rainy season. They accepted, and from then on were given their food in the king's palace.

Before long a certain holiday took place. It was celebrated by drinking alcohol, which the people thought would bring good luck. The King of Benares thought, "Good wine is not usually available to monks who live simply in the forests. I will treat them to some as a special gift." So he gave the 500 forest monks a large quantity of the very best tasting wine.

The monks were not at all accustomed to alcohol. They drank the king's wine and walked back to the garden. By the time they got there, they were completely drunk. Some of them began dancing, while others sang songs. Usually they put away their bowls and other things neatly. But this time they just left everything lying around, here and there. Soon they all passed out into a drunken sleep.

When they had slept off their drunkenness, they awoke and saw the messy condition they'd left everything in. They became sad and said to each other, "We have done a bad thing, which is not proper for holy men like us." Their embarrassment and shame made them weep with regret. They said, "We have done these unwholesome things [*akusala-kamma*-s] only because we are away from our holy teacher."

At that very moment the 500 forest monks left the pleasure garden and returned to the Himalayas. When they arrived they put away their bowls and other belongings neatly, as was their custom. Then they went to their beloved master and greeted him respectfully.

He asked them, "How are you, my children? Did you find enough food and lodgings in the city? Were you happy and united?"

They replied, "Venerable master, we were happy and united. But we drank what we were not supposed to drink. We lost all our common sense and self-control. We danced and sang like silly monkeys. It's fortunate we didn't turn into monkeys! We drank wine, we danced, we sang, and in the end we cried from shame."

The kind teacher said, "It is easy for things like this to happen to pupils who have no teacher to guide them. Learn from this, do not do such things in the future."

From then on they lived happily and grew in goodness.

After telling this story, the Buddha identified the births in this way:

"The 500 forest monks at that time are my disciples today. And their teacher was I who am today the Buddha."

The moral: "A pupil without a teacher is easily embarrassed."

The Curse of Mittavinda
(*Mittavinda-Jātaka, Mittavindaka-Jātaka*)

The Buddha told this story while he was living in Jetavana monastery with regard to a disobedient monk. The incidents of this story's telling are the same as those for the first Jātaka of the ninth book, the *Gijjha-Jātaka* [No. 427].

[A certain young monk, immediately after his ordination, became careless in his duties, his fulfillment of good qualities, and did not pay attention to elder monks' admonitions. He said to them, "Don't tell me how to behave. I know what to do and what not to do."

One day, the monks in the preaching hall, having heard of his disobedience, were discussing his behavior. The Buddha heard of it from the monks. On hearing of it, the Buddha summoned that monk, and the Buddha warned him, "Oh monk, in your previous life also you did not listen to elders' advice and because of that you were blown to your death by *veramba* winds.][25]

Here, the Buddha admonished this monk, "Long ago you, too, were disobedient. And because of that a cutting wheel of blades was given to you." And the Buddha told this story of the past:

Chapter 1. Jealousy

Once upon a time, there was a monk who lived in a tiny monastery in a little village. He was very fortunate that the village rich man supported him in the monastery. He never had to worry about the cares of the world. His alms food was always provided automatically by the rich man.

---

25 *Veramba* winds are strong high winds that blow from four directions at the same time.

So the monk was calm and peaceful in his mind. There was no fear of losing his comfort and his daily food. There was no desire for greater comforts and pleasures of the world. Instead, he was free to practice the correct conduct of a monk, always trying to eliminate his faults and do only wholesome deeds. But he didn't know just how lucky he was!

One day an elder monk arrived in the little village. He had followed the path of Truth [Dhamma] until he had become perfect and faultless.

When the village rich man saw this unknown monk, he was very pleased by his gentle manner and his calm attitude. So he invited him into his home. He gave him food to eat, and he thought himself very fortunate to hear a short teaching from him. He then invited him to take shelter at the village monastery. He said, "I will visit you there this evening, to make sure all is well."

When the perfect monk arrived at the monastery, he met the village monk. They greeted each other pleasantly. Then the village monk asked, "Have you had your lunch today?" The other replied, "Yes, I was given lunch by the supporter of this monastery. He also invited me to take shelter here."

The village monk took him to a room and left him there. The perfect monk passed his time in meditation.

Later that evening, the village rich man came. He brought fruit drinks, flowers and lamp oil, in honor of the visiting holy man. He asked the village monk, "Where is our guest?" He told him what room he had given him.

The man went to the room, bowed respectfully, and greeted the perfect monk. Again he appreciated hearing the way of Truth as taught by the rare faultless one.

Afterwards, as evening approached, he lit the lamps and offered the flowers at the monastery's lovely temple shrine. He invited both monks to lunch at his home the next day. Then he left and returned home.

In the evening, a terrible thing happened. The village monk, who had been so contented, allowed the poison of jealousy to creep into his mind. He thought, "The village rich man has made it easy for me here. He provides shelter each night and fills my belly once a day.

"But I'm afraid this will change because he respects this new monk so highly. If he remains in this monastery, my supporter may stop caring for me. Therefore, I must make sure the new monk does not stay."

Thinking in this way, he lost his former mental calm. His mind became disturbed due to his jealousy – the fear of losing his comfort and his daily food. This led to the added mental pain of resentment against the perfect monk. He began plotting and scheming to get rid of him.

Late that night, as was the custom, the monks met together to end the day. The perfect monk spoke in his usual friendly way, but the village monk would not speak to him at all.

So the wise monk understood that he was jealous and resentful. He thought, "This monk does not understand my freedom from attachment to families, people and comforts. I am free of any desire to remain here. I am also free of any desire to leave here. It makes no difference. It is sad this other one cannot understand nonattachment. I pity him for the price he must pay for his ignorance."

He returned to his room, closed the door, and meditated in a high mental state throughout the night.

The next day, when it was time to go collect alms food from the supporter of the monastery, the village monk rang the temple gong. But he rang it by tapping it lightly with his fingernail. Even the birds in the temple courtyard could not hear the tiny sound.

Then he went to the visiting monk's room and knocked on the door. But again he only tapped lightly with his fingernail. Even the little mice inside the walls could not hear the silent tapping.

Having done his courteous duty in such a tricky way, he went to the rich man's home. The man bowed respectfully to the monk, took his alms bowl, and asked, "Where is the new monk, our visitor?"

The village monk replied, "I have not seen him. I rang the gong, I knocked at his door, but he did not appear. Perhaps he was not used to such rich food as you gave him yesterday. Perhaps he is still asleep, busily digesting it, dreaming of his next feast! Perhaps this is the kind of monk who pleases you so much!"

Meanwhile, back at the monastery, the perfect monk awoke. He cleaned himself and put on his robe. Then he calmly departed to collect alms food wherever he happened to find it.

The rich man fed the village monk the richest of food. It was delicious and sweet, made from rice, milk, butter, sugar and honey. When the monk had eaten his fill, the man took his bowl, scrubbed it clean, and sweetened it with perfumed water. He filled it up again with the same wonderful food. He gave it back to the monk, saying, "Honorable monk, our holy visitor must be worn out from traveling. Please take my humble alms food to him." Saying nothing, he accepted the generous gift for the other.

By now the village monk's mind was trapped by its own jealous scheming. He thought, "If that other monk eats this fantastic meal, even if I grabbed him by the throat and kicked him out, he still would never leave! I must secretly get rid of this alms food. But if I give it to a stranger, it will become known and talked about. If I throw it away in a pond, the butter will float on the surface and be discovered. If I throw it away on the ground, crows will come from miles around to feast on it, and that too would be noticed. So how can I get rid of it?"

Then he saw a field that had just been burned by farmers to enrich the soil. It was covered with hot glowing coals. So he threw the rich man's generous gift on the coals. The alms food burned up without a trace. And with it went his peace of mind!

For, when he got back to the monastery, he found the visitor gone. He thought, "This must have been a perfectly wise monk. He must have known I was jealous – afraid of losing my favored position. He must have known I resented him and tried to trick him into leaving. I wasted alms food meant for him. And all for the sake of keeping my own belly full! I'm afraid something terrible will happen to me! What have I done?" So, afraid of losing his easy daily food, he had thrown away his peace of mind.

For the rest of his life the rich man continued to support him. But his mind was filled with torment and suffering. He felt doomed like a walking starving zombie, or a living hungry ghost.

When he died, his torment continued. For he was reborn in a hell world, where he suffered for hundreds of thousands of years.

Finally, there too he died, as all beings must. But the results of his past actions were only partly completed. So he was reborn as a demon, 500 times! In those 500 lives, there was only one day when he got enough to eat, and that was a meal of afterbirth dropped by a deer in the forest!

Then he was reborn as a starving stray dog – another 500 times! For the sake of a full monk's belly in a past life, all these 500 lives were also filled with hunger, and quarreling over food. Only a single time did he get enough to eat, and that was a meal of vomit he found in a gutter!

Finally most of the results of his actions were finished. Only then was he so very fortunate enough to be reborn as a human being. He was born into the poorest of the poor beggar families of the city of Kāsi, in northern India. He was given the name, Mittavinda.

From the moment of his birth, this poor family became even more poor and miserable. After a few years, the pain of hunger became so great, that his parents beat him and chased Mittavinda away for good. They shouted, "Be gone forever! You are nothing but a curse!"

Poor Mittavinda! So very long ago he had not known how lucky he was. He was contented as a humble village monk. But he allowed the poison of jealousy to enter his mind – the fear of losing his easy daily food. This led to the self-torture of resentment against a perfect monk, and to trickery in denying him one wholesome gift of alms food. And it took a thousand and one lives for the loss of his comfort and daily food to be completed. What he had feared, his own actions had brought to pass!

Chapter 2. Greed

Little did poor Mittavinda know that his lives of constant hunger were about to come to an end. After wandering about, he eventually ended up in Benares.

At that time the Enlightenment Being was living the life of a world-famous teacher in Benares. He had 500 students. As an act of charity, the people of the city supported these poor students with food. They also paid the teacher's fees for teaching them.

Mittavinda was permitted to join them. He began studying under the great teacher. And at last, he began eating regularly.

But he paid no attention to the teachings of the wise master. He was disobedient and violent. During 500 lives as a hungry dog, quarreling had become a habit. So he constantly got into fist fights with the other students.

It became so bad that many of the students quit. The income of the world-famous teacher dwindled down to almost nothing. Because of all his fighting, Mittavinda was finally forced to run away from Benares.

He found his way to a small remote village. He lived there as a hard-working laborer, married a very poor woman, and had two children.

It became known that he had studied under the world- famous teacher of Benares. So the poor villagers selected him to give advice when questions arose. They provided a place for him to live near the entrance to the village. And they began following his advice.

But things did not go well. The village was fined seven times by the king. Seven times their houses were burned. And seven times the town pond dried up.

They realized that all their troubles began when they started taking Mittavinda's advice. So they chased him and his family out of the village. They shouted, "Be gone forever! You are nothing but a curse!"

While they were fleeing, they went through a haunted forest. Demons came out of the shadows and killed and ate his wife and children. But Mittavinda escaped.

He made his way to a seaport city [Gambhīra]. He was lonely, miserable and penniless. It just so happened that there was a kind generous rich merchant living in the city. He heard the story of Mittavinda's misfortunes. Since they had no children of their own, he and his wife adopted Mittavinda. For better or worse they treated him exactly as their own son.

His new mother and father were very religious. They always tried to do wholesome things. But Mittavinda still had not learned his lesson. He did not accept any religion, so he often did unwholesome things.

Some time after his father's death, his mother decided to try and help him enter the religious life. She said, "There is this world and there is the one to come. If you do bad things, you will suffer painful results in both worlds."

But foolish Mittavinda replied, "I will do whatever I enjoy doing and become happier and happier. There is no point considering whether what I do is wholesome or unwholesome. I don't care about such things!"

On the next full moon holy day, Mittavinda's mother advised him to go to the temple and listen all night long to the wise words of the monks. He said, "I wouldn't waste my time!" So she said, "When you return I will give you a thousand gold coins."

Mittavinda thought that with enough money he could enjoy himself constantly and be happy all the time. So he went to the temple. But he sat in a corner, paid no attention, and fell asleep for the night. Early the next morning he went home to collect his reward.

Meanwhile his mother thought he would appreciate wise teachings. Then he would bring the oldest monk home with him. So she prepared delicious food for the expected guest. When she saw him returning alone, she said, "Oh my son, why didn't you ask the senior monk to come home with you for breakfast?"

He said, "I did not go to the temple to listen to a monk or to bring him home with me. I went only to get your thousand gold coins!" His disappointed mother said, "Never mind the money. Since there is so much delicious food prepared – only eat and sleep!" He replied, "Until you give me the money I refuse to eat!" So she gave him the thousand gold coins. Only then did he gobble up the food until all he could do was fall asleep.

Mittavinda did not think a thousand gold coins were enough for him to constantly enjoy himself. So he used the money to start a business, and before long he became very rich. One day he came home and said, "Mother, I now have 120,000 gold coins. But I am not yet satisfied. Therefore I will go abroad on the next ship and make even more money!"

She replied, "Oh my son, why do you want to go abroad? The ocean is dangerous and it is very risky doing business in a strange land. I have 80,000 gold coins right here in the house. That is enough for you. Please don't go, my only son!"

Then she held him to keep him from leaving. But Mittavinda was crazy with greed. So he pushed his mother's hand away and slapped her face. She fell to the floor. She was so hurt and shocked that she yelled at him, "Be gone forever! You are nothing but a curse!"

Without looking back, Mittavinda rushed to the harbor and set sail on the first departing ship.

Chapter 3. Pleasure

After seven days on the Indian Ocean, all the winds and currents stopped completely. The ship was stuck! After being dead in the water for seven days, all on board were terrified they would die.

So they drew straws to find out who was the cause of their bad luck and frightening misfortune. Seven times the short straw was drawn by Mittavinda!

They forced him onto a tiny bamboo raft, and set him adrift on the open seas. They shouted, "Be gone forever! You are nothing but a curse!" And suddenly a strong wind sent the ship on its way.

But once again Mittavinda's life was spared. This was a result of his wholesome actions as a monk, so many births ago. No matter how long it takes, actions cause results.

Sometimes an action causes more than one result, some pleasant and some unpleasant. It is said there are Asura-s who live through such mixed results in an unusual way.

Asura-s are unfortunate ugly gods. Some of them are lucky enough to change their form into beautiful young dancing girl goddesses. These are called Apsaras-es.

They enjoy the greatest pleasures for seven days. But then they must go to a hell world and suffer torments as hungry ghosts for seven days. Again they become Apsaras goddesses – back and forth, back and forth – until both kinds of results are finished.

While floating on the tiny bamboo raft, it just so happened that Mittavinda came to a lovely Glass Palace. There he met four very pretty Apsaras-es. They enjoyed their time together, filled with heavenly pleasures, for seven days.

Then, when it was time for the goddesses to become hungry ghosts, they said to Mittavinda, "Wait for us just seven short days, and we will return and continue our pleasure."

The Glass Palace and the four Apsaras-es disappeared. But still Mittavinda had not regained the peace of mind thrown away by the village monk, so very long ago. Seven days of pleasure had not satisfied him. He could not wait for the lovely goddesses to return. He wanted more and more. So he continued on, in the little bamboo raft.

Lo and behold, he came to a shining Silver Palace, with eight Apsaras goddesses living there. Again he enjoyed seven days of the greatest pleasure. These Apsaras-es also asked him to wait the next seven days, and disappeared into a hell world.

Amazing as it may seem, the greedy Mittavinda went on to seven days of pleasure in a sparkling Jewel Palace with 16 Apsaras-es. But they too disappeared. Then he spent seven days in a glowing Golden Palace with 32 of the most beautiful Apsaras-es of all.

But still he was not satisfied! When all 32 asked him to wait seven days, again he departed on the raft.

Before long he came to the entrance of a hell world filled with suffering tortured beings. They were living through the results of their own actions. But his desire for more pleasure was so strong that Mittavinda thought he saw a beautiful city surrounded by a wall with four fabulous gates. He thought, "I will go inside and make myself king!"

After he entered, he saw one of the victims of this hell world. He had a collar around his neck that spun like a wheel, with five sharp blades cutting into his face, head, chest and back. But Mittavinda was still so greedy for pleasure that he could not see the pain right before his eyes. Instead he saw the spinning collar of cutting blades as if it were a lovely lotus blossom. He saw the dripping blood as if it were the red powder of perfumed sandalwood. And the screams of pain from the poor victim sounded like the sweetest of songs!

He said to the poor man, "You've had that lovely lotus crown long enough! Give it to me, for I deserve to wear it now." The condemned man warned him, "This is a cutting collar, a wheel of blades." But Mittavinda said, "You only say that because you don't want to give it up."

The victim thought, "At last the results of my past unwholesome deeds must be completed. Like me, this poor fool must be here for striking his mother. I will give him the wheel of pain." So he said, "Since you want it so badly, take the lotus crown!"

With these words the wheel of blades spun off the former victim's neck and began spinning around the head of Mittavinda. And suddenly all his illusions disappeared – he knew this was no beautiful city, but a terrible hell world; he knew this was no lotus crown, but a cutting wheel of blades; and he knew he was not king, but prisoner. Groaning in pain he cried out desperately, "Take back your wheel! Take back your wheel!" But the other one had disappeared.

Just then the king of the gods arrived for a teaching visit to the hell world. Mittavinda asked him, "Oh king of gods, what have I done to deserve this torment?" The god replied, "Refusing to listen to the words of monks, you obtained no wisdom, but only money. A thousand gold coins did not satisfy you, nor even 120,000. Blinded by greed, you struck your mother on your way to grabbing greater wealth still.

"Then the pleasure of four Apsaras-es in their Glass Palace did not satisfy you. Neither eight Apsaras-es in a Silver Palace, nor 16 in a Jewel Palace. Not even the pleasure of 32 lovely goddesses in a Golden Palace was enough for you! Blinded by greed for pleasure you wished to be king. Now, at last, you see your crown is only a wheel of torture, and your kingdom is a hell world.

"Learn this, Mittavinda – all who follow their greed wherever it leads are left unsatisfied. For it is in the nature of greed to be dissatisfied with what one has, whether a little or a lot. The more obtained, the more desired – until the circle of greed becomes the circle of pain."

Having said this, the god returned to his heaven world home. At the same time the wheel crashed down on Mittavinda. With his head spinning in pain, he found himself adrift on the tiny bamboo raft.

Soon he came to an island inhabited by a powerful she-devil. She happened to be disguised as a goat. Being hungry, Mittavinda thought nothing of grabbing the goat by a hind leg. And the she-devil hiding inside kicked him way up into the air. He finally landed in a thorn bush on the outskirts of Benares!

After he untangled himself from the thorns, he saw some goats grazing nearby. He wanted very badly to return to the palaces and the dancing girl Apsaras-es. Remembering that a goat had kicked him here, he grabbed the leg of one of these goats. He hoped it would kick him back to the island.

Instead, this goat only cried out. The shepherds came, and captured Mittavinda for trying to steal one of the king's goats.

As he was being taken as a prisoner to the king, they passed by the world-famous teacher of Benares. Immediately he recognized his student. He asked the shepherds, "Where are you taking this man?"

They said, "He is a goat thief! We are taking him to the king for punishment!" The teacher said, "Please don't do so. He is one of my students. Release him to me, so he can be a servant in my school." They agreed and left him there.

The teacher asked Mittavinda, "What has happened to you since you left me?"

He told the story of being first respected, and then cursed, by the people of the remote village. He told of getting married and having two children, only to see them killed and eaten by demons in the haunted forest. He told of slapping his generous mother when he was crazy with the greed for money. He told of being cursed by his shipmates and being cast adrift on a bamboo raft. He told of the four palaces with their beautiful goddesses, and how each time his pleasure ended he was left unsatisfied. He told of the cutting wheel of torture, the reward for the greedy in hell. And he told of his hunger for goat meat, that only got him kicked back to Benares without even a bite to eat!

The world-famous teacher said, "It is clear that your past actions have caused both unpleasant and pleasant results, and that both are eventually completed. But you cannot understand that pleasures always come to an end. Instead, you let them feed your greed for more and more. You are left exhausted and unsatisfied, madly grasping at goat legs! Calm down, my friend. And know that trying to hold water in a tight fist, will always leave you thirsty!"

Hearing this, Mittavinda bowed respectfully to the great teacher. He begged to be allowed to follow him as a student. The Enlightenment Being welcomed him with open arms.

* * *

At the end of this Jātaka story, the Buddha identified the births in this way:

"Mittavinda then, was this disobedient monk. And I who have become the Buddha was the teacher who gave him advice."

The moral: "In peace of mind, there is neither loss nor gain."

$$\boxed{83}$$

A Hero Named Jinx
[Friendship]
(*Kālakaṇṇi-Jātaka*)

This story was told by the Buddha while he was dwelling in Jetavana monastery with regard to a friend of the millionaire Anāthapiṇḍika's named 'Jinx' [Kālakaṇṇi],[26] to whom Anāthapiṇḍika remained faithful from childhood despite his name, and who at one point saved Anāthapiṇḍika's wealth from robbers.

When Anāthapiṇḍika told the Buddha the incident, the Buddha said, "This is not the first time that a man named Jinx has saved his friend's wealth from robbers. The exact same thing happened as well in the past." And at Anāthapiṇḍika's request, the Buddha told the story of the past:

Once upon a time, there was a very rich man who was well-known for wholesomeness. He had a good friend who had the somewhat strange name, Jinx [Kālakaṇṇi]. They had been the best of friends ever since they were little children making mud-pies together. They had gone to the same schools and helped each other always.

After graduating, Jinx fell on hard times. He couldn't find a job and earn a living. So he went to see his lifelong friend, the prosperous and successful rich man. He was kind and comforting to his friend Jinx, and was happy to hire him to manage his property and business.

After he went to work in the rich man's mansion, pretty soon his strange name became a household word. People said, "Wait a minute, Jinx," "Hurry up, Jinx," "Do this, Jinx," "Do that, Jinx."

After a while some of the rich man's neighbors went to him and

---

26 Literally, the name means 'one with black ears.' To be "black-eared" is an unlucky quality. It is a bad omen that spoils luck. Hence, 'Jinx.'

said, "Dear friend and neighbor, we are concerned that misfortune may strike. Your mansion manager has a very strange and unlucky name. You should not let him live with you any longer. His name fills your house, with people saying, 'Wait a minute, Jinx,' 'Hurry up, Jinx,' 'Do this, Jinx,' 'Do that, Jinx.' People only use the word 'jinx' when they want to cause bad luck or misfortune. Even house spirits and fairies would be frightened by hearing it constantly and would run away. This can only bring disaster to your household. The man named Jinx is inferior to you – he is miserable and ugly. What advantage can you possibly get by keeping such a fellow around?"

The rich man replied, "Jinx is my best friend! We have supported and cared for each other ever since we were little tots making mud-pies together. A lifelong trustworthy friend is of great value indeed! I could not reject him and lose our friendship just because of his name. After all, a name is only for recognition.

"The wise don't give a name a second thought. Only fools are superstitious about sounds and words and names. They don't make good luck or bad luck!" So saying, the rich man refused to follow the advice of his busybody neighbors.

One day he went on a journey to his home village. While he was away, he left his friend Jinx in charge of his mansion home.

It just so happened that a gang of robbers heard about this. They decided it would be a perfect time to rob the mansion. So they armed themselves with various weapons and surrounded the rich man's home during the night.

Meanwhile, the faithful Jinx suspected that robbers might attack. So he stayed up all night to guard his friend's possessions. When he caught sight of the gang surrounding the house, he woke up everybody inside. Then he got them to blow shell horns and beat drums and make as much noise as possible.

Hearing all this, the bandits thought, "We must have been given bad information. There must be many people inside and the rich man must still be at home." So they threw down their clubs and other weapons, and ran away.

The next morning the people from the mansion were surprised to see the discarded weapons. They said to each other, "If we didn't have such a wise house protector, all the wealth in the mansion would certainly have been stolen. Jinx has turned out to be a hero! Rather than bringing bad luck, such a strong friend has been a blessing to the rich man."

When the master of the house returned home his neighbors met him and told him what had happened. He said, "You all advised against letting my friend stay with me. If I had done as you said, I'd be penniless today!

"Walking together for just seven steps is enough to start a friendship. Continuing for 12 steps forms a bond of loyalty. Remaining together for a month brings the closeness of relatives. And for longer still, the friend becomes like a second self. So my friend Jinx is no jinx – but a great blessing!"

At the conclusion of this Jātaka story, the Buddha identified the births:

"The Venerable Ānanda was the faithful Jinx of those days. And I, myself, was the rich man."

The moral: "The longer the friendship, the greater its rewards."

A Question From a Seven-year-old
[Six Worthy Ways]
(Atthasadvāra-Jātaka)

The Buddha told this story while living in Jetavana temple with regard to a boy who was very wise and understanding.

When the boy was seven years old he came to his father, who was a wealthy man of Sāvatthi, and asked his father what were the doors to spiritual well being. His father did not know the answer, but knew that the Buddha would. So, taking perfumes and flowers, he went to the Buddha, kneeled down before him and related to the Buddha the boy's question. The Buddha replied that he had answered the very same question from his son in former days. But due to re-becoming [puna-bbhava], the answer has become clouded over in his mind. And at the father's request, the Buddha told this story of the past:

Once upon a time there was a rich man living in Benares, in northern India. He had a son who was intelligent, curious and eager to learn. Even though he was only seven years old, he was determined to find out what is really valuable.

One day the little boy asked his father, "What are the ways to gain the most valuable things in life?"

His father said, "Only worthy ways lead to worthwhile goals. These are the six worthy ways [*atthasa-dvāra-s*]:

- keep yourself healthy and fit;
- be wholesome in every way;
- listen to those with more experience;
- learn from those with more knowledge;
- live according to Truth [Dhamma];
- act with sincerity, not just energy."

The boy paid close attention to his father's words. He tried hard to practice these ways from then on. As he grew up and became wise, he realized that the six worthy ways, and the most valuable things in life, could not be separated.

The Buddha then identified the births, saying:

"This child was the same as the little boy in those days. And I, myself, was the father."

The moral: "'A serious question deserves a serious answer.'"

A Lesson From a Snake
[The Value of Goodness]
(Sīlavīmaṁsana-Jātaka)

The Buddha told this story while living in Jetavana monastery with regard to an honored Brahmin adviser of the king of Kosala who put to the test his reputation for goodness in order to determine what it was that the king admired in him. On determining that it was his goodness that the king honored, he decided to go to the Buddha in Jetavanārāma and to enter the monkhood. By application, he gained spiritual insight and became free of defilement, becoming an Arahant [saint].

One evening, the monks assembled in the preaching hall were talking about this. When the Buddha entered and asked them what they were talking about before he came there, he said, "Oh monks, the actions of this Brahmin in putting to the test his reputation for goodness, and afterward renouncing the world and working out his salvation, was done as well by the wise in the past." And saying this, the Buddha told this story of the past:

Once upon a time, King Brahmadatta of Benares had a very valuable adviser priest. He came from a rich noble family. He was intelligent and full of knowledge. He was generous with his wealth and knowledge, holding nothing back. People thought of him as a kind and good person.

By practicing the Five Training Steps [pañca-sīla-s, the first five sikkhā-pada-s], he trained his mind to avoid the five unwholesome actions [akusala-kamma-s]. He discovered that giving up each unwholesome action made him better off in its own way:

- destroying life, since you have to kill part of yourself in order to kill someone else;

- taking what is not given, since this makes the owner angry at you;
- doing wrong in sexual ways, since this leads to the pain of jealousy and envy;
- speaking falsely, since you can't be true to yourself and false to another at the same time;
- losing your mind from alcohol, since then you might hurt yourself by doing the other four.

Seeing how he lived, King Brahmadatta thought, "This is truly a good man."

The priest was curious to learn more about the value of goodness. He thought, "The king honors and respects me more than his other priests. But I wonder what it is about me that he really respects most. Is it my nationality, my noble birth or family wealth? Is it my great learning and vast knowledge? Or is it because of my goodness? I must find the answer to this."

Therefore, he decided to perform an experiment in order to answer his question. He would pretend to be a thief!

On the next day, when he was leaving the palace, he went by the royal coin maker. He was stamping out coins from gold. The good priest, not intending to keep it, took a coin and continued walking out of the palace. Because the money maker admired the famous priest highly, he remained sitting and said nothing.

On the following day the make-believe thief took two gold coins. Again the royal coin maker did not protest.

Finally, on the third day, the king's favorite priest grabbed a whole handful of gold coins. This time the money maker didn't care about the priest's position or reputation. He cried out, "This is the third time you have robbed his majesty the king." Holding onto him, he shouted, "I've caught the thief who robs the king! I've caught the thief who robs the king! I've caught the thief who robs the king!"

Suddenly a crowd of people came running in, yelling, "Aha! You pretended to be better than us! An example of goodness!" They slapped him, tied his hands behind his back, and hauled him off to the king.

But on their way, they happened to go by some snake charmers. They were entertaining some bystanders from the king's court with a poisonous cobra. They held him by the tail and neck, and coiled him around their necks to show how brave they were.

The tied up prisoner said to them, "Please be careful! Don't grab that cobra by the tail. Don't grab him by his neck. And don't coil that poisonous snake around your own necks. He may bite you and bring your lives to a sudden end!"

The snake charmers said, "You ignorant priest, you don't understand about this cobra. He is well mannered and very good indeed. He is not bad like you! You are a thief who has stolen from the king. Because of your wickedness and criminal behavior, you are being carried off with your hands tied behind your back. But there's no need to tie up a snake who is good!"

The priest thought, "Even a poisonous cobra, who doesn't bite or harm anyone, is given the name 'good' [su-sīla]. In truth, goodness is the quality people admire most in the world!"

When they arrived at the throne room, the king asked, "What is this, my children?" They replied, "This is the thief who stole from your royal treasury." The king said, "Then punish him according to the law."

The adviser priest said, "My lord king, I am no thief!" "Then why did you take gold coins from the palace?" asked the king.

The priest explained, "I have done this only as an experiment, to test why it is you honor and respect me more than others. Is it because of my family background and wealth, or my great knowledge? Because of those things, I was able to get away with taking one or two gold coins. Or do you respect my goodness most of all? It is clear that by grabbing a handful of coins I no longer had the name 'good'. This alone turned respect into disgrace!

"Even a poisonous cobra, who doesn't harm anyone, is called 'good'. There is no need for any other title!"

To emphasize the lesson he had learned, the wise priest recited:

"High birth and wealth and even knowledge vast, I find,
  Are less admired than goodness is, by humankind."

The king pardoned his most valuable adviser priest. He asked to be allowed to leave the king's service in the ordinary world and become a forest monk. After refusing several times, the king eventually gave his permission.

The priest went to the Himalayas and meditated peacefully. When he died he was reborn in a heaven world.

The Buddha said:

"My disciples today were the king's followers in those days. And I, myself, who have today become the Buddha was the adviser priest."

The moral: "People prize goodness most of all."

A Priest Who Worshipped Luck
[Superstition]
(*Maṅgala-Jātaka*)

The Buddha told this story while living in the Bamboo Grove temple with regard to a Brahmin who was skilled in prognostication from pieces of cloth.

An exactly similar situation as happened to the holy man in the Jātaka story happened to the Buddha himself with regard to this Brahmin and his son when the Buddha saw with his divine eye [*dibba-cakkhu*] that the Brahmin and his son were predestined to attain Arahant-ship [freedom from defilement].

The Buddha told this Brahmin that in the past, too, he held such superstitions. And at the Brahmin's request, the Buddha told this story of the past:

Once upon a time, the Enlightenment Being was born into a high-class family in northwestern India. When he grew up, he realized his ordinary life could not give him lasting happiness. So he left everything behind and went to live in the Himalayas as a forest monk. He meditated and gained knowledge and peace of mind.

One day he decided to come down from the forests to the city of Rājagaha. When he arrived he stayed overnight in the king's pleasure garden.

The next morning he went into the city to collect alms food. The king saw him and was pleased with his humble and dignified attitude. So he invited him to the palace. He offered him a seat and gave him the best foods to eat. Then he invited him to live in the garden for good. The holy man agreed, and from then on he lived in the king's pleasure garden and had his meals in the king's palace.

At that time there was a priest in the city who was known as 'Lucky Cloth' [Dussalakkhaṇa-brāhmaṇa].[27] He used to predict good or bad luck by examining a piece of cloth.

It just so happened that he had a new suit of clothes. One day, after his bath, he asked his servant to bring the suit to him. The servant saw that it had been chewed slightly by mice, so he told the priest.

Lucky Cloth thought, "It is dangerous to keep in the house these clothes that have been chewed by mice. This is a sure sign of a curse that could destroy my home. Therefore, I can't even give them to my children or servants. The curse would still be in my house!

"In fact, I can't give these unlucky clothes to anyone. The only safe thing to do is to get rid of them once and for all. The best way to do that is to throw them in the corpse grounds, the place where dead bodies are put for wild animals to eat.

"But how can I do that? If I tell a servant to do it, desire will make him keep the clothes, and the curse will remain in my household. Therefore, I can trust this task only to my son."

He called his son to him and told all about the curse of the clothes that were slightly chewed by mice. He told him not even to touch them with his hand. He was to carry them on a stick and go throw them in the corpse grounds. Then he must bathe from head to foot before returning home.

The son obeyed his father. When he arrived at the corpse grounds, carrying the clothes on a stick, he found the holy man sitting by the gate. When Lucky Cloth's son threw away the cursed suit, the holy man picked it up. He examined it and saw the tiny teeth marks made by the mice. But since they could hardly be noticed, he took the suit with him back to the pleasure garden.

---

27 Literally, 'a Brahmin, or priest, who believes in prognosticative marks on cloth.'

After bathing thoroughly, his son told Priest Lucky Cloth what had happened. He thought, "This cursed suit of clothes will bring great harm to the king's favorite holy man. I must warn him." So he went to the pleasure garden and said, "Holy one, the unlucky cloth you have taken, please throw it away! It is cursed and will bring harm to you!"

But the holy man replied, "No, no, what others throw away in the corpse grounds is a blessing to me! We forest meditators are not seers of good and bad luck. All kinds of Buddhas and Enlightenment Beings have given up superstitions about luck. Anyone who is wise should do the same. No one knows the future!"

Hearing about the truly wise and enlightened ones made Priest Lucky Cloth see how foolish he had been. From then on he gave up his many superstitions and followed the teachings of the humble holy man.

When the Buddha had finished relating the story, he identified the births:

"The father and son in the past were the same as today. And I, myself, was the holy man."

The moral: "A fool's curse can be a wise man's blessing."

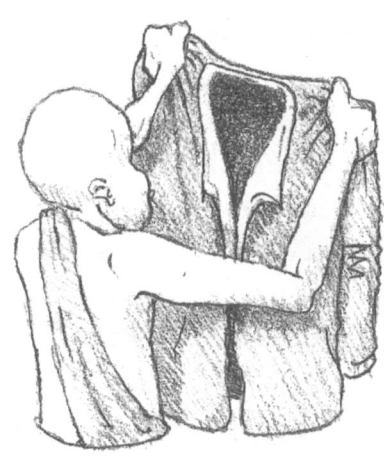

The Bull Called Tit-for-Tat
[All Deserve Respect]
(Sārambha-Jātaka)

The Buddha told this story while at Sāvatthi about wrongful speech.

A certain monk used to abuse others with rough speech. The Buddha asked this monk, "Do you use rough words?" The monk answered him, "Yes, I do." The Buddha then said, "Oh my dear, it is not good to use rough words. Rough words are not liked even by animals. This was so even in the past." And the Buddha then told the story of 'The Bull Called Delightful,' the *Nandivisāla-Jātaka* [No. 28], with the difference that the story here was about a bull named 'Tit-for-Tat' [Sārambha].

Once upon a time, in the country of Gandhāra in northern India, there was a city called Takkasilā. In that city the Enlightenment Being was born as a certain calf. Since he was well bred for strength, he was bought by a high-class rich man. He became very fond of the gentle animal, and called him 'Tit-for-Tat' [Sārambha]. He took good care of him and fed him only the best.

When Tit-for-Tat grew up into a big fine strong bull, he thought, "I was brought up by this generous man. He gave me such good food and constant care, even though sometimes there were difficulties. Now I am a big grown up bull and there is no other bull who can pull as heavy a load as I can. Therefore, I would like to use my strength to give something in return to my master."

So he said to the man, "Sir, please find some wealthy merchant who is proud of having many strong bulls. Challenge him by saying that your bull can pull one hundred heavily loaded bullock carts."

Following his advice, the high-class rich man went to such a merchant and struck up a conversation. After a while, he brought up the idea of who had the strongest bull in the city.

The merchant said, "Many have bulls, but no one has any as strong as mine." The rich man said, "Sir, I have a bull who can pull one hundred heavily loaded bullock carts." "No, friend, how can there be such a bull? That is unbelievable!" said the merchant. The other replied, "I do have such a bull, and I am willing to make a bet."

The merchant said, "I will bet a thousand gold coins that your bull cannot pull a hundred loaded bullock carts." So the bet was made and they agreed on a date and time for the challenge.

The merchant attached together one hundred big bullock carts. He filled them with sand and gravel to make them very heavy.

The high-class rich man fed the finest rice to the bull called Tit-for-Tat. He bathed him and decorated him and hung a beautiful garland of flowers around his neck.

Then he harnessed him to the first cart and climbed up onto it. Being so high-class, he could not resist the urge to make himself seem very important. So he cracked a whip in the air, and yelled at the faithful bull, "Pull, you dumb animal! I command you to pull, you big dummy!"

The bull called Tit-for-Tat thought, "This challenge was my idea! I have never done anything bad to my master, and yet he insults me with such hard and harsh words!" So he remained in his place and refused to pull the carts.

The merchant laughed and demanded his winnings from the bet. The high-class rich man had to pay him the one thousand gold coins. He returned home and sat down, saddened by his lost bet, and embarrassed by the blow to his pride.

The bull called Tit-for-Tat grazed peacefully on his way home. When he arrived, he saw his master sadly lying on his side. He asked, "Sir, why are you lying there like that? Are you sleeping? You look sad." The man said, "I lost a thousand gold coins because of you. With such a loss, how could I sleep?"

The bull replied, "Sir, you called me 'dummy'. You even cracked a whip in the air over my head. In all my life, did I ever break anything, step on anything, make a mess in the wrong place, or behave like a 'dummy' in any way?" He answered, "No, my pet."

The bull called Tit-for-Tat said, "Then sir, why did you call me 'dumb animal', and insult me even in the presence of others? The fault is yours. I have done nothing wrong. But since I feel sorry for you, go again to the merchant and make the same bet for two thousand gold coins. And remember to use only the respectful words I deserve so well."

Then the high-class rich man went back to the merchant and made

the bet for two thousand gold coins. The merchant thought it would be easy money. Again he set up the one hundred heavily loaded bullock carts. Again the rich man fed and bathed the bull, and hung a garland of flowers around his neck.

When all was ready, the rich man touched Tit-for-Tat's forehead with a lotus blossom, having given up the whip. Thinking of him as fondly as if he were his own child, he said, "My son, please do me the honor of pulling these one hundred bullock carts."

Lo and behold, the wonderful bull pulled with all his might and dragged the heavy carts, until the last one stood in the place of the first.

The merchant, with his mouth hanging open in disbelief, had to pay the two thousand gold coins. The onlookers were so impressed that they honored the bull called Tit-for-Tat with gifts. But even more important to the high-class rich man than his winnings, was his valuable lesson in humility and respect.

When the Buddha ended this story, he added:

"The high-class rich man at that time is today Ānanda. The Brahmin's wife became Uppalavaṇṇā. And the bull Tit-for-Tat was I who have become the Buddha."

The moral: "Harsh words bring no reward. Respectful words bring honor to all."

The Phony Holy Man
[Hypocrisy]
(Kuhaka-Jātaka)

The Buddha told this story while he was living in Jetavana temple. The details of its narration will be told in the fourteenth book in the *Uddāla-Jātaka* [No. 487].

[The Buddha told this story while living in Jetavana temple about a monk who even though he had dedicated himself to the Buddha's teachings, was nevertheless dishonest.

The monks gathered one evening in the preaching hall were discussing this. When the Buddha entered, he asked them what they were talking about before he came. The Buddha then said, "Such is not so only now. This man was deceitful before, as well." And at the monks' request, the Buddha told a Jātaka story.]

Once upon a time there was a man who looked and acted just like a holy man. He wore nothing but rags, had long matted hair, and relied on a little village to support him. But he was sneaky and tricky. He only pretended to give up attachment to the everyday world. He was a phony holy man.

A wealthy man living in the village wanted to earn merit by doing good deeds. So he had a simple little temple built in the nearby forest for the holy man to live in. He also fed him the finest foods from his own home.

He thought this holy man with matted hair was sincere and good, one who would not do anything unwholesome. Since he was afraid of bandits, he took his family fortune of 100 gold coins to the little temple.

He buried it under the ground and said to the holy man, "Venerable one, please look after this my family fortune."

The holy man replied, "There's no need to worry about such things with people like me. We holy ones have given up attachment to the ordinary world. We have no greed or desire to obtain the possessions of others."

"Very well, Venerable one," said the man. He left thinking himself very wise indeed, to trust such a good holy man.

However, the wicked holy man thought, "Aha! This treasure of 100 gold coins is enough for me to live on for the rest of my life! I will never have to work or beg again!" So a few days later he dug up the gold and secretly buried it near the roadside.

The next day he went to the wealthy villager's home for lunch as usual. After eating his fill he said, "Most honorable gentleman, I have lived here supported by you for a long time. But holy ones who have given up the world are not supposed to become too attached to one village or supporter. It would make a holy man like me impure! Therefore, kindly permit me to humbly go on my way."

The man pleaded with him again and again not to go, but it was useless. "Go then, Venerable sir," he agreed at last. He went with him as far as the boundary of the village and left him there.

After going on a short way himself, the phony holy man thought, "I must make absolutely sure that stupid villager does not suspect me. He trusts me so much that he will believe anything. So I will deceive him with a clever trick!" He stuck a blade of dry grass in his matted hair and went back.

When he saw him returning, the wealthy villager asked, "Venerable one, why have you come back?" He replied, "Dear friend, this blade of grass from the thatched roof of your house has stuck in my hair. It is most unwholesome and impure for a holy one such as myself to 'take what is not given'."

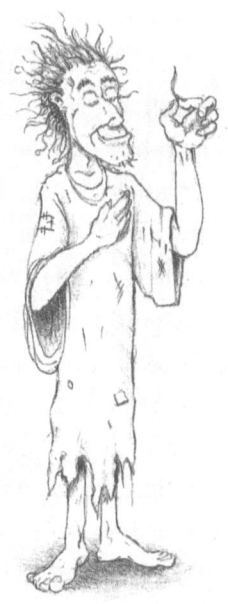

The amazed villager said, "Think nothing of it, your reverence. Please put it down and continue on your way. Venerable ones such as you do not even take a blade of grass that belongs to another. How marvelous! How exalted you are, the purest of the holy. How lucky I was to be able to support you!" More trusting than ever, he bowed respectfully and sent him on his way again.

It just so happened that the Enlightenment Being was living the life of a trader at that time. He was in the midst of a trading trip when he stopped overnight at the village. He had overheard the entire conversation between the villager and the 'purest of the holy'. He thought, "That sounds ridiculous! This man must have stolen something far more valuable than the blade of dry grass he has made such a big show of returning to its rightful owner."

The trader asked the wealthy villager, "Friend, did you perhaps give anything to this holy-looking man for safekeeping?" "Yes, friend," he replied, "I trusted him to guard my family fortune of 100 gold coins." "I advise you to go see if they are where you left them," said the trader.

Suddenly worried, he ran to the forest temple, dug up the ground, and found his treasure gone. He ran back to the trader and said, "It has been stolen!" "Friend," he replied, "No one but that so-called holy man could have taken it. Let's catch him and get your treasure back."

They both chased after him as fast as they could. When they caught up with him they made him tell where he had hidden the money. They went to the hiding place by the roadside and dug up the buried treasure.

Looking at the gleaming gold the Bodhisatta said, "You hypocritical holy man. You spoke well those beautiful words, admired by all, that one is not to 'take what is not given'. You hesitated to leave with even a blade of grass that didn't belong to you. But it was so easy for you to steal a hundred gold coins!" After ridiculing the way he had acted in this way, he advised him to change his ways for his own good.

The Buddha then identified the births, saying:

"The dishonest monk of today was the hypocritical holy man of the past. And I who have today become the Buddha was the trader in those days."

The moral: "Be careful of a holy man who puts on a big show."

One Way Hospitality
[Ingratitude]
(Akataññu-Jātaka)

The Buddha told this story while living at Jetavana monastery with regard to the millionaire Anāthapiṇḍika and a country merchant with whom Anāthapiṇḍika corresponded, but the two of whom had never met.

An exactly similar situation as happened to the Benares merchant and a country merchant in the Jātaka story, happened to Anāthapiṇḍika with this country merchant.

When Anāthapiṇḍika, thinking this would be a good story to tell the Buddha, told him the whole story, the Buddha said, "This is not the first time, sir, that this country merchant has acted in this way. He was just the same in the past." And at Anāthapiṇḍika's request, the Buddha told the story of the past:

Once upon a time there were two merchants who wrote letters back and forth to each other. They never met face to face. One lived in Benares and the other lived in a remote border village.

The country merchant sent a large caravan to Benares. It had 500 carts loaded with fruits and vegetables and other products. He told his workers to trade all these goods with the help of the Benares merchant.

When they arrived in the big city they went directly to the merchant. They gave him the gifts they had brought. He was pleased and invited them to stay in his own home. He even gave them money for their living expenses. He treated them with the very best hospitality. He asked about the well being of the country merchant and gave them gifts to take back to him. Since it is easier for a local person to get a good price, he saw to it that all their goods were fairly traded. They returned home and told their master all that had happened.

Later on, the Benares merchant sent a caravan of 500 carts to the border village. His workers also took gifts to the country merchant. When they arrived he asked, "Where do you come from?" They said they came from the Benares merchant, the one who wrote him letters.

Taking the gifts, the country merchant laughed in a very discourteous way and said, "Anyone could say they came from the Benares merchant!" Then he sent them away, giving them no place to stay, no gifts, and no help at all.

The caravan workers went downtown to the marketplace and did the best they could trading without local help. They returned to Benares and told their master all that had happened.

Before too long, the country merchant sent another caravan of 500 carts to Benares. Again his workers took gifts to the same merchant. When his workers saw them coming, they said to him, "We know just how to provide suitable lodgings, food and expense money for these people."

They took them outside the city walls to a good place to camp for the night. They said they would return to Benares and prepare food and get expense money for them.

Instead they rounded up all their fellow workers and returned to the campsite in the middle of the night. They robbed all 500 carts, including the workers' outer garments. They chased away the bullocks, and removed and carried off the cartwheels.

The villagers were terrified. They ran back home as fast as their legs could carry them.

The city merchant's workers told him all they had done. He said, "Those who forget gratitude and ignore simple hospitality wind up getting what they deserve. Those who do not appreciate the help they have received soon find that no one will help them anymore."

At the conclusion of this story, the Buddha identified the births:

"The country merchant of the past was this country merchant today. And the merchant of Benares was I who am today the Buddha."

The moral: "If you don't help others, you can't expect them to help you."

91

Poison Dice
[Deception]
(*Litta-Jātaka*)

The Buddha told this story while living in Jetavana temple with regard to the thoughtless use of things.

At one time, the monks of that day were thoughtless in their use of the four requisites [*catu-paccaya*-s]. These are clothing, food, shelter, and medicine. Such thoughtlessness barred their escape from the cycle of re-becoming [*puna-bbhava*]. Knowing this, the Buddha set forth rules with regard to their careful usage. The Buddha said, "Thoughtless use of the four requisites is like taking deadly poison. And there are, indeed, those in the past who by their thoughtlessness did inadvertently take poison." Saying this, the Buddha told a Jātaka story of the past:

Once upon a time there was a rich man living in Benares who was addicted to gambling. He played dice with another gambling addict, a man whose mind worked in tricky ways.

While the rich gambler was very honest and above board, the tricky one was dishonest. When he kept on winning he kept on playing. But when he began to lose he secretly put one of the dice in his mouth and swallowed it. Then he claimed it was lost and stopped the game.

The rich gambler began to notice this trick. Then one day he decided to teach him a lesson. He smeared poison on the dice and let it dry so it was invisible. He took these dice to the usual place and said, "Let's play dice!"

His friend agreed. They set up the gambling board and began to play. As usual the tricky one began by winning every throw of the dice. But as soon as he began to lose he sneaked the dice into his mouth.

Seeing this the rich gambler said, "Swallow now, and then something you don't expect will happen. Your own dishonesty will make you suffer much."

After swallowing the poison dice the trickster fell down sick and fainted. The rich gambler, who was basically good at heart, thought, "Enough is enough. Now I must save his life."

He made a medical mixture to cause vomiting. He made him swallow it, and he threw up the poison dice. He gave him a drink made with clear butter, thick palm syrup, honey and cane sugar. This made the trickster feel just fine again.

Afterwards he advised him not to deceive a trusting friend again. Eventually both gamblers died and were reborn as they deserved.

At the end of this Jātaka story, the Buddha said:

"I, myself, was the honest rich gambler in the past."

The moral: "Deceiving a friend may be hazardous to your health."

$\boxed{92}$

The Mystery of the Missing Necklace
(Mahāsāra-Jātaka)

The Buddha told this story while living in Jetavana monastery with regard to the Venerable Ānanda.

At one time, the wives of King Pasenadi of Kosala asked the king for someone to preach the Buddha's doctrine [Dhamma] to them in the harem. The king consented.

When the king went to the Buddha, he heard the praises of a lay brother named Chattapāni, who was seated at the Buddha's feet at the time. On another day, when the king happened to see Chattapāni on his way to Jetavanārāma, he summoned him and asked him whether he would agree to preach the Dhamma to his harem. But Chattapāni responded that such was the prerogative of the monks.

Recognizing the force of this remark, the king called his wives together, told them of his intention to ask the Buddha to send one of his disciples to instruct them and asked them whom they would prefer. The ladies chose the Venerable Ānanda.

King Pasenadi then went to the Buddha and relayed his wives' wishes. And the Buddha consented to Ānanda becoming their teacher. The Buddha having so consented, Ānanda then began to regularly instruct the king's wives.

One day when Ānanda went to the palace to instruct the ladies, he found them troubled and dejected. He learned from them that the jewel from the king's turban was missing, and everyone was being considered a suspect by the king's ministers. Ānanda thereupon went to the king and suggested that there was a way to find the jewel without worrying everyone. Ānanda suggested that the king call together everyone he suspected and give them each a wisp of straw or a lump of clay, telling them to put it in such-and-such a place the next day at daybreak. The person who took the jewel would put it in the straw or clay, and so bring it back. If it is brought back the first day, well and good. If not, the same thing ought to be done a second and third day. In this way, a large number of people will escape worry, and the king will get his jewel back.

When the elder Ānanda came again on the third day, and the jewel had still not been brought back, he suggested that a large water pot filled with water be placed in the corner of the courtyard with a screen put before it. The king was to give an order that all who frequent the area, men and women alike, are to remove their outer garments and one-by-one wash their hands behind the screen, coming back only afterwards. This the king did.

The thief, seeing that Ānanda was not letting things rest, decided then to give up the jewel. He hid the jewel on his person, and going behind the screen, dropped it in the water. When everyone was gone, the pot was emptied, and the jewel was found.

The story of how Ānanda's cleverness had recovered the jewel spread about. And one evening, the monks in the preaching hall were discussing it. When the Buddha entered and found out what it was they were discussing, he said, "Not only today, but also in the past, the wise through their cleverness have recovered what was stolen, showing that it had fallen into the hands of an animal, and in so doing saved a lot of trouble." And the Buddha told this story of the past:

Chapter 1. One Crime Leads to Another

Once upon a time, King Brahmadatta was ruling in Benares in northern India. After completing his education, the Enlightenment Being became one of his ministers.

One day the king went on an outing to his pleasure garden. A big crowd from the court went with him. They visited many parts of the lovely park. Near a cool forest they came upon a beautiful clear pond. The king decided to go for a swim. So he dove into the water. Then he invited all the ladies of his harem to join him in the refreshing pond.

Laughing together, the harem women took off all their ornaments and jewelry – from their heads, necks, ears, wrists, fingers, waists, ankles and toes. Along with their outer clothing, they handed all these over to their servant girls for safekeeping. Then they jumped into the pond with King Brahmadatta.

The king had given one of his favorite queens a very valuable pearl necklace. She was so fond of it that she called it by a pet name, 'Most Precious' [Mahāsāra].

It just so happened that a curious she-monkey had been watching all this from a branch of a nearby tree. Peering between the green leaves, she had paid very close attention. When she had caught sight of the Most Precious pearl necklace, her eyes had nearly popped out of her head!

Imagining how grand she would look wearing the queen's beautiful necklace, she patiently watched the servant girl who was guarding it. In the beginning the girl watched very carefully. But the heat of the day soon made her drowsy. When the she-monkey saw her start to snooze, she swung down from the tree as fast as the wind. In a flash she grabbed the necklace called Most Precious, put it around her neck, and ran back up the tree.

Afraid that the other monkeys would see it, the little thief hid the gleaming pearl necklace in a hollow of the tree. Then she sat guarding her loot, remaining silent and pretending to be as innocent as a nun!

In a minute or two the servant girl awoke from her accidental nap. Frightened, she immediately looked over the queen's possessions. When she saw the necklace was missing she yelled out in terror, "Help! Help! Some man has taken the queen's pearl necklace, the one called Most Precious!"

After running to her side, security guards went and reported the theft to the king. He ordered them to stop at nothing, and to catch the thief immediately. Frightened of the king's wrath, the guards began dashing madly around the pleasure garden searching for the thief.

At that very moment there happened to be a poor man walking just outside the garden. He was on his way back to his far-off home village after paying his meager taxes to the royal treasury. The commotion from inside the park scared him and he started running away.

Unfortunately, the security guards saw him running and said to each other, "That must be the thief!" They rushed through the garden gate and after a short chase easily captured the innocent man. They began beating him as they shouted, "You no good thief! Confess that you robbed the queen's pearl necklace, the one she calls Most Precious."

The poor man thought, "If I say I didn't take it, these men will beat me to death for sure. But if I confess, they will have to take me to the king." So he said, "Yes, I admit it, I took the necklace." Hearing this the security guards handcuffed him and hauled him off to the king.

After being told of the man's confession, the king asked him, "Where is the Most Precious necklace now? What have you done with it?"

Being a somewhat clever fellow, the prisoner replied, "My lord king, I am a very poor man indeed. I have never in my life owned anything at all valuable, not a Most Precious bed or a Most Precious chair – and certainly not a Most Precious pearl necklace. It was your majesty's own Chief Financial Adviser who made me steal this Most Precious. I gave it to him. He alone knows where it is now."

King Brahmadatta summoned his Chief Financial Adviser and asked, "Did you take Most Precious from this man's hands?" "Yes my lord," said he. "Where is it now?" asked the king. "I gave it to the Royal Teacher Priest."

The Royal Teacher Priest was called for and asked about the stolen necklace. He claimed, "I gave it to the Official Court Musician."

He in turn was summoned and questioned. He answered, "I gave Most Precious to a high-class prostitute."

When she was identified and brought to the king, he demanded to know what she had done with the queen's pearl necklace. But she alone replied, "Your majesty, I don't know anything about a pearl necklace!"

As the sun began to set, the king said, "Let us continue this investigation tomorrow." He handed the five suspects over to his ministers and returned to his palace for the night.

Chapter 2. The Mystery Is Solved

Meanwhile, the royal minister who happened to be the Enlightenment Being had seen and heard all that had taken place in the pleasure garden. He realized that the mystery could be solved only by careful examination. Jumping to conclusions could lead to the wrong answers. So he started examining and analyzing the situation in his mind.

He thought, "The necklace was lost inside the pleasure garden. But the poor villager was captured outside the pleasure garden. The gates had strong guards standing watch. Therefore, the villager could not have come in to steal the necklace. Likewise, no one from inside the garden could have gotten out through the guarded gates with the stolen necklace. So it can be seen that none of these people could have gotten away with Most Precious, either from inside or outside!

"What a mystery! The poor man who was first accused must have said he gave it to the Chief Financial Adviser just to save himself. The Chief Financial Adviser must have thought it would go easier for him if the Royal Teacher Priest were involved. The priest must have blamed the Official Court Musician so that music would make their time in the palace dungeon pass more pleasantly. And the Official Court Musician probably thought that being with the high-class prostitute would take away the misery of prison life. So he said he gave the necklace to her.

"After examining carefully, it is easy to see that all five suspects must be innocent. But the garden is full of monkeys who are known to cause mischief. No doubt some she-monkey thought Most Precious would set her above the rest, and the necklace is still in her hands."

So he went to the king and said, "Your excellency, if you hand over the suspects to me, I will do the investigation for you." "By all means, my wise minister," said the king, "examine into it yourself."

The minister called for his servant boys. He told them to keep the five suspects together in one place. They were to hide nearby, listen to all that was said, and then report back to him.

When the five prisoners thought they were alone they began talking freely to each other. First the Chief Financial Adviser said to the poor villager, "You little crook! We never saw each other before. So when did you give the stolen Most Precious to me?"

He replied, "My lord sir, most exalted adviser to the great king, I have never had anything of any value whatsoever, not even a broken-down bed or chair. I certainly have not seen any such Most Precious necklace! I don't know what you people are talking about. Being scared to death by the king's guards, I only mentioned you in the hope that one as important as you could free us both. Please, my lord, don't be angry at me."

The Royal Teacher Priest said to the Chief Financial Adviser, "You see, this man admits he has not given it to you, so how could you have given it to me?" He replied, "We are both in high positions. I thought that if we got together and backed each other up, we could settle this matter."

The Official Court Musician asked, "Oh Royal Teacher Priest, when did you give the queen's pearl necklace to me?" "I thought that if you were imprisoned with me," said the priest, "your music would make it much more pleasant. That's why I lied."

Then the woman said to the Official Court Musician, "You miserable crook! When did I come to you? When did you come to me? We have never met each other before. So when could you possibly have given me the stolen Most Precious?" He said to her, "Oh dear young lady, please don't be angry with me. I only accused you so that when we five are imprisoned together, your being with us will make us all happy."

Not being either a poor frightened stranger or a slippery government official, the high-class prostitute was the only one who had told the truth. So there was no one to accuse her of shifting the blame.

Of course the wise minister's servants had been eavesdropping on the entire conversation. When they reported it all back to him, he realized his suspicion was confirmed – some she-monkey must have taken the necklace. So he thought, "I must come up with a plan to get it back."

First he had a bunch of cheap imitation jewel ornaments made. Then he had several she-monkeys captured in the royal pleasure garden. He had them decorated with the imitation ornaments – necklaces on their necks, and bracelets on their wrists and ankles. Then they were released in the garden. The minister ordered his servants to watch all the she-monkeys carefully. When they saw anyone with the missing pearl necklace, they were to scare her into dropping it.

The she-monkey who had taken Most Precious was still guarding it in the hollow of the tree. The other she-monkeys strutted back and forth saying, "See how fine we look. We have these beautiful necklaces and bracelets." She couldn't stand seeing and hearing this. She thought, "Those are nothing but worthless imitations." To show them all up, she put on her own neck the Most Precious necklace of real pearls.

Immediately the servants frightened her into dropping it. They took it to their master, the wise minister. He took it to the king and said, "Your majesty, here is the pearl necklace, the one called Most Precious. None of the five who admitted to the crime was really a thief. It was taken instead by a greedy little she-monkey living in your pleasure garden."

The amazed king asked, "How did you find out it was taken by a she-monkey? And how did you get it back?" The minister told the whole story.

The king said, "You were certainly the right one for the job. In times of need, it is the wise who are appreciated most." Then he rewarded him by showering him with wealth, like a heavy rain of the seven valuables – gold, silver, pearls, jewels, lapis lazuli, diamonds and coral.

* * *

The story having been told, the Buddha identified the births:

"Ānanda was the king in those days. And I who am today the Buddha was the wise minister."

The moral: "Theft from greed, lies from fear, truth from examining."

93

The Careless Lion
[Circumspection]
(Vissāsabhojana-Jātaka)

The Buddha told this story while living in Jetavana temple with regard to taking reliable gifts [dāna] trustingly.

At that time, the monks used to take food, clothing, and other requisites from their relatives without any consideration of circumstances or consequences. The Buddha, seeing this, decided to admonish the brotherhood [Saṅgha] against it, saying that such acceptance of things given without circumspection is like taking poison. And poison kills, whether it is given by a relative or stranger. The Buddha added that in the past, there were those who took poison without thinking because it was offered by those who were dear to them, and they thereby met their end. And the Buddha told this story of the past:

Once upon a time, the Five Training Steps [pañca-sīla-s, the first five sikkhā-pada-s] were not yet known in the world. There was a very wealthy man living in Benares who owned a large herd of cattle. He hired a man to look after them.

During the time of year when the rice paddies were filled with the green growing rice plants, the herdsman took the cattle to the forest to graze. From there he brought the milk and butter and cheese to the rich man in Benares.

It just so happened that being in the forest put the cattle in a very frightening situation. There was a meat-eating lion living nearby. Sensing the presence of the lion kept the cattle in constant fear. This made the cows tense and high-strung, leaving them too weak to give more than a little milk.

One day the owner of the cattle asked the herdsman why he was bringing such a small amount of milk and butter and cheese. He replied,

"Sir, cows need to be calm and contented to give much milk. Due to a nearby lion, your cows are always afraid and tense. So they give hardly any milk."

"I see," said the rich man. Thinking like an animal trapper, he asked,

"Is the lion closely connected to atny other animal?" The herdsman answered, "Sir, there happens to be a variety of deer living in the forest. They are called 'minideer' [Sinh. *mīmina*] because they are so small. Even the adults only grow to be about one foot tall. The lion has become very friendly with a certain minideer doe."

The rich man of Benares said, "So that my cows will be at peace and able to give their usual milk, this is what you are to do. Capture the lion's friend and rub poison all over her body. Then wait a couple days before releasing her. She will be like bait in a trap for the lion. When he dies, bring his body to me. Then my cows will be safe and happy again."

The herdsman followed his boss's orders exactly. When the lion saw his favorite minideer doe, he was so overjoyed that he threw all caution to the wind. Without even sniffing the air around her, he immediately began licking her excitedly all over. Because of too much joy and not enough caution, he fell into the poisonous trap. The poor lion died on the spot.

The Buddha said:

"The rich man in those days was I who am today the Buddha."

The moral: "Too much of a good thing can be dangerous."

94

The Holy Man Who Tried To Be Too Holy
[Extremism]
(*Lomahaṁsa-Jātaka*)

The Buddha told this story while he was at Pāṭikārāma, near Vesāli, with regard to Sunakkhatta.

Sunakkhatta, having left the Buddha's order [Saṅgha], became an adherent of Korakkhattiya and went about Vesāli vilifying the Buddha and declaring that his doctrines did not lead to the destruction of suffering. When Sāriputta reported this to the Buddha, the Buddha responded that he had tested the efficacy of severe asceticism 90 aeons [Kappa-s] ago, and had found it wanting. And at Sāriputta's request, the Buddha told this story of the past:

Once upon a time, the Enlightenment Being lived in a world where most religions were very similar. They taught that the way to remove suffering from the mind was to make the body suffer instead. As strange as it seems, most people thought that the holiest of the holy were the ones who tortured their bodies the most! Since everyone seemed to agree with this, the Bodhisatta decided to find out for himself if it was true.

He stopped living as an ordinary everyday person and became a holy man according to the custom of the times. This meant that he gave up everything, even his clothes. He went naked, with his body covered only by dust and dirt.

So he wouldn't be spoiled by the taste of good food, he forced himself to eat only filthy things – dirt, ashes, urine and cow dung.

So he could concentrate without being interrupted by anyone, he went to live in the most dangerous part of the forest. If he did see a human being, he ran away like a timid deer.

In the wintertime he spent his days under the trees and his nights out in the open. So in the daytime he was soaked by the cold water dripping from the icicles hanging from the tree branches. And at night he was covered by the falling snow. In this way, in winter, he made his body suffer the most extreme cold in both day and night.

In the summertime he spent his days out in the open and his nights under the trees. So in the daytime he was burned by the most severe rays of the sun. And at night he was blocked from the few cooling breezes of the open air. In this way, in summer, he made his body suffer the most extreme heat in both day and night.

This was how he struggled, trying to bring peace to his mind. He was so determined that he lived his entire life in this way.

Then, just as he was about to die, he saw a vision of himself reborn in a hell world. The vision struck him like lightning, and instantly he knew that all the ways he had tortured his body were completely useless! They had not brought him peace of mind. Lo and behold, as he gave up his false beliefs and held on to the truth [Saccaṁ], he died and was reborn in a heaven world!

The Buddha said:

"I was the naked ascetic at that time."

~~~~~~

The moral: "Even at the very last moment, 'The truth shall make you free.'"

~~~~~~

95

Clear-sighted the Great, King of the World
[Impermanence]
(*Mahāsudassana-Jātaka*)

The Buddha told this story to the Venerable Ānanda as he lay on his deathbed in the town of Kusinārā with regard to Ānanda's saying that the Buddha ought not suffer his end in such a sorry little suburban town in the jungle, but rather in Rājagaha or some other large city. The Buddha responded that in the past, in the days of the Universal Monarchy of King Clear-sighted the Great [Mahāsudassana], this town was then a mighty city surrounded by jeweled walls. And at Ānanda's request, the Buddha told this story of the past, and pronounced the *Mahāsudassana Sutta*.[28]

It is said that there are two ways to practice religion. One is to live apart from the ordinary everyday world as a monk, a nun or a holy one. Those who are sincere in this way have as their highest goal the direct experience of complete Truth – full Enlightenment [Nibbāna].

The other way to practice religion is within the ordinary world. Those who are sincere in this way have as their highest goal the harmony of an undivided world, living peacefully under a perfectly wholesome ruler – a 'King of the World' [*cakkavattin*].

Once upon a time the Enlightenment Being was born and given the name 'Clear-sighted' [Sudassana]. As he grew up he developed ten rules of good government [*dasa-rāja-dhamma*-s]: absence of hidden ill will, absence of open hostility, harmlessness, self-control, patience, gentleness, charity, generosity, straightforwardness and goodness.

The people of the world began to notice the wholesomeness and fairness of Clear-sighted, who lived strictly according to these rules.

---

28 The *Mahāsudassana Sutta* is the 17th Sutta of the *Dīghanikāya*.

Gradually those in his vicinity volunteered to live under his authority as king, rather than under the dishonest politicians of the time.

As his reputation spread, every king in the world came to Clear-sighted and said, "Come, oh lord. You are welcome. My kingdom is your kingdom. Advise me how to rule in your name."

Then Clear-sighted said, "Do not destroy life. Do not take what is not given. Do not behave wrongly in sexual desires. Do not speak falsely. Do not take alcohol that clouds the mind. My commands to the world are only these five.[29] As long as these five are obeyed, my sixth rule is freedom for all to follow local customs and religions."

After all the people on earth had come to live under his peaceful rule, he became known as Clear-sighted the Great [Mahāsudassana], King of the World. His royal city, the capital of the whole world, was called Kusāvatī. It was a beautiful and prosperous city with four magnificent gates – one golden, one silver, one jade and one crystal.

Outside the gates, Kusāvatī was surrounded by seven rows of palm trees – a row with golden trunks and silver leaves and fruits; a row with silver trunks and golden leaves and fruits; a row with cat's-eye trunks and crystal leaves and fruits; a row with crystal trunks and cat's-eye leaves and fruits; a row with agate trunks and coral leaves and fruits; a row with coral trunks and agate leaves and fruits; and finally a row with trunks and leaves and fruits of every kind of jewel found in the world!

When breezes blew through these marvelous palms the sweet sounds of gentle music were heard throughout the city. This music was so enticing and pleasant that some of the citizens were enchanted into stopping their work and dancing for joy!

Clear-sighted the Great, King of the World, had a couch encrusted with jewels from the wonderful palms. After a long, righteous and peaceful reign, he lay on the rich couch for the last time. He knew that his end was near.

---

29 These are the *pañca-sīla*-s, the first five of the ten *sikkhā-pada*-s, or 'Training Steps.'

Of all his 84,000 queens, the one who loved him most was called, 'Most-pleasant' [Subhaddā]. Sensing the state of his mind she said, "You rule over all the cities of the world, including this beautiful Kusāvatī with its four magnificent gates and seven rows of marvelous palms. Think about this and be happy!"

The King of the World said, "No, my dear queen, don't say that. Instead you should advise me to give up attachment to the cities of the world and all they contain." Surprised, she asked, "Why do you say this, my lord?" "Because today I will die," he said.

Then Queen Most-pleasant started to cry, wiping away the tears as they flowed. And all the other 84,000 queens also broke into tears. And the king's ministers and his whole court, both men and women, could not keep from weeping and sobbing. All eyes overflowed with tears.

But King Clear-sighted the Great said, "Your tears are useless. Be at peace." Hearing this the wailing subsided and his subjects became silent. Then he said to Queen Most-pleasant, "Oh my queen, do not cry, do not lament. Anything that comes into being, whether it be a kingdom including the whole world, or just a tiny sesame seed – it cannot last forever. Anyone who comes into being, whether it be the King of the World, or the poorest petty thief – all must decay and die. Whatever is built up, falls apart. Whatever becomes, decays. The only true happiness is in the moment when becoming and decaying are not."

In this way the Enlightenment Being got them to think about what most people don't want to think about – that all things come to an end. He advised them to be generous and wholesome. Then the King of the World, like everyone else, died. He was reborn as a god in a heaven world, where in time, like everyone else, he died.

The story told, the Buddha identified the births:

"Queen Most-pleasant in those days is today Rāhula's mother. Rāhula then was the king's eldest son. The king's ministers and courtiers are today the Buddha's disciples. And King Clear-sighted the Great was I who am today the Buddha."

The moral: "'All good things come to an end.'"

The Prince and the She-devils
(Telapatta-Jātaka)

The Buddha told this story while living in a forest near the town of Desakā in the Sumbhā country, with regard to the *Janapadakalyāṇi Sutta*.[30] The Buddha said on that occasion that if the fairest maiden in all the countryside were to dance and sing in public, and a man were told that if he carried a bowl filled to the brim with oil through the crowd he would win the maiden, but that if he spilt one single drop he would lose his head, that man would not turn his attention to anything else or grow slack in his efforts. In the same way monks ought to cultivate mindfulness [*sati*] relating to the body.

The Buddha then said that this task was easy as the man was escorted along by one who threatened him with a drawn sword. But in past days, it was a truly hard task for the good to preserve right mindfulness and to curb their passions so as not to look at celestial beauty in all its perfectness. Yet even so, they won out, and in so doing won a kingdom.

And saying this, the Buddha told an old story:

Chapter 1. Five Meals in the Forest

Once upon a time King Brahmadatta was ruling in Benares, in northern India. The Enlightenment Being was born as the last of his 100 sons and grew up to be a wise young man.

In those days there were Silent Buddhas [Pacceka-Buddha-s] who came to the palace to receive alms food. They were called Buddhas

---

30 The *Janapadakalyāṇi Sutta*, or *Janapada Sutta* appears in the *Mahāvagga* of the *Saṁyuttanikāya*, Book 3, Chapter 2, Section 10. (Book 3 of the *Mahāvagga* is the 47th chapter of the *Saṁyuttanikāya* as a whole.)

because they were enlightened – they knew the Truth [Dhamma] and experienced life as it really is, in every present moment. They were called Silent because they did not preach the Truth. This was because they knew it was a time when no one would be able to understand it. However, being filled with sympathy for the unhappiness of all beings, the Silent Buddhas wished to help anyone who asked them.

One day the young prince was thinking about his 99 older brothers and wondering if he had any chance to become King of Benares. He decided to ask the Silent Buddhas about it.

The next day the Silent Buddhas came as usual to collect alms food in the palace. The prince brought purified water and washed their feet. When they had sat down he gave them appetizers to eat. Before giving the next course he said to them, "I am 100th in line to the throne. What are the odds that I will become King of Benares?"

They replied, "Oh prince, with so many older brothers there is almost no chance you will ever be king here. However, you might become King of Takkasilā. If you can get there in seven days you can become king. But on your way there is a dangerous forest. You must take the road passing through it, since it would take twice as long to go around it.

"That forest is known as 'Devils Woods' [Yakkha-vana], because it is filled with all kinds of devils – he-devils, she-devils, and even little children-devils! The she-devils spend most of their time by the roadside. They use magic to make buildings and entire cities appear along the way.

"The buildings have ceilings decorated with stars, and gorgeous rich couches surrounded by silk curtains of many colors. Sitting on these couches, the she-devils make themselves look like the sweetest, most pleasant of goddesses. With words dripping with honey they attract travelers saying, 'You look tired. Come in, sit down, have something to drink and then be on your way.'

"Those who are persuaded to come in are invited to sit down. Then the she-devils use their beautiful physical appearance to trap their visitors with their own burning desires. After giving in to their desires, the strangers are killed by the she-devils and eaten while their blood is still hot!

"In this way those who are attracted by sight are trapped by the physical forms of women. Those who are attracted by sound are trapped by their singing voices and music. Those attracted by smell are trapped by the divine perfumes they wear. Those attracted by taste are trapped by the heavenly tasting delicacies they offer. Those attracted by touch are trapped by their soft luxurious beds and velvet couches.[31]

"But if you, fair prince, can control all five senses, and force yourself to avoid looking at those beautiful enticing she-devils, only then can you become King of Takkasilā in seven days."

The grateful Bodhisatta replied, 'Thank you, Venerable ones. I will follow your advice. After hearing such warnings, how could I take the chance of looking at them?"

Then he asked the Silent Buddhas to give him special charms to protect him on his dangerous journey through Devils Woods. So they chanted protective blessings onto a string and some sand. He accepted the charms and paid his farewell respects to them, and then to his royal parents.

Returning to his own home he announced to his household servants, "I am going to Takkasilā to win the kingship. You are to remain here." But five of them said, "We also wish to go with you." "No," said he, "you can't come with me. I have been warned that on the way there are beautiful she-devils who trap people who can't resist the desires coming from their own five senses. Then they kill their victims and eat them while their blood is still hot. It is far too dangerous for you. I will rely only on myself and travel alone."

But the five would not listen. They said, "If we go with you, oh prince, we will force ourselves to keep from looking at those beautiful she-devils. We will accompany you to Takkasilā." "If you insist, then so be it," said the prince, "but keep your determination strong."

---

31 Desires that arise from sight, sound, smell, taste, and touch are known as the 'five sensual desires' [*pañca-kāma-guṇa-s*].

The she-devils were waiting for them in Devils Woods. They had already magically formed beautiful villages and cities with lovely houses and palaces along the way.

It just so happened that one of the prince's five servants was easily enchanted by the sight of the curves and figures of the bodies of women. So he began to fall behind in order to admire them. The worried prince asked, "Why do you delay, my friend?" "My feet ache," said the man, "let me sit and rest a while in one of these mansions. Then I will catch up with you." "My good friend," said the prince, "those are she-devils. Don't chase after them!"

Nevertheless, blinded by the temptation of the sense of sight, the man replied, "My lord, I can't turn away. Whatever will happen, let it happen!" Giving him one last warning, the prince continued on with the other four.

The one who remained behind went closer to the beautiful looking forms he was so attracted to. After pleasing themselves fully with the man, the she-devils killed him and ate him on the spot!

Then they went farther into Devils Woods and created another mirage of a beautiful mansion. They sat inside and began singing the sweetest melodies, accompanied by the lovely sounds of all kinds of musical instruments. One of the prince's followers was enchanted by the sound of beautiful music. So he too fell behind and was gobbled up by the still hungry she-devils.

Farther down the road they created another magic mansion filled with the scents of all kinds of divine perfumes. This time the man who loved sweet smells fell behind and was eaten as well.

Next the she-devils created a fabulous restaurant filled with foods having the most heavenly flavors. Here the lover of the tastes of the finest delicacies wandered in and was devoured in turn.

Then the she-devils went still farther down the road, created soft luxurious beds and velvet couches, and sat on them. The last of the prince's followers was one who loved the touch of the softest fabrics and the most luxurious comfort. So he too fell behind and met his death, and was quickly eaten by the ravenous she-devils.

These events left the Enlightenment Being all alone in Devils Woods. A certain she-devil thought, "Aha! This one is very strong-minded indeed. But I am even more determined. I will not stop until I have tasted his flesh!" So she alone stubbornly followed him, even though the other devils gave up the chase.

As she got closer to the edge of Devils Woods, some woodsmen saw her and asked, "Lovely lady, who is it that walks on ahead of you?" "We are newlyweds," replied the lying demon. "He is my too pure husband, who ran away from me on our wedding night. That's why I'm chasing after him."

The woodsmen caught up to the prince and asked, "Noble sir, this delicate flower-like golden-skinned young maiden has left her family to live with you. Why don't you walk with her, instead of making her chase after you?"

The prince replied, "Good people, she is not my wife. She is a devil. She killed the five men who followed me and ate them while their blood was still hot!"

Whereupon the lovely looking devil said, "See how it is, gentlemen. Anger can make husbands call their own wives devils and hungry ghosts! Such is the way of the world."

Continuing to follow the prince, the determined she-devil magically made herself look pregnant. Then she seemed to be a first-time mother carrying her make-believe baby on her hip. Whoever saw the pair questioned them just as the woodsmen had. Each time the Bodhisatta repeated, "She is not my wife. She is a devil. She killed the five men who followed me and ate them while their blood was still hot!"

Chapter 2. A Feast in the Palace

Finally they arrived at Takkasilā. The she-devil made her 'son' disappear and followed alone.

At the city gate the prince stopped and went into a rest house. Because of the magic power of the charmed sand and string he had gotten from the Silent Buddhas, the she-devil was not able to follow him inside. She stayed outside and made herself look as beautiful as a goddess.

The King of Takkasilā happened to see her as he was going to his pleasure garden. Overwhelmed by her beauty, he decided he must have her. He sent a servant to ask if she was married. When he did so, she replied, "Yes, my husband is inside this rest house."

Hearing this, the prince called out from within, "She is not my wife. She is a devil. She killed the five men who followed me and ate them while their blood was still hot!" And once again she said, "See how it is, sir. Anger can make husbands call their own wives devils and hungry ghosts! Such is the way of the world."

The servant returned to the king and told him what both had said. To which the king replied, "Un-owned goods belong to the king." So he sent for the she-devil and seated her on a royal elephant. After the procession returned to the palace, he made her his number one queen.

That evening the king had a shampoo and bath, ate his supper, and went to bed. The demon had her supper, made herself look even more beautiful than before, and followed the king to his bed. After pleasing him, she turned on her side and began to weep.

The king asked, "Why are you crying, my sweetheart?" "My lord," said she, "you picked me up from the roadside. In this palace there are many jealous women. They will say, 'She has no mother or father, no family or country. She was found on the side of the road.' Don't let them make fun of me like that, my lord. Give me power over the whole kingdom so none will dare challenge me."

"My lovely," replied the king, "I have no such power over the whole kingdom. My authority is only over those who revolt or break the law." But since he was so pleased by her physical charms, the king continued, "My sweetheart, I will grant you complete authority over all who dwell within my palace."

Satisfied with this, the new queen waited until the king was asleep. Then she secretly ran off to her home in the city of devils. She gathered together the she-devils, he-devils, and even the hungry little children-devils. Then she took them all back to the palace. She killed her new husband, the king, and gobbled him up – all except his bones! The other devils ate all the rest who lived in the palace – even the dogs and chickens! Only bones were left behind.

The next morning the people found the palace doors locked. Worried, they broke through the windows with axes, went inside, and found human and animal bones scattered around. Only then did they realize that the man in the rest house was right, that the king's new queen was a flesh-eating devil.

Meanwhile, the Enlightenment Being had protected himself from the murderous she-devil during the night. He had spread the charmed sand on the roof of the rest house and wound the charmed string around the outside walls. At dawn he was still awake inside, standing alertly with sword in hand.

After cleaning up the mess in the palace the citizens discussed the situation among themselves. They said, "The man in the rest house must be master of his senses, since he did not even look at the she-devil's dangerous beauty. If such a noble, determined and wise man were ruling our country, we all would prosper. Let us make him our new king."

In unanimous agreement they went to the rest house and invited the prince to be their king. When he accepted, they escorted him to the palace, seated him on a pile of jewels, and crowned him king.

He ruled righteously, following the ten rules of good government [*dasa-rāja-dhamma*-s]. He avoided the four ways of going astray – prejudice [*upanāha*], anger [*kodha*], fearfulness [*dosa*] and foolishness [*moha*]. And he always remembered the advice of the Silent Buddhas, that had led him to the kingship. Unlike his five unfortunate followers, he had resisted the blind desire for the pleasures of the five senses. Only then could he benefit all his subjects with his wise rule.

* * *

The Buddha said:

"The citizens of the kingdom are today the Buddha's followers. And I was the prince who won the kingdom."

The moral: "Living only for pleasures of their senses, fools are devoured."

97

A Man Named Bad
[Self Acceptance]
(Nāmasiddhi-Jātaka)

The Buddha told this story while he was living in Jetavana monastery with regard to a monk who thought that luck went with a name, and who wished to change his name.

This monk, named 'Bad' [Pāpaka], asked his teachers to change his name to one of better omen. But his teachers told him that a name only served to denote a thing, and did not impute qualities. He continued in his request, though, till the entire community of monks knew of it.

One evening, the monks in the preaching hall were discussing this matter. When the Buddha entered and found out what they were talking about, he said, "Oh monks, this is not the first time that this brother has believed that luck went with names. He was equally dissatisfied with the name he had in former days, as well." And the Buddha told this story of the past:

Once upon a time there was a world-famous teacher in Takkasilā, in northwestern India. He had 500 high-class students who learned sacred teachings from him.

It just so happened that one of these high-class students had been named 'Bad' [Pāpaka] by his parents. One day he thought, "When I am told, 'Come Bad', 'Go Bad', 'Do this Bad', it is not nice for me or others. It even sounds disgraceful and unlucky."

So he went to the teacher and asked him to give him a more pleasant name, one that would bring good fortune rather than bad. The teacher said, "Go, my son, go wherever you like and find a more fortunate name. When you return, I will officially give you your new name."

The young man named Bad left the city, and traveled from village to village until he came to a big city. A man had just died and Bad asked what his name was. People said, "His name was Alive [Jīvaka]." "Alive also died?" asked Bad. The people answered, "Whether his name be Alive or whether it be Dead, in either case he must die. A name is merely a word used to recognize a person. Only a fool would not know this!" After hearing this, Bad no longer felt badly about his own name – but he didn't feel good about it either.

As he continued on his way into the city, a debt-slave girl was being beaten by her masters in the street. He asked, "Why is she being beaten?" He was told, "Because she is a slave until she pays a loan debt to her masters. She has come home from working, with no wages to pay as interest on her debt." "And what is her name?" he asked. "Her name is Rich [Dhanapālī]," they said. "By her name she is Rich, but she has no money even to pay interest?" asked Bad. They said, "Whether her name be Rich or whether it be Poor, in either case she has no money. A name is merely a word used to recognize a person. Only a fool would not know this!" After hearing this, Bad became even less interested in changing his name.

After leaving the city, along the roadside he met a man who had lost his way. He asked him, "What is your name?" He replied, "My name is Tourguide [Panthaka]." "You mean to say that even a Tourguide has gotten lost?" asked Bad. Then the man said, "Whether my name be Tourguide or whether it be Tourist, in either case I have lost my way. A name is merely a word used to recognize a person. Only a fool would not know this!"

Now completely satisfied with his own name, Bad returned to his teacher.

The world-famous teacher of Takkasilā asked him, "How are you, my son? Have you found a good name?" He answered, "Sir, those named Alive and Dead both die, Rich and Poor may be penniless, Tourguide and Tourist can get lost. Now I know that a name is merely a word used to recognize a person. The name does not make things happen, only deeds do. So I'm satisfied with my name. There's no point in changing it."

The teacher summarized the lesson his pupil had learned this way – "By seeing Alive as dead, Rich as poor, Tourguide as lost, Bad has accepted himself."

The Buddha then identified the births:

"This brother who is today dissatisfied with his name, was the similarly dissatisfied high-class student of the past. The 500 high-class students are today the Buddha's disciples. And the world-famous teacher was I who am today the Buddha."

The moral: "'A rose by any other name would smell as sweet.'"

98

A Man Named Wise
[Cheating]
(Kūṭavāṇija-Jātaka)

The Buddha told this story while living in Jetavana temple with regard to a scheming merchant of Sāvatthi.[32]

There were two merchants in partnership in Sāvatthi who traveled with their merchandise and then came back with the proceeds. One was very cunning and the other was very honest and well educated.

At one point, the cunning merchant thought to himself, "My partner, for the entire duration of the last trip, ate only very coarse food and slept in very uncomfortable surroundings. Now that he is home again and can eat good food, he will gorge himself and die of indigestion. Then I will divide what we have made into three portions, giving one to his orphans and keeping two for myself." And with this in mind, he had put off day by day the division of the profits.

Finding that it was in vain to press for a division of the profits, the honest merchant took some flowers, incense and lamps, and went to see the Buddha. The Buddha received him kindly, and said, "Why, friend, have I not seen you for a long time?" And the merchant told the Buddha what was going on. Hearing the explanation, the Buddha said to him, "Not only now, but even in the past this man was a cunning rogue." And at the merchant's request, the Buddha told the past story:

Once upon a time, the Enlightenment Being was born in a merchants' family in Benares, in northern India. He was given the name

---

32 The "story of the present" here is the same as in Jātaka No. 218, also titled Kūṭavāṇija-Jātaka. The Jātaka story itself, however, is different.

Wise [Paṇḍita]. When he grew up he began doing business with a man whose name just happened to be Verywise [Atipaṇḍita].

It came to pass that Wise and Verywise took a caravan of 500 bullock carts into the countryside. After selling all their goods they returned to Benares with their handsome profits.

When it came time to split their gains between them, Verywise said, "I should get twice as much profit as you." "How come?" asked Wise. "Because you are Wise and I am Verywise. It is obvious that Wise should get only half as much as Verywise."

Then Wise asked, "Didn't we both invest equal amounts in this caravan trip? Why do you deserve twice as much profit as I?" Verywise replied, "Because of my quality of being Verywise." In this way their quarrel went on with no end in sight.

Then Verywise thought, "I have a plan to win this argument." So he went to his father and asked him to hide inside a huge hollow tree. He said, "When my partner and I come by and ask how to share our profits, then you should say, 'Verywise deserves a double share.'"

Verywise returned to Wise and said, "My friend, neither of us wants this quarrel. Let's go to the old sacred tree and ask the tree spirit to settle it."

When they went to the tree Verywise said solemnly, "My lord tree spirit, we have a problem. Kindly solve it for us." Then his father, hidden inside the hollow tree, disguised his voice and asked, "What is your question?" The man's cheating son said, "My lord tree spirit, this man is Wise and I am Verywise. We have done business together. Tell us how to share the profits." Again disguising his voice, his father responded, "Wise deserves a single share and Verywise deserves a double share."

Hearing this solution, Wise decided to find out if it really was a tree spirit speaking from inside the tree. So he threw some hay into it and set it on fire. Immediately Verywise's father grabbed onto a branch, jumped out of the flames and fell on the ground. He said in his own voice, "Although his name is Verywise, my son is just a clever cheater. I'm lucky that the one named Wise really is so, and I've escaped only half-toasted!"

Then Wise and Verywise shared their profits equally. Eventually they both died and were reborn as they deserved.

The Buddha then said:

"The scheming merchant of today was the same as the scheming merchant in this Jātaka story. And I was the honest merchant named Wise."

The moral: "A cheater may be clever but not wise."

Achieving Nothing
[No Thing]
(Parosahassa-Jātaka)

The Buddha told this story while he was living in Jetavana monastery with regard to Sāriputta's wisdom.

On a certain occasion, the monks gathered in the preaching hall were discussing how Sāriputta had expounded the meaning of a pithy saying of the Buddha. On entering the hall and being told by the monks what it was they were talking about, the Buddha said, "This is not the first time, oh monks, that the meaning of a pithy saying of mine has been brought out by Sāriputta. He did the same in the past." And saying this, the Buddha told the story:

Once upon a time the Bodhisatta – the Enlightenment Being – was born into a high-class family in northern India. When he grew up he gave up the ordinary desires of the everyday world and became a holy man. He went to the Himalayan Mountains where 500 other holy men became his followers.

He meditated throughout his long life. He gained supernatural powers – like flying through the air and understanding people's thoughts without their speaking. These special powers impressed his 500 followers greatly.

One rainy season, the chief follower took 250 of the holy men into the hill country villages to collect salt and other necessities. It just so happened that this was the time when the master was about to die. The 250 who were still by his side realized this. So they asked him, "Oh most holy one, in your long life practicing goodness and meditation, what was your greatest achievement?"

---

33 Compare also Candābha-Jātaka [No. 135].

Having difficulty speaking as he was dying, the last words of the Enlightenment Being were, "No Thing [*Akiñcanaṁ*]." Then he was reborn in a heaven world.

Expecting to hear about some fantastic magical power, the 250 followers were disappointed. They said to each other, "After a long life practicing goodness and meditation, our poor master has achieved 'nothing'." Since they considered him a failure, they burned his body with no special ceremony, honors, or even respect.

When the chief follower returned he asked, "Where is the holy one?" "He has died," they told him. "Did you ask him about his greatest achievement?" "Of course, we did," they answered. "And what did he say?" asked the chief follower. "He said he achieved 'nothing'," they replied, "so we didn't celebrate his funeral with any special honors."

Then the chief follower said, "You brothers did not understand the meaning of the teacher's words. He achieved the great knowledge of 'No Thing'. He realized that the names of things are not what they are. There is what there is, without being called 'this thing' or 'that thing'. There is no 'Thing'." In this way the chief follower explained the wonderful achievement of their great master,[34] but they still did not understand.

Meanwhile, from his heaven world, the reborn Enlightenment Being saw that his former chief follower's words were not accepted. So he left the heaven world and appeared floating in the air above his former followers' monastery. In praise of the chief follower's wisdom he said,

"The one who hears the Truth [Saccaṁ] and understands automatically, is far better off than a thousand fools who spend a hundred years thinking and thinking and thinking."[35]

---

34 Such is frequently described as an attribute of an Arahant, or one without defilements. It is taken to mean that he is above such impurities of character as passion for a thing [*rāga*], anger on account of this or that thing [*dosa*] and delusion as to the nature of things [*moha*].

35 The import of the Pāli title of this story, *Parosahassa-Jātaka* [The Story of More than a Thousand] is given in this verse. The import is '... more than a thousand fools.' So also, Jātaka 101, *Parosata-Jātaka* [The Story of More than a Hundred], refers to the period of time that the fools spend thinking.

By preaching in this way, the Great Being encouraged the 500 holy men to continue seeking Truth [Saccaṁ]. After lives spent in serious meditation, all 500 died and were reborn in the same heaven world with their former master.

The Buddha said:

"Sāriputta was the chief follower in the past. And I, myself, was the Great Being."

The moral: "When the wise speak, listen!"

A Mother's Wise Advice
[Nonviolence]
(Asātarūpa-Jātaka, Aghātarūpa-Jātaka)

The Buddha told this story while he was in Kuṇḍadhāna Forest near the city of Kuṇḍiya with regard to Suppavāsā, the daughter of the king of Koliya. At that time, she had carried a child in her womb for seven years, was in the seventh day of giving birth and was having great pains. In spite of this suffering, she thought of the Buddha and his message regarding the end of sufferings. Such thoughts, indeed, were a consolation to her in her pain. So she sent her husband to the Buddha to hear a greeting from her and to tell him of her condition.

Her message having been given to the Buddha, the Buddha blessed her, wishing that she grow strong again and give birth to a healthy child. And at the moment of his words, so she did.

When her husband returned home, he found that she had delivered the child already and he marveled at the Buddha's powers.

Now that the child was born, Suppavāsā was anxious to show her bounty for seven days to the Buddha and his retinue, so she sent her husband back to invite them. But at the same time, the Buddha had received an invitation from the layman who supported the Venerable Moggallāna. Wishing to gratify Suppavāsā's charitable desires, the Buddha sent Moggallāna to explain the matter, and accepted the hospitality of Suppavāsā for seven days.

On the seventh day, she dressed up her newly born son, whose name was Sīvalī, and had him bow before the Buddha and the monks. When, in due course, he was brought before Sāriputta, the elder kindly asked the infant whether all was well with him. "How could it be, Venerable sir?" said the child. "I have had to wallow in blood for seven long years!"

Joyfully, Suppavāsā exclaimed that her child, only seven days old, was discussing religion with one of the Buddha's chief disciples, Sāriputta. The Buddha asked her whether she would like to have another such child, and she said, "Seven more, if they would be like him."

At the age of seven, Sīvalī joined the monkhood. And when he reached the age of 20, so that he was able to, he became a full-fledged monk. In due course, he gained Arahant-ship [sainthood].

One day, the monks in the preaching hall were discussing Sīvalī's achievements and the circumstances of his birth, wondering what deeds were the cause of this. When the Buddha entered and questioned the monks as to the subject of their conversation, he said that Sīvalī was seven years in the womb and seven days in birth all because of his own past deeds. And similarly, Suppavāsā's seven years of pregnancy and seven days in labor resulted from her past deeds. And at the monks' request, the Buddha told the story of the past:

Once upon a time, the son of Brahmadatta was ruling righteously in Benares, in northern India. It came to pass that the King of Kosala made war, killed the King of Benares, and made the queen become his own wife.

Meanwhile, the queen's son escaped by sneaking away through the sewers. In the countryside he eventually raised a large army and surrounded the city. He sent a message to the king, the murderer of his father and the husband of his mother. He told him to surrender the kingdom or fight a battle.

The prince's mother, the Queen of Benares, heard of this threat from her son. She was a gentle and kind woman who wanted to prevent violence and suffering and killing. So she sent a message to her son – "There is no need for the risks of battle. It would be wiser to close every entrance to the city. Eventually the lack of food, water and firewood will wear down the citizens. Then they will give the city to you without any fighting."

The prince decided to follow his mother's wise advice. His army blockaded the city for seven days and nights. Then the citizens captured their unlawful king, cut off his head, and delivered it to the prince. He entered the city triumphantly and became the new King of Benares.

The Buddha then said:

"Sīvalī was the prince who in the past blockaded the city and became king. Suppavāsā was his mother. And I who have become the Buddha was his father, king of Benares."

The Buddha added:

"It was as a result of blockading the city for seven days that Sīvalī was in the womb for seven years and was seven days in birth. It was similarly on account of his previous deeds that he gained Arahant-ship. And it was because Suppavāsā sent her message bidding her son to take the city by blockade, that she was doomed to a seven-year pregnancy and to seven days of labor."

The moral: "Every deed receives its just deserts."

Also,

"Kind advice is wise advice."

Appendix A

Who Was the Bodhisatta?

Some who tell these stories say that they are about past lives of the Buddha, the Enlightened One. Before he became enlightened as the Buddha, he was called the Bodhisatta, the Enlightenment Being. Look at the list below to see who is said to be the Bodhisatta in each story.

51. King Goodness the Great
52. King Fruitful
53. The richest man in Benares
54, 85. A caravan leader
55. Prince Five-Weapons
56. A poor farmer
57. Mr. Monkey
58. A prince of monkeys
59. A drummer father living in a small country village
60. The son of a conch-blower living in a small country village
61. A very well-known teacher
62. A king who loved to gamble
63. The Buttermilk Wise Man
64, 65. A well-known teacher
66. A holy man from a rich high-class family
67. The king
68. A son to the same couple in many births
69. A doctor who was an expert at treating snake bites
70. The Shovel Wise Man
71. A world-famous teacher and holy man
72. The Elephant King Goodness

73. A holy man living humbly in a little hut
74. A very wise tree spirit who was the leader of a large clan
75. The fish who worked a miracle
76. The meditating security guard
77. A humble forest monk
78. The barber
79. A traveling merchant
80. A dwarf, bent over and partly hunchbacked
81. A homeless holy man and teacher
82. The world-famous teacher
83. A very rich man
84. A rich father living in Benares
85, 54. A caravan leader
86. A very valuable adviser priest
87. A forest monk
88. The bull called Tit-for-Tat
89. A trader
90. The Benares merchant
91. A rich man living in Benares who was addicted to gambling
92. The wise minister
93. A very wealthy man living in Benares
94. The holy man who tried to be too holy
95. Clear-sighted the Great, King of the World
96. The last of King Brahmadatta's 100 sons
97. A world-famous teacher
98. An honest merchant named Wise
99. The master holy man
100. The son of Brahmadatta ruling righteously in Benares

Appendix B

An Arrangement of Morals

The morals from the stories are arranged below, according to the Ten Perfections.

The Enlightenment Being – the Bodhisatta – developed each of them along his way to realizing the full enlightenment of the Buddha. This can be used as a different order for reading the stories.

Moral	Story	Page
Generosity		
If you don't help others, you can't expect them to help you.	90	189
The ungrateful stops at nothing, and digs his own grave.	72	94
Poor indeed is the rich man who won't part with a penny.	78	132
Wholesomeness – Morality		
Keep sober – and keep your common sense.	53	32
A pupil without a teacher is easily embarrassed.	81	150
Deceiving a friend may be hazardous to your health.	91	192
People prize goodness most of all.	86	174
Desire enslaves. Wisdom liberates.	66	76
Giving up attachment to the ordinary world – Renunciation		
Only one possession is enough to keep the mind from finding freedom.	70	87

Moral	Story	Page
It's easier to gain power than to give it up.	52	9
Wickedness between women and men brings unhappiness to both.	61	55

Wisdom

Beware of the panic-stricken man. What he can do is more dangerous than what scared him in the first place.	77	116
A cheater may be clever but not wise.	98	222
It's a fortunate brother who has an intelligent sister.	67	81
One way or another, we're all related.	68	83
Seduction can be dangerous to men and women both.	63	67
You can't force someone to be good.	62	60
"Don't bite off more than you can chew."	56	44
Too much of a good thing can be dangerous.	93	202
It pays to be careful.	58	49
"Appearances can be deceiving."	80	144
"A rose by any other name would smell as sweet."	97	219
"A serious question deserves a serious answer."	84	172
A fool's curse can be a wise man's blessing.	87	178
Fools are deaf to wise words.	74	107
When the wise speak, listen!	99	225
Theft from greed, lies from fear, truth from examining.	92	194
The wise are led by common sense. Fools follow only hunger.	54, 85	35

Moral	Story	Page
The only weapon you need is hidden inside you.	55	39
The bad intentions of foolish people are easily overcome by the wile of noble ones.	57	46
Every deed receives its just deserts	100	228

Energy – Perseverance

"Don't put off until tomorrow what you can do today."	71	91

Patience

Understanding relieves anger.	64, 65	73
Overdoing leads to a downfall.	59, 60	52

Truthfulness

Be careful of a holy man who puts on a big show.	89	185
No one defends a betrayer of trust.	79	141
Even at the very last moment, "The truth shall make you free."	94	204

Determination

Determination wins respect.	69	85
It pays to have a holy man around.	76	113
Living only for pleasures of their senses, fools are devoured.	96	211
Refusing to harm others, the good heart wins over all.	51	1

Loving-kindness

The longer the friendship, the greater its rewards.	83	168
Gratitude is a reward, which is itself rewarded.	73	100

Moral	Story	Page
Kind advice is wise advice.	100	228
True innocence relieves the suffering of many.	75	110
Evenmindedness – Equanimity		
Harsh words bring no reward. Respectful words bring honor to all.	88	181
A good loser is a true gentleman	57	46
"All good things come to an end."	95	207
In peace of mind, there is neither loss nor gain.	82	155

KING SIX TUSKER
AND
THE QUEEN WHO HATED HIM
CHADDANTA-JĀTAKA
(No. 514)

INTERPRETED BY
KURUNEGODA PIYATISSA MAHA THERA

STORY TOLD BY
TODD ANDERSON

2nd EDITION, REVISED AND ENLARGED BY
KURUNEGODA PIYATISSA MAHA THERA AND
STEPHAN HILLYER LEVITT

Interpreter's Introduction to the 1ˢᵗ Edition

The reader is presented here with a Jataka story written very much as it is told in the Sinhalese translation of the Pali original (*Sinhala Jataka Pot Vahanse* – Colombo: Jinalankara Press, 1928). The standard English translation was also used as a reference (The Jataka or Stories of the Buddha's Former Lives, ed. E. B. Cowell – London: Pali Text Society, 1981, 6 vols.).

In our version my friend the storyteller wanted me to interpret in the same way as the Sinhalese storyteller. This is in contrast to the occasional summarizing which we did in our previously published Prince Goodspeaker and King Fruitful, which we were pleased to hear were so touching to many of the readers.

In Chaddanta Jataka it is interesting to read the long descriptions of the forest elephants and their lifestyle. Even today it is known that elephants respect their elders, much as they and humans did in the ancient time of our story.

The generosity and patience of the Enlightenment Being (Bodhisatta) are presented in an emotional and respectful way that can be felt by the listener.

In earlier times a capable reader used to read out loud in the middle of a listening crowd. Long descriptions enhanced the storytelling and generated an emotional response. Those feelings enriched their lives with wholesome qualities and virtues. In this way they used their time to cultivate high human values. The good results of good deeds and the bad results of bad deeds were firmly registered and cultivated by listening to such stories in the past. This contributed to building a good society.

In the Sinhalese version the enriched language is highly emotional and sensational. Unfortunately this cannot be fully captured in English. Our presentation is an attempt to show modern readers one way that ancestors taught human morals.

The picture on the front cover is from the north gateway of the ancient stupa in Sanchi, India, depicting a scene from the Chaddanta Jataka. Our thanks to Ven. Dedunupitiye Somaratana, the Incumbent, for providing this photograph.

We thank all our readers and listeners as well as The Corporate Body of the Buddha Educational Foundation of Taiwan.

May all beings be well and happy!

Kurunegoda Piyatissa
October 18, 1996

Buddhist Literature Society Inc.
New York Buddhist Vihara
84-32 124th Street
Kew Gardens
New York, NY 11415 U.S.A.

$$\boxed{514}$$

King Six Tusker and the Queen
Who Hated Him
(*Chaddanta-Jātaka*)

The Buddha told this story while dwelling in Jetavanārāma with regard to a nun who was from a good family of Sāvatthi. One day, while listening to a sermon by the Buddha, she admired his extreme beauty of form and wondered whether she had ever been his wife. Immediately, the memory of her life as 'Little Grace' [Cūla-subhaddā], consort of King 'Six Tusker' [Chaddanta], came back to her and she laughed from joy. But on further recollecting that she had caused the great elephant king's death, she burst into sobs and wept aloud. On seeing this, the Buddha broke into a smile. When asked by the assembly of monks why he was smiling, the Buddha said, "Oh monks, this young nun wept on recalling a sin she once committed against me." And saying this, the Buddha then told this story of the past.

Chapter 1. Rebirth of the Bodhisatta

Once upon a time there were 8,000 noble elephants who were able to fly through the air whenever they wished. They lived in the Himalayan Mountains near a lake that was 800 miles [Yojana-s] long and 800 miles wide. Since it had six bays that were shaped like elephant tusks, it was called the Lake of Six Tusks [Chaddanta-vāpi].

It just so happened that the king of this elephant nation had a son. He was pure white in color, with a bright red mouth and red feet. Even among these fantastic elephants he was no ordinary elephant baby. This was not his first life or his first birth. Millions of years before, he had been a follower of a long-forgotten teaching 'Buddha' – a fully 'Enlightened One'. He had wished with all his heart to become a Buddha just like his beloved master.

He was reborn in many lives – sometimes as poor animals, sometimes as long-living gods and sometimes as human beings. He always tried to learn from his mistakes and develop the 'Ten Perfections' [dasa-pāramitā-s]: energy, determination, truthfulness, wholesomeness, giving up attachment to the ordinary world, even-mindedness, wisdom, patience, generosity, and of course – loving-kindness. This was so he could purify his mind and remove the three root causes of unwholesomeness [akusala-mūla-s] – craving, anger and the delusion of a separate self – and someday replace them with the three purities [ti-pārisuddhi-s] – nonattachment [alobha], loving-kindness [adosa] and wisdom [amoha].

This 'Great Being' had been a humble follower of the forgotten Buddha. His goal was to gain the same enlightenment of a Buddha – the experience of complete Truth. So people call him 'Bodhisatta', which means 'Enlightenment Being'. No one really knows about the millions of lives lived by this great hero. But many stories have been told – including this one about a magnificent elephant. After many more rebirths, he would become the Buddha who is remembered and loved in all the world today.

When the elephant prince grew up he reached a height of 132 feet [Hattha-s]. He was 180 feet long from trunk to tail. His trunk alone was 87 feet long and as bright and strong as a silver chain. Because he happened to have six tusks he was known as 'Six Tusker' [Chaddanta]. These were gigantic – 45 feet long and 22 feet around. And they shone brilliantly in six colors – blue, yellow, red, white, crimson and all the first five at once. After his father died he became the new king of the 8,000 noble elephants.

It is said that elephants are very intelligent, and these were more so than usual. They were even wise enough that the entire nation had come to honor and serve the 500 Silent Buddhas [Pacceka-Buddha-s] who also lived in the Himalayas at that time.

They were called Buddhas because they were enlightened. This means that they no longer experienced themselves, the ones called 'I' or 'me', as being in any way different from all life living itself. So they were able to experience life as it really is, in every present moment.

Being one with all life, they were filled with compassion and sympathy for the unhappiness of all beings. So they wished to teach and help them to be enlightened just as they were. But the time of our story was a most unfortunate time, a very sad time. It was a time when no one else was able to understand the Truth [Dhamma] and experience life as it really is. And since these Buddhas knew this, that was why they were Silent insofar as teachings go.

Chapter 2. Home and Family

In the middle of the Lake of Six Tusks, for a diameter of 192 miles it was free of all plant life and as clear, clean and bright as a magic jewel. Around this vast open center there grew seven circular thickets – white lilies, blue, red and white lotuses, white and red lilies, and finally edible white water lilies that are especially loved by elephants.

Outside the seven thickets was another circle of mixed water lilies and lotuses. Then, in elephant-hip-deep water there was a circle of red rice paddy at the outer edge of the lake. Along the shore there was a thicket of different kinds of shrubs, with delicate and sweet-smelling flowers that were blue, yellow, red and white. That made a total of ten circular thickets, each one extending outward for 16 miles.

Then came a circle of bean plants, followed by circles of morning glories, cucumbers, pumpkins, squash and other creeping plants. Then came forests of sugar cane as big as palm trees, bananas the size of elephant tusks, Sal trees and jackfruit trees with fruits as big as water jars. There were forests of very sweet-tasting tamarinds and wood-apple trees. Next was a big forest of many kinds of trees. Finally there was a huge circle of bamboo trees.

But that was not all! Surrounding the bamboo forest were seven encircling mountains. First was Golden Mountain [Suvaṇṇa-pabbata] – 112 miles high, then Jewel Mountain [Maṇi-passa-pabbata] – 96 miles high, Sunshine Mountain [Sūriya-pabbata] – 80 miles high, Moon Mountain [Canda-pabbata] – 64 miles high, Reflecting Water Mountain [Uddaka-passa-pabbata] – 48 miles high, Big Dark Mountain [Mahā-kāla-pabbata] – 32 miles high, and finally the outer circle called Little Dark Mountain [Cūla-kāla-pabbata] – only 16 miles high! The highest inner Golden Mountain surrounded the Lake of Six Tusks country like the rim of a gigantic golden bowl, so that the light reflecting from it made the lake shine like the young sun at dawn.

At the end of the northeast tusk of the lake stood a huge banyan tree. Its trunk was 25 miles across and 112 miles high, and it had 8,000 banyan roots growing down from its branches. It was as beautiful as a mountain of jewels.

On the west side of the Lake of Six Tusks was a golden cave extending into Golden Mountain for 192 miles. King Six Tusker spent the spring in this cave with his entire nation of 8,000 elephants, including his two queens. The first was called 'Great Grace' [Mahā-subhaddā] and the second, 'Little Grace' [Cūla-subhaddā].

The Elephant King spent the summer months under the hanging roots of the huge banyan tree, enjoying the cool breezes blowing from the Lake of Six Tusks. One day he was informed that the great forest of Sal trees was in full bloom. Wishing to enjoy the beautiful fragrance of the large blossoms he went to the blooming Sal forest, followed by all the other elephants. He just happened to bump his forehead against one of the flower-laden trees. Queen Little Grace was standing upwind, so the heavier twigs and leaves and biting red ants in their little leaf houses fell on her royal body. Queen Great Grace happened to be standing downwind, so the lighter flower petals and sweet-smelling pollen were blown onto her royal body.

Because of her own ignorance Queen Little Grace misinterpreted these events. Instead of accepting the simple fact of objects falling on her body causing minor discomfort which passed quickly, she imagined that a self living inside her had been insulted. To defend this self-image she automatically and immediately got angry at the Great Being, King Six Tusker. She thought, "He dropped dirty twigs and leaves and red ant houses on me, but on his favorite wife, the number one queen, he dropped lovely flower petals and sweet pollen. I'll get even with him!" And she tied this anger to herself and herself to it, determined not to let it go.

A few days later the nation of 8,000 elephants went down to bathe in the Lake of Six Tusks. Two young elephant calves took fragrant roots of *Usīra*-bushes in their trunks and respectfully washed King Six Tusker. They thoroughly rubbed his thick elephant skin, a job as big as if they were washing Mount Kelāsa.

When they were finished and the king came out of the lake, they bathed the two beautiful queens in the same way. They too left the water and stood by his side. Then the entire nation of 8,000 elephants went into the lake, played in the water, picked various lotuses and decorated their king and queens with the flowers.

It just so happened that one elephant, while swimming in the lake, saw a marvelous lotus with seven flowers one inside the other reaching high above the water. The lucky elephant plucked it up and offered it to King Six Tusker. He held it in his trunk and sprinkled the sweet-smelling pollen on his forehead. Then he gave the seven-flowered lotus to his number one queen, Great Grace.

When she saw this, Queen Little Grace thought, "Even this great seven-flowered lotus he gave to his more loved one, not to me." She used this thought to build up hatred, which she tied to herself and herself to it, determined not to let it go.

One day not long after, the Enlightenment Being mixed together sweet fruits and lotus roots which he sprinkled with lotus nectar. This he put into the alms bowls of the 500 Silent Buddhas.

Meanwhile, Queen Little Grace had collected many big and little fruits which she also gave as alms to the Buddhas. Still holding onto her hatred, she silently dedicated the blessing of her gift to her own craving for vengeance. Wishing with all her might she thought, "When this present life comes to an end may I be reborn in the royal family of the kingdom of Madda as the Princess Grace [Subhaddā]. When I grow up may I become the number one queen of the King of Benares. Able to please his mind, may I become his favorite so I can do whatever I want. With such power may I speak to the king and get him to send a hunter to kill this king of elephants with a poisoned arrow and bring me his tusks that shine with six colors!"

From that time on she did not eat or drink. Soon she became dehydrated and died.

Chapter 3. The Hate-filled Queen

Rebirth took place as Grace, daughter of the Queen of Madda. When she grew up she married the King of Benares and became his favorite wife, the most pleasing to his mind. She came to be in charge of all the king's 16,000 wives.

Remembering her previous life Queen Grace thought, "My great wish is coming true. Now I have the power to request the tusks of the Elephant King be brought to me!" She rubbed medicinal oils on her skin, dressed in dirty clothes and lay in bed as if sick.

The king began asking for his favorite queen. When told she was ill he went to her bed, massaged her back and said, "Oh queen whose body once glowed, why are you grieving? Your color has paled and your large eyes have faded. You are like a once beautiful garland that has been crushed."

She replied, "My lord, I seem to be in a nightmare with a fantastic craving that cannot be satisfied. I fear if my wish is not granted I must die!"

"Whatever joys and luxuries are desired in this world I can provide," said the king, "so tell me your wish and I will grant it."

"Great king, granting my wish will not be easy. First summon all the hunters in your kingdom and then I will tell my fantastic craving."

The king left her chamber and ordered the drums be beaten to call all the hunters. Soon they arrived, of course bringing suitable gifts for the king. There were 60,000 of them in all.

Sitting by an open window the king told Queen Grace, "My dear queen, all the clever and fearless hunters, knowers of forests and beasts, have come to me. Whatever you want me to do for you can now be done."

The queen addressed the crowd, "Hunters, listen to me well. In a dream I have seen a certain pure white elephant with six magnificent tusks. It is those tusks which I crave and if I do not get them I will surely die!"

Some of the hunters answered her, "Neither we nor our parents nor our grandparents ever saw or heard of such an elephant with six tusks. Tell us please, according to your dream, in what direction is this elephant to be found?"

Queen Grace looked at all the hunters carefully. She saw one who had wide feet, calf muscles as big and round as alms bowls, large knees and ribs, a thick beard and brown-stained teeth. He was the biggest of them all and was so covered with scars from old wounds that he was the ugliest too. He stood out easily in the crowd. Known as 'Top Dog' [Sonuttara], some storytellers say this was not the first lifetime in which he became an enemy of the Enlightenment Being. "This big ugly one will do just fine," thought the queen.

With the king's permission she took Top Dog to the top of the seven-storied palace. She opened the northern window, pointed towards the Himalayas and said, "There in the North, when you have passed seven mountains you will come to a golden cliff full of flowers that are loved by human-headed bird beings [Kinnara-s]. Look down from the top of that golden peak and you will see on the other side a banyan tree as big as a green cloud, with 8,000 hanging roots. The pure white Elephant King with six tusks is under that tree. He cannot be conquered by anybody since he is protected by 8,000 elephants who ride on the wind to strike with their long sharp tusks. His powerful elephant guards are angered by even a change in the wind. If they see a man their rage blows hot air from their trunks and turns him into ashes."

This was enough to frighten even Top Dog. "Your highness," he replied, "in your royal family there is plenty of gold, silver, pearls, lapis lazuli and precious jewels. Why do you need the ivory from those tusks? Is it really that you want that elephant killed? Or in truth do you aim to get me killed?"

"When I remember what that elephant did to me," she said, "I am filled with jealousy and it makes my heart burn with frustration. Oh hunter, grant me the vengeance I crave and five of the richest villages in the kingdom shall be yours! Oh hunter my friend, I have given alms to Silent Buddhas and dedicated the benefit to my own greatest wish – to have that six tusker killed and keep his biggest pair of tusks for myself. This was not a dream, but a mighty promise that must now come to pass. By the power of that promise, go and have no fear!"

Top Dog agreed, saying, "As you wish, your majesty. Now please tell me where he lives exactly, and where he sleeps. What road does he take to go bathing and where does he bathe? Tell me what you can about his lifestyle."

Remembering her previous life as an elephant she said, "Very near the giant banyan tree there is a big lake with crystal clear water and a beautiful bathing place. Flowers bloom there, served by honeybees. When the Elephant King finishes his bath his skin is as white as a pure white lotus and he dresses in blue lotus garlands. Happily he returns home following his beloved Queen Great Grace."

"I will kill the king elephant," said Top Dog, "and bring you his tusks." The queen was filled with joy and gave him a thousand gold coins. She said, "Now go home and in seven days' time be ready to begin the journey."

The queen summoned blacksmiths and told them, "We need an ax, a hatchet, a shovel, a pick, a hammer, a bamboo cutter, a grass cutter, an iron staff, a saw, an iron pole and a grappling hook. Make them quickly and bring them to me."

Then she called leather workers and ordered them, "We need a bag as big and strong as a water jar, ropes and straps strong enough to tie an elephant, sandals big enough to fit an elephant, and a big umbrella. Make them quickly from the strongest leather and bring them to me."

After all these things were made and brought to the queen, she added fire sticks and other necessities. She put everything in the big leather bag, making it as heavy as a huge water jar filled with water.

After the week had passed, Top Dog returned and bowed before the queen. Having the strength of five elephants, he tucked the heavy leather bag easily under his arm. After taking leave of the king and queen he left the palace, loaded up his chariot and rode out of the city. After going through many villages and towns he crossed the border of the kingdom of Benares. He went through vast forests and, after sending home the crowds that followed him, he arrived in the land where no people live.

Chapter 4. The Hunt

Top Dog used the grass cutter to get through a jungle of grass, and the bamboo cutter for basil and reed thickets. After first piercing the biggest trees with the pick, he used the ax to chop his way through a forest. Then he made a bamboo ladder and climbed it to the top of an impenetrable bamboo thicket, which he crossed by using a bamboo pole that he stretched over it.

Coming to a muddy swamp he walked over it using two wooden planks, one after the other, over and over again. Then he made a canoe and paddled it across a flooded area.

At last he arrived at the foot of the great circle of mountains. He climbed by throwing the grappling hook and leather rope up, tying the bottom to a peg he had hammered into the mountain, and pulling himself up the rope to the hook. Then he hammered another peg into the mountain, tied it to the rope, pulled out the grappling hook and threw it farther up the slope. Hitting the rope beneath him sharply he dislodged the lower peg, gathered it in, and pulled himself up to the hook. He repeated this over and over again until he reached the summit.

He climbed down the other side by hammering the peg into the mountain and tying the leather rope to it as well as to the big leather bag. Then he sat inside the bag and lowered it downwards – just like a spider hanging by a thread from his cobweb. On the other hand, there were some places where he simply grabbed hold of the big leather umbrella and used it like a parachute to fly down like a graceful bird (or at least, so it is said).

After climbing up and down the first six mountains, he finally came to the innermost Golden Mountain, which just so happened to be 112 miles high! He climbed to the top and found Kinnara-s living there, as had been foretold by Queen Grace. These are winged beings who look human from the waist up and birdlike from the waist down. They are innocent creatures who generally avoid talking with people – since they consider them to be mostly liars.

Looking down the other side of Golden Mountain, Top Dog saw the giant banyan tree, as big as a cloud, with its 8,000 roots hanging down. He saw too the white Elephant King with six tusks, who could not be conquered by anyone, guarded by 8,000 strong fighting elephants with sharp tusks and able to fly like the wind. Nearby he saw the great lake filled with beautiful lotuses served by millions of bees. And he saw the path the king was accustomed to following to go for his bath.

Urged on by the hateful desire for vengeance of the wicked queen, he climbed down the inner cliff face of Golden Mountain. He reached the dwelling of King Six Tusker seven years, seven months and seven days after starting out.

Top Dog thought out his plan – "I will make a pit, hide inside it, shoot the Elephant King and bring him to the end of his life!" So he went into the forest, collected wood and cut down trees to make posts.

While the elephants were bathing in the lake he dug a pit with the shovel he had brought, hiding the dug-up dirt by sprinkling it in the water. He set the posts in the bottom of the pit to support planks which he covered with dirt and brush, leaving only a hole the size of an arrow and an entrance for himself at the far end.

At dawn he attached a false hair bun on top of his head like Indian holy men wear. He disguised himself further by wearing holy yellow robes. Then he hid inside the pit with his bow and poison-tipped arrow.

When the Enlightenment Being passed by, Top Dog, with the terrible wish to kill in his heart, shot him with the poison arrow. The king elephant trumpeted a great cry of pain. All the other elephants began trumpeting just as loudly from fear. Trampling grass and trees alike into powder, the 8,000 fled in eight directions.

The king was driven by his great pain into wanting to kill his attacker. He followed the line of flight of the arrow and saw the hunter hiding in the pit. Then he noticed the yellow robes, the kind worn by perfect men whom the good would never blame.

Suddenly he said, "Whoever is stained, not having tamed his mind, and is dishonest, is not worthy of that yellow robe. But one who has cleaned his stains by concentrating his mind, and is honest and wholesome, is worthy to wear the yellow robe." By giving this teaching to his enemy, the Great Being blew out the fire of anger within himself. Then he asked, "My friend, why do you want to kill me? Or were you persuaded by another to kill me?"

Top Dog replied, "Queen Grace, favorite of the King of Benares and respected by the royal family, saw you in a dream. It was she who rewarded me and said, 'I want his tusks. Go get them and bring them to me!'"

Realizing this must be a deed of the re-born Little Grace, the Enlightenment Being decided he must suffer the pain of losing his tusks for her sake. And furthermore he thought, "She doesn't want anything to do with my tusks. She wants me dead!"

Then he said to Top Dog, "She knows that my parents' and grandparents' and great grandparents' tusks have been saved by us here after their deaths. She specifically wants my tusks because her hatred makes her want me dead. All right, get started hunter – take your saw and cut off my tusks while I still live. Then go tell the hate-filled queen the elephant died because of them."

With saw in hand the hunter approached. But since the great Elephant King was 132 feet tall, appearing to be as big as a mountain, he could not reach the tusks. Then the Great Being lay on the ground and bowed his head.

The hunter got onto the trunk that was as bright and strong as a silver chain. He climbed up until he stood on the forehead just as if he had conquered the peak of holy Mount Kelāsa. Then he climbed down the forehead, put his foot into the mouth, stuck his knee up against the cheek and inserted the long saw into the mouth. He began drawing the saw with both hands. The great white elephant felt severe pain as his mouth filled up with blood. The hunter shifted back and forth but could not cut the mighty tusks.

Accepting the pain, Six Tusker spit out the blood and asked, "My friend, can't you cut it yourself?" "No, my lord," said the man. Still alert in his mind, he continued, "Then take my trunk that I am now too weak to raise, and put it on the saw." After the hunter did so, the elephant helped him saw off his own tusks, as easily as if they were the tender parts of a palm tree.

Then the Great Being said, "Friend hunter, it is not because I do not like them that I give you these tusks. And neither is it because I wish for a superior rebirth – as Māra, god of death, or as Sakka, king of the gods, or even as Brahma, greatest of all gods. Instead I wish only to give the most perfect gift possible – for the benefit of the unfortunate queen and all other beings."

After giving his six tusks of six colors to Top Dog he asked, "How long did it take you to get here?" "It took me seven years, seven months and seven days," he replied. "Go my friend, you may reach Benares in seven days by the magic of these magnificent tusks!"

After Top Dog was out of sight, and before Great Grace and the other elephants returned, the Bodhisatta died.

Then the 8,000 elephants who had fled in eight directions returned. Along with Queen Great Grace they saw the great corpse. They wept and cried out to the Silent Buddhas, true friends of the Great Being, "Sirs, the one who used to give you the Four Necessities [*catu-paccaya*-s] – food, clothing, shelter and medicine – has died from a poison-soaked arrow. Come and see his dead body."

All 500 Silent Buddhas flew miraculously through the air and landed at the place of death. Two strong young elephants lifted the body of their king and made it bow down respectfully to the Silent Buddhas. Then they burned the body on a gigantic funeral fire. All night long the Silent Buddhas chanted in honor of the Enlightenment Being.

The next morning the 8,000 elephants blew out the funeral fire. Filled with grief they wept, threw dirt on their heads, and returned to their homes following Queen Great Grace.

Chapter 5. The Victorious Queen

Even before the seventh day, Top Dog arrived in the suburbs of Benares carrying the graceful tusks – beautiful and matchless in the world, brightening the forests with their golden radiance. He sent word ahead to the queen, "I have killed the elephant and brought you his tusks."

When he got to the city he went to Queen Grace and said, "Your majesty, the elephant for whom your heart was filled with hatred, the one you told me to find and kill, he has indeed been killed by me. Have no doubt of the death of that Elephant King, for here are his tusks." And he gave them over to her.

The tusks, which were beautiful and shining with six colors, she received on her bejeweled fan and placed on her lap. On seeing the tusks of her husband of a previous life she thought, "This beautiful Elephant King was killed by me, for on my command Top Dog killed him with a poison-soaked arrow." With her mind focused on the Great Being she suffered her full measure of pain and remorse. Unable to bear the pain of her overwhelming grief, her heart broke and she died on that very same day.

* * *

This Jātaka story having been told, the Buddha made the story clear by saying:

"Queen Grace is today this nun. Top Dog is today Devadatta. And I who am today the Buddha was King Six Tusker."

At the end of the Buddha's telling of the story, many people attained the stream entrance state of mind [*sotāpatti*]. And the nun, by spiritual insight, attained Arahant-ship [sainthood] and freed herself from all future pain and rebirth.

The moral: "Ignorance breeds hatred."

Also,

"Suffering is the first truth."

ABOUT PARIYATTI

Pariyatti is dedicated to providing affordable access to authentic teachings of the Buddha about the Dhamma theory (*pariyatti*) and practice (*paṭipatti*) of Vipassana meditation. A 501(c)(3) non-profit charitable organization since 2002, Pariyatti is sustained by contributions from individuals who appreciate and want to share the incalculable value of the Dhamma teachings. We invite you to visit www.pariyatti.org to learn about our programs, services, and ways to support publishing and other undertakings.

Pariyatti Publishing Imprints

Vipassana Research Publications (focus on Vipassana as taught by S.N. Goenka in the tradition of Sayagyi U Ba Khin)

BPS Pariyatti Editions (selected titles from the Buddhist Publication Society, copublished by Pariyatti)

MPA Pariyatti Editions (selected titles from the Myanmar Pitaka Association, copublished by Pariyatti)

Pariyatti Digital Editions (audio and video titles, including discourses)

Pariyatti Press (classic titles returned to print and inspirational writing by contemporary authors)

Pariyatti enriches the world by

- disseminating the words of the Buddha,
- providing sustenance for the seeker's journey,
- illuminating the meditator's path.

www.ingramcontent.com/pod-product-compliance
Lightning Source LLC
Chambersburg PA
CBHW050357260626
47156CB00003B/770